TWISTING FATES

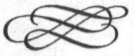

LEIGH CREEK

ECC PUBLISHING LLC

Copyright © 2026 by Leigh Creek (Elizabeth C. Cabrera). 1st Edition.

Visit the author's website at www.authorleighcreek.com.

All rights reserved.

No part of this publication may be reproduced, distributed, or transmitted in any form or by any means, including information storage and retrieval systems, photocopying, recording, or any other electronic or mechanical methods without prior written permission from the author and publisher, except for the use of brief quotations in a book review. For permission requests, contact ECC Publishing at eccpublishing@gmail.com.

This book was not created with generative artificial intelligence (gen AI), and the author does not support gen AI in any way. No portion of this publication/work may be reproduced, translated, transmitted, and/or copied to train gen AI technologies, systems, programs, or models in any form or by any means without the express written permission of the copyright holder. Any unauthorized use of this material will be subject to legal action.

This is a work of fiction. Names, characters, places, and incidents either are the products of the author's imagination or are used fictitiously. Any resemblance to actual persons, living or dead, business, companies, events, or locales, is entirely coincidental.

Paperback ISBN: 979-8-9880600-7-9

Ebook ISBN: 979-8-9880600-6-2

Book Cover by Amanda Hawkins at Eternal Geekery.

Edited by Jamie at copyediting.by.jamie@gmail.com

Formatted and Published by ECC Publishing (the imprint of Elizabeth C. Cabrera)

❀ Formatted with Vellum

CONTENT WARNINGS

For the full, detailed list of content warnings for this book, please visit the author's website:
   www.authorleighcreek.com/twisting-fates

To everyone whose favorite desert is cinnamon roll men...

CHAPTER 1

"If these weather patterns are indicative of the next few months, this could be the most active tornado season we've had in the past decade." Addie plastered her best TV smile on and parroted the words from the prompt. The flashing studio lights above her burned into her skin as she pointed at the green screen behind her—like pinprick knives that she could never quite get used to, even after these past few years under them.

Nothing about what she said surprised her, as she had been the one to add it to the script before the cameras started rolling. She'd been monitoring it for the past two weeks—so closely that she'd barely slept in days. The lingering reminder of her recent lack of showers wafted up to invade her nose. She continued talking to the invisible crowd in front of her through the camera lens, but the smell persisted.

No, recently Addie had opted to remain glued to her meteorology setup at her job with the local TV station. She'd been studying the upcoming weather patterns for weeks leading to this but hadn't wanted to announce it live until she had been one hundred percent sure of her forecast. And the minute she'd seen the trajectory of this system, it became abundantly clear that this system would make for a dangerous season.

The lights above her cut off suddenly as the camera focused back on the two news anchors behind the main desk. It mercifully cut her air time off for today's shift with a sort of finality that only could be found in a busy and bustling station.

Her colored contacts abruptly shifted from the changing of the light, and she had to blink a few times to focus. Now that she was off air, she could finally run to the hair and makeup area to take them out. *Good riddance.*

The producer waved the *off the air* signal behind the camera, and Addie trotted off stage. She all but ripped the mic setup off and handed it off as quickly as she could. It felt like shedding a fake layer of muck that she'd grown to despise over the years, and she let out a quick sigh of relief.

Channel 5 at 5 had been her home since she'd moved back to Kansas a few years ago, but being in front of the camera wasn't *exactly* what she'd dreamed up for herself. It felt so fake sometimes, standing all prim and proper with a TV-ready exaggerated smile etched into her features, but it paid the bills.

Addie would've loved if—when someone heard the name *Adelyn Walters*—it held some genuine weight behind it in the Kansas weather community. She'd worked her ass off getting her doctorate in meteorology, so it would be nice to be known for something *other* than '*Oh hey, are you that weather girl with the spooky eyes?*'

The reminder of her *spooky* eyes made her eyes feel heavier than usual under the weight of colored contacts, more aware of the fact that her own eye color had to be faked because of a few '*She looks like she's possessed*' comments from viewers. If she had it her way, she'd toss them out and never wear them again. If she could, she'd throw everything that reminded her of this place out the window. But she couldn't.

You can't quit right now.

Shoving the displeasure aside, her thoughts returned to the weather room. Her eyes had been glued to the streams of data and projections from the moment she'd arrived at the station hours earlier, all the way up until a producer had yanked her away to go on the air. Her skin practically itched with the need to get back as quickly as possible, so she could review the latest data.

This time of year was optimal for this kind of weather, with atmospheric patterns that were off the charts and ever-changing with each passing moment. Every computer model forecast that she'd seen the past two weeks, every Doppler radar image, told her that it was shaping up to be the most active season that she'd seen in her career.

The last time she'd seen a weather system like this, it had been back when she'd been studying the super outbreaks of 1997 and 2003 back in school.

Her forecast today was the first time she'd mentioned anything about the system bearing toward them—and for a reason. If there was anything she'd learned in her years with tornadoes and anyone who called Tornado Alley home, it was to not say anything with finality until absolutely necessary. The people that lived in this region were a sturdy bunch, but they heard the warnings and sirens so often that they hardly paid them attention.

There was zero questioning this one—it was going to wreak havoc across the state by the end of this season. It wouldn't be a matter of whether there *would* be any deadly tornadoes that cropped up out of this but how *many*.

Addie's stomach growled angrily at her, a familiar cramping sensation forcing her to slow her pace. Before she could make her way across the room, someone bumped her hip with theirs.

"Where exactly do you think you're going, missy?"

She recognized that voice anywhere and smiled, despite her mood. "To the weather room. Where do you think?"

Addie didn't have to turn to see the wide-set grin plastered on Evie's face. So bright and beaming that, despite the fact that it was well into the afternoon, she was too sleep-deprived to handle.

"No," Evie corrected, currently guiding Addie away from her intended destination. "We're heading to that meeting we were invited to."

The camerawoman and friend, whose arm snaked up to link the

two, was the definition of naturally energetic. Practically skipping as she immediately directed Addie in the opposite direction.

Addie frowned, trying to remember. "Meeting?"

"Yes, the one from that email from this morning?"

Admittedly, Addie *had* seen an email from their boss come in that morning, but she hadn't had a chance to look. She'd been knee deep in emails and correspondent data she'd been getting from her colleagues over at the National Weather Center in Oklahoma.

"Is it one that can wait?" she asked, but her friend just lifted a shoulder noncommittally in response.

Addie craned her neck to look up at Evie, hoping she would see the scowl etched into Addie's face, but found her attempt unsuccessful. Evie gleefully ushered Addie along, her effort made easier by the simple fact that Addie would never have the strength to protest her.

Her friend batted her long eyelashes, catching a ceiling light just right to cause a twinkle in her chestnut eyes, which pleaded for cooperation.

Addie groaned. "Fine. But aren't you supposed to be on camera three?"

Evie's dark-black hair swished over her shoulder with a flick. "It must be something really fun, then, if they're willing to give me a break from camera work!"

The large conference room door clicked shut behind them, filling the large space with a hollow silence that was in complete contrast with the hustle and bustle of the station. The rest of the station was filled to the brim with bright, iridescent lighting, wires running along every inch of floor space, and dark contrasting walls designed to highlight the main set more—making the quiet, naturally lit conference room feel like a safe haven by comparison.

As Addie took a seat next to Evie, she grabbed her phone from where she'd tucked it. If they had a moment for her to check her email —for whatever it was that she'd walked into—she would take it. She scrolled through the emails on her phone, but as she had been waiting on some of the latest numbers to include in tomorrow's report, her inbox was flooded. Page upon page of forecast projections and weather patterns from her contacts at the *National Weather Center* filled it to the brim.

Where was this damned thing?

Ah, there. She was about to tap the message when the door swung open with a loud bang.

Addie nearly dropped her phone, playing a quick game of hot potato as her boss and one of the other producers waltzed in.

"Good to see you outside of the weather room for a change," John said with a grin, one she returned with a fake smile of her own.

Addie suspected that his wife's opinion of John often reflected her own—evidenced by the wrinkled shirt he was wearing from once again sleeping one too many nights in the break room. If he was just an asshole on set, that would be one thing. Most people were assholes on set, but Addie speculated his *glowing* personality wasn't hindered under the weight of his responsibilities.

With that goofy-ass grin he flashed everybody, perched below the permanent deep bags underneath his eyes, it was about the only thing that prevented her from all out sucker punching him in the face. All the guys at the station *loved* John. He was one of the boys.

Her boss wasn't the worst guy she'd ever encountered ... but he didn't exactly rank in the ten best ones either. Like a mantra, she continuously had to remind herself whenever he gave her *constructive criticism* on her appearance that she needed this job and couldn't afford to tell him exactly what she thought of him. Still, there were only so many ways he could phrase *'You're lucky you're pretty'* before she'd started having to excuse herself to the bathroom and scream into her arm.

The other producer, someone she had hardly spoken to more than a handful of times, was an unknown. He was shorter and less rotund than John, but he had a weaselly look about him, with his slicked back jet-black hair and a sneer etched into his features. She quickly scanned to find a name tag, knowing damn well there wouldn't be one, on the off chance his name would materialize in her head before she said something stupid.

"Let's cut to the chase; we're on a tight schedule as it is," the producer announced as he plopped into the seat next to John. "The higher-ups want you to head the weather documentary."

Addie blinked a few times. "Come again?"

She vaguely remembered them mentioning something about a documentary a few months ago at one of their quarterly meetings, but her name hadn't been anywhere *near* that project. In fact, it was her coworker, Sally, who had been there for fifteen years, who was the only name mentioned in the same sentence as that documentary.

When the hell had *she* been named the lead for this?!

"It's a huge ask from the higher-ups, and you've been selected to head the project. They've already put a lot of money toward this to get the edge on Channel 9. Don't want to wait until they get word and start putting together a team of their own," he continued, a glint catching the light against his wide spectacles nearly the size of saucers. Reflected through them, Addie was able to see the loose chestnut curls fluffed around her head reflected back at her.

There must've been some mistake. "But … I can't just *leave* right now…. What about Sally? Wasn't she the lead?"

"Well, unfortunately, she backed out today," John interjected, giving the producer a pointed look before continuing. "Her daughter was in an accident last night, so she's taking some personal time to help take care of her."

Addie's hand instinctively flew to her chest. "Oh my God, poor Sally! Is her daughter okay? What happened? Is she—"

"They're all fine, but we need someone to fill her role," the producer interrupted, agitation creeping into his voice, "and they didn't want to miss this system. You're the only other person they wanted."

Talk about whiplash.

Addie nearly fell off her chair from how far forward she propped herself. *"Me?* They wanted me to fill in for Sally?"

"You used to also chase tornadoes back in the day, didn't ya?" the producer, whose name continued to escape her, chimed.

Ah, there it is. Addie highly doubted that her ratings were high enough to be the determining factor for replacing Sally. There was only one other on-staff meteorologist, but between the two, she was the only one with any chasing experience.

Addie nodded without looking away from John. "Yeah, before I came to work here. But that was ... that was several years ago now."

"It's more experience than anyone else." The producer shrugged. "We have the files for you to take with you to review, and your team lead is waiting in the conference room downstairs to meet you. He'll take you two to meet the rest of your team."

"My team?"

The producer nodded. "You'll be joining a chase team that we've already selected."

"Great, I don't get to choose a team either," Addie mumbled, more to herself than to the others. She wasn't nearly as quiet as she'd hoped when the producer clucked his tongue at her. Addie sat back as she chewed on her lower lip, not caring if she smudged the bright-red lipstick that they'd smeared on her earlier in the process.

John cleared his throat before the producer could reply. "We thoroughly vetted all of the teams that applied for the project in advance. We had it narrowed down between two teams that are highly qualified, but I promise that you'll be working with the best of the best. And you'll have Evie with you for filming, so you won't be completely on your own."

Addie glanced at her friend. "Evie?"

"We originally had someone else for this," John continued, "but because of your friendship and chemistry together on set, the execs agreed to let us switch to Evie. They figured it would make it easier to work in the field."

Evie's mouth opened as if she were about to speak, but instead she adjusted herself in the seat next to her. If so much hadn't already been going on, Addie would've commented on how odd that was, knowing Evie was *never* one to hold back if she had something to say. But she filed that away to deal with later as the matter at hand played out.

There was a lot to consider, and she didn't have nearly enough time to factor in *everything* that was needed.

As selfish as it was to think, at least she wouldn't be alone. It would be worse having to be dragged off with some new team completely on her own, but having Evie, her friend, with her, would help soften that discomfort.

Despite that flicker of appreciation, she also knew that Evie didn't have any experience with storm chasing. There was no doubt in Addie's mind that Evie was easily the most skilled camerawoman she'd ever met, but filming storm chasing was a completely different beast.

She exchanged a look with Evie, who appeared to be just as out-of-water as she felt. They had that in common at the moment.

"When do we get started?" she asked, trying to think of the million checklist-type items she'd have to get done to prepare for something like this.

The producer huffed and slid a folder across the table to her. "Here's the file for your team. You pack up and leave with the team lead today."

Addie eyed the folder. "You're joking."

"Not even a little," John said, aiming a glare in the producer's direction again. "We only found out about Sally backing out this morning. But with the system advancing so quickly, they want you in the field as soon as possible."

"That's ... That's pretty quick...." Addie said. Quick was an understatement. All she had with her were the clothes on her back and her laptop bag she'd left over in the weather room.

The producer folded his arms across his chest. "Do you have any affairs you need to arrange?"

Honestly, Addie couldn't think of a single thing that she needed to take care of. Her life the past year or so had mostly been made up of running back and forth between her apartment and the station, copious amounts of takeout, and grabbing the occasional coffee with Evie in her free time.

There weren't any events coming up that she would have to cancel or reschedule. She didn't have any living relatives to speak of that would care if she was there or not. And it wasn't exactly like she had any friends outside of work who would miss her. Her *landlady* wouldn't even miss her because all of her bills were on autopay.

It was rather sad if she thought about it.

"No," she answered simply.

"Good," the producer stated, the eye roll apparent in his tone. "Then we can head downstairs and get you on your way."

"I don't ... I don't know. This is all so sudden..." she stammered out, watching her boss and the producer already rising from their seats.

"The execs have already spent a good amount of money on this project," the producer drawled, a lilt to his tone that Addie didn't care for one bit. "If you were to tell them no ... I don't know if they'd feel too generous when the next round of layoffs comes around...."

She had to hand it to him: That was about as subtle as a freight train careening through Times Square, but the point had been made.

It wasn't the first time she'd heard that veiled threat.

Beeping medical equipment flashed in her memory, as bright as the day it had happened last year, the line on the monitor flatlining and leaving her completely on her own. And no way to pay...

She clenched her lower lip with her teeth, hoping it would prevent her from saying something.

"Alrighty then," she allowed. "Let's get this show on the road, I guess."

The producer nodded and threw her a wink. "Atta girl."

Addie decided immediately that on principle alone, she refused to learn his name.

John shot her a sympathetic smile. "I'll be with you to introduce you to the lead. He's a very nice guy. I think he's about your age, so you should get along pretty well."

Fortunately for her sanity, the producer parted ways with them as they left the conference room, heading back to set.

John remained, ushering them down the hall to the stairwell with an air of sympathy that felt palpable. She could tell from the look in his eyes that he was just about as pleased with this whole arrangement as she was, a frown carving lines into his face.

Evie stuck close to Addie's side. Her usually confident friend appeared a bit more on edge than usual, though Addie couldn't blame her. She'd been thrown into the deep end, just as much as Addie had.

"What's his name?" Addie asked as they entered the hallway from the stairwell. "The team lead we're going to meet?"

"His name is Benjamin Borack."

John opened the door for her before the name could register, ushering her into the conference room.

The second she saw him, recognition flared to life. He turned upon hearing the door open, freezing almost immediately as his eyes landed on her.

Wow, talk about a blast from the past. It had been, what … five years since she'd last seen him at graduation?

He looked almost the same as he did back then, though he was several shades tanner than she remembered. His paler olive complexion was now enriched with a warm, almost golden hue. His fluffy, jet-black hair was more pristinely cut now, not nearly as disheveled and unkempt as she'd remembered. Instead, it was neatly clean cut along the sides, while the hair up top effortlessly styled into a cascade of tamed waves.

It was definitely him, though.

This was her team lead for the next few months?

John looked between the two, clearing his throat. "Uh, I take it you two know each other?"

Understatement of the century. There was no way Addie could have forgotten the one man who'd nearly destroyed her career before it had started.

"We've met," the two said simultaneously.

CHAPTER 2

"If it isn't Adelyn Walters. How long has it been?" Ben said slowly, the surprise in his expression slowly morphing into something friendlier as his eyes roved over her. He pushed the rim of his glasses up his nose as he came over to greet them, extending a hand toward her.

How someone could look so familiar yet so foreign at the same time baffled her. What baffled her more was the fact that despite everything he'd put her through, she *still* found him just as attractive as she did all those years ago. More so, in fact. *Frustratingly* so.

Ben had always been on the tall side, with the top of her head barely reaching his shoulders, but he had been lanky. The school-boy kind of lanky that a lack of proper nutrition, while cramming for grad school, would do to a person.

He certainly wasn't lanky now.

Lean muscle peeked out from beneath the dark-blue button-up that he was wearing, contrasting the memory in her mind of his thinner frame. His shoulders were broader than she remembered—just enough for her to notice but not enough to make him look like an entirely different person.

He had managed to tame the mess of jet-black curls on top of his head. Instead of letting it fall haphazardly every which way, it was now neatly trimmed on the sides with longer, textured waves on top. It still looked tousled like it once had, but it was more stylish now. Even the fringe that swept down his forehead was neater, coming down to just above his thick black eyebrows.

He'd upgraded the thin, borderline flimsy glasses he used to sport to a pair of dark, thick-rimmed ones. They didn't hide the bright flash of amber eyes staring at her from the other side, like she would've thought from such a style—it only managed to magnify them.

He looked put together. Professional.

Nothing like the messy smart-ass she remembered—but *handsome*.

Images of the wild girl with a tangle of brunette curls flashed in her mind, causing nostalgia to cloud her vision. It felt like a lifetime ago, though in reality the last time she'd ever really felt like herself had been three years ago when she'd started at the station. Her hair color was just about the only thing that hadn't changed about her—though now it was tamed back into stylish ponytails and updos that better suited life behind the camera. Symbolic, if she really thought about it.

"Graduation day, I think," she replied, shaking the hand he extended to her.

His handshake was firm, confident. It wasn't like the producer's was, or some of the other men she worked with on a regular basis. Theirs was a meek, gentle handshake that a lot of men gave when they were afraid of damaging tiny little womanly hands—as if they were all peaches just shy of a bruise.

Despite the encouraging handshake, however, Addie fought the urge to squeeze his hand with a vice-like grip.

His smile widened. "That long? I feel like it was just yesterday that you were telling me to go fuck myself."

Ah, there he is.

She gave in to her previous desires and squeezed his hand harder just before releasing it, satisfied when he sucked his teeth in a mild wince.

"You and Addie went to school together?" Evie asked, flanking her. Addie then remembered that she and Ben weren't alone, and that strangling him in front of her coworker and boss wasn't likely the best path for her. Though that didn't stop her from shooting a glare at him in warning to keep his mouth shut.

But of course, she should have known better. It *was* Ben after all.

Ben's smile widened. "We did. Same grad school program. She kicked my ass regularly, I'm afraid."

John raised an eyebrow across the room but didn't say anything. Evie appeared enraptured by the conversation. Addie, on the other hand, wanted nothing more than for the earth to open and swallow her up. Maybe then she could get out of this awkward-as-hell situation.

Addie felt a long-dormant twitch flicker above her right eyebrow. The one that had been miraculously cured after she'd graduated. She rubbed it with her thumb, but annoyance immediately curdled her gut at the smug look that Ben shot her from her periphery.

"It was so easy to do, too," she commented, satisfied when Ben's jaw clenched. "And a lot of fun."

Ben nodded, rocking on his feet. "Yeah, but it made me a better chaser. *Thank you* for that."

She hummed low in her throat, unable to prevent herself from snatching the low-hanging fruit practically dangling right in front of her. "Not enough to be valedictorian, though?"

Ben's smile widened further, the smug kind that let her know she'd successfully hit his pride. "I still think that extra credit from Dr. Harding pushed you into that spot."

That smile fluttered something dormant in her gut, catching her off guard. How the hell could she even *think* about that after everything? She'd dealt with those feelings a long time ago, hadn't she? A once upon a time desire that was quashed before it could see the light of day. But there it was, a longing that flamed to life as she looked up at the man in front of her. An annoying fly buzzing about that she'd have to learn to swat away once again. She shrugged. "If that's what helps you sleep at night."

"Though it would've been hard to beat you, Addie," he continued, his voice lowering. "Pretty sure you lived in the library most of the time and had the number for every TA we had on speed dial."

"You would know, wouldn't you?" she spat, the venom behind the statement practically hissed between her teeth. Knowing flashed in Ben's eyes as his smile waned, giving Addie a small sense of satisfaction.

The adult version of herself knew that at some point, she and Ben would have to talk things out like civilized people. The grad school version of herself would've already had him pinned to the floor.

It was in moments like this that she genuinely *missed* that version of herself.

Evie, silent up to this point, looked like she was about to burst. An excited grin and gleam in her eyes that tore Addie's attention away from Ben. She turned just as Evie reached over to sling her arm around Addie, hugging her into her tall frame.

"I'm gonna have a *lot* of fun asking you about what Addie was like when she wasn't quite as much of a stick-in-the-mud," Evie said.

Okay, ouch.

"Just because I'm not out on the town every other night," Addie cut in, lips tugging downward in a frown, "doesn't mean I'm a stick-in-the-mud."

It just meant that she, reality TV, and YouTube were well acquainted—on the odd chance she wasn't setting up shop in the weather room.

"When was the last time you went out and did something fun?" Evie asked, already knowing the answer as a self-satisfied grin split across her face. When Addie glowered at her, she laughed. "I rest my case."

Ben chuckled and ran a hand through his hair, his fingers temporarily disappearing through the thick black waves. "A stick-in-the-mud, huh?"

Addie spun. "I'm *not* a stick-in-the-mud!"

Ben ignored her, directing his attention to Evie. "The Addie I went to school with was a firecracker, for sure."

Addie's cheeks warmed, suddenly hoping that Ben wouldn't share everything. There had been more than a few sleep-deprived antics that she wished, in hindsight, she hadn't done.

She was a different person back then. More carefree and ... well, fun. But that was before she'd had to take life a bit more seriously.

"Some things haven't changed," John said, covering a laugh with a cough when Addie aimed a glare at him.

Traitors, the both of them.

"Anyway, I assume you have all the details on what to expect for this documentary?" Addie asked, turning her attention back to Ben.

"Yeah, Sally told me last week during our call," Ben said, directing his attention over to John. "It's been ... great ... catching up ... but is Sally coming down soon?"

John stepped forward, his arms folded across his chest. "There's been a bit of a change with that. Sally won't be joining you."

Ben furrowed his eyebrows. "Is—is she alright? Are we postponing the documentary or—"

John held up a hand. "No, the execs aren't patient enough to postpone this. Your team will still get paid for the contract. We'll just be switching up who we send with you."

Ben's eyes drifted back to Addie, who was now finally able to give him an amused grin. "Please tell me it's not her."

Addie would be more insulted, but this was as much news to him as it had been for her, so she tried not to hold it against him. *Tried* being the operative word, when her temper over this whole affair kicked in. "I'm more than capable, thank you."

Ben grimaced. "I'm sure, but is there anyone else you could possibly send? Someone that preferably wouldn't bite me?"

The silence around them was deafening before Evie blanched. "You've *bitten* him before?"

Addie folded her arms across her chest and averted her gaze. "Only once."

Twice, but Ben didn't comment on that. He instead shot a pleading gaze over to John, as if he were calling for his mother to come rescue him from a bully.

John, on the other hand, was trying to hide another laugh, this time behind the stack of files he'd been carrying. He wouldn't be of any help to Ben, or Addie for that matter.

Evie had joined him but was much less subtle about it, openly giggling behind her hand.

Not a single person was on her side, and she just about wanted to throw her hands up in the air and say to hell with all of them.

"I'm afraid you're stuck with her," John finally managed when he was able to subdue his laughter enough to talk. "She's the only other meteorologist on our team with any storm-chasing experience, and she's more than capable. I'll take them to pick their things up. In the meantime, you'll go in to chat with a few of the producers to sort out some of the details. When I bring them back, you're all free to go."

A groan reverberated from Ben as he turned back to Addie, rubbing the back of his neck.

"The feeling's mutual," she grumbled.

Classic rock blasted over the radio, the beat in tune with every bump in the winding road. Addie and Evie barely had time to run home and pack a bag before they'd been all but handed off to Ben for the foreseeable future.

No one had said much since they'd gotten out on the road. The silence had stretched taut between the three of them, with Ben cranking up the radio just to fill the gaps.

What *could* be said at a moment like this? All previous issues aside —Ben and his team had been effectively screwed in this deal. The team that Ben *thought* he was getting was now just Addie and Evie. Whatever they'd planned with Sally was out the window.

Both Addie and Evie had been given an all-or-nothing assignment that meant relinquishing the next few months of their lives for work— so no one was in a particularly good spot with all of this.

Granted, Addie's life outside of work wasn't all that thrilling these days, so her getting thrown on this assignment wasn't the end of the world. Evie, on the other hand, had a much more active social life outside of work. Recently, however, Evie had been hanging around the station with Addie, so she wasn't sure if there was some other change going on with her friend. And with the outbreak looming over all of them, she hadn't had time to ask.

Addie hadn't wanted to start off this whole project on *such* a sour note, but no words came to her to placate the situation.

Addie clutched the handle in the front seat, holding on for what felt like dear life. It had been quite some time since she'd gone out into the middle of nowhere like this. The open fields of Kansas seemed to stretch on for miles, and the constant jostling made her stomach clench uncomfortably from the lack of practice. It had been such a routine back then, but her stomach preferred the steady ground of the newsroom.

Ben finally turned to grin at her before lowering the volume on the radio. "Nauseous?"

Addie laughed uncomfortably. "I'm out of practice for these roads."

Without taking his eyes off the road, he reached into the center console and fished out a pack of gum. A few pieces were already missing from the peppermint-flavored pack, but she eagerly accepted it.

"It still gets to me sometimes on longer treks," Ben answered before she could ask. "The gum helps."

"Thanks," she said before she popped one into her mouth, letting the taste settle on her tongue before continuing. "So, how many people do you have on your team?"

Ben smirked at her before his gaze returned to the road. "It wasn't in our file?"

It had been, of course, but she'd barely had time to look at it. It had been packed away in her bag thrown in the trunk.

Addie shrugged. "How would I know? I didn't get a chance to look. I'd only just been handed it when I walked into that conference room."

"So, you've known about this about as long as I have?"

She could feel his eyes on her, but she stared ahead. The gum was certainly helping, the peppermint a perfect calming balm to the rising nausea, but she didn't want to jinx it. "It would seem that way."

Ben laughed, but there was no humor in it. "The next few weeks are going to be a *scream*."

Addie mumbled a protest under her breath, folding her arms across her chest and sinking further down in her seat. She allowed her gaze to fall on the wind turbines in the open fields to her right as she ignored the scent of Ben's aftershave, which permeated the vehicle.

He was absolutely right, though.

She wasn't thrilled about being tossed to the wolves, even less so about Evie getting thrown in with her just because she had made the cardinal sin of being *her* friend, but she would be damned if she allowed this to fall apart.

"So, your team," she prompted again. "How many?"

The line of Ben's jaw worked before relaxing. "Right now, there are five of us. We're relatively small compared to some of the bigger company-based chasers, but we're efficient and we get results."

Addie nodded as a sudden gust of wind whooshed from behind her, causing her hair to tangle around her face. Evie, in the backseat, was apparently having the time of her life. She had the window rolled down and was sticking her head outside. She sort of reminded Addie of a golden retriever, with the only difference being the long streaks of Evie's black hair.

Ben nodded in her direction. "Has she ever been on a chase before?"

"Not that I know of."

"Great," he sighed. "I have a camerawoman with no chase experience and *you*. This should be fun."

Addie sucked in deep breath, calming her instinct to lash out that years of practice at the station had taught her. Something about his tone pricked her the wrong way. Addie pulled herself up and whirled in her seat to face him. She was tempted to tell him that this hadn't exactly been her idea to begin with, but she resisted the urge. The last thing his ego needed was to hold some sort of advantage over her, including the fact that she could lose her job if she didn't do this documentary to the best of her ability.

As much as she hated it at times, she couldn't afford to lose it either. The mountain of unpaid medical bills stacking up on her kitchen counter kept her rooted in place, and forced the TV-ready smile on her face. She lowered her voice so that Evie couldn't hear her. "Say what you want about me, but you leave *her* alone. Got it?"

Ben surprised her by immediately grinning. A genuine smile that warmed his entire face up with it, bringing back that handsome quality that she'd seen earlier. "Glad to see not all of that spark has faded there, firecracker."

"I have plenty of *spark*, thank you very much," she snapped, resisting the urge to slap him. "And don't call me that!"

"I beg to differ, but don't worry." He shrugged casually, the motion drawing her eyes to the muscles in his broad shoulders before she quickly glanced away. "We'll take care of her. I'm a stickler for safety —as you'll soon find out—so we'll make sure she knows where she can set up to get the footage she needs."

If Addie squinted—through the plume of dirt that curtained their path and the tall grass that tickled the underbelly of the car—she could start to make out what appeared to be a large white vehicle ahead. Memories of such a sight flooded Addie's senses, and she could practically feel the stalks of wheat against her skin.

It wasn't exactly uncommon for storm chasers like Ben and his team to have an RV camper on standby. Most serious teams did, ones that weren't just chasing for the hell of it, though seeing those kinds of thrill-seeking adrenaline junkies was becoming more and more common with the popularization of tornado movies and documentaries.

Addie's old team had a camper as well, though smaller in size from the one Addie could see more and more as the car carved a path through the grass.

"Is that your team's camper?" she asked.

"Yes, ma'am, it is," Ben replied, pulling out into the clearing just on the other side of the camper. "Our engineer, Grace, was able to remodel an old RV to house all of our navigating and research equipment."

Ben had hardly put the car in park when the first of the team members rushed at them. A tall blonde woman, shorter than Evie by a hair, took a few long strides and grabbed her hand as she exited the car with a bright smile. "It's so nice to meet you! Ben's—"

"Grace, that isn't Sally," Ben interrupted. "Sally and her cameraman couldn't make it. This is their replacement. Our camera-woman, Evelyn Daniels, and Adeyln Walters, our meteorologist."

The woman, Grace, turned and only beamed further, her blonde ponytail swinging wildly with her movement. "Ohmygosh, is this *the* Adeyln Walters? The one you went to school with?"

Addie raised an eyebrow in Ben's direction. Things just got more interesting. "I am. How did you know that?"

"We've heard that name plenty of times, trust me." Grace nodded. "He used to say that you were the devil in—"

"Oh, Grace, I was *just* telling Addie about the renovations you did to the RV," Ben said quickly. "You should show her around after they've both met everyone and we've hashed out the plan."

Ben strode toward the RV with Evie and Addie's bags, his long legs making quick work of it, and disappeared through the door before anyone could protest. All the better. Addie wanted to find out more about what all he'd been telling people about her when two men, nudging each other playfully, started to walk over.

"Hey, welcome to the team!" the first of the two said as he extended a hand. "I'm Ryan."

He wasn't much taller than herself, and that was oddly comforting, as it seemed the two of them formed a sort of involuntary duo of the shortest people on the team. Addie was used to being the shortest person in the room, so having someone about the same height was nice.

She accepted his hand, feeling the rough calluses on his skin. It somehow matched his rough, square jawline, which was peppered with a dark-brown five o'clock shadow that lingered from what she suspected to have been a long day on the road. The dark-brown curls tousled atop his head matched his eyes, as well as the patches of dirt caked onto the knees of his jeans. Everything about him read rough and tough, but the smile he angled in her direction indicated otherwise.

She offered a smile of her own. "Nice to meet you, Ryan."

The other man stepped forward, instead opting to give a simple wave instead of a handshake. "I'm Tony."

Addie was struck by the intense ice-blue color of his eyes, never having seen that color before in person. They were almost hypnotic, though the way he couldn't seem to maintain eye contact with her for longer than a few seconds at a time managed to quickly break the spell they cast.

He was almost as tall as Ben but hunched over so much that he practically curled in on himself like an armadillo on a hot Texas asphalt. A shame, really, as he was quite handsome.

Whereas Ryan gave off the rough-and-tumble vibe she expected in this part of the country, Tony gave off a more Hollywoodesque look that felt out of place. He reminded her of one of those TV doctors she watched in the increasingly little amount of free time she had—complete with the sharp angles of his nose and jaw that practically screamed *heartbreaker*. He looked more like a Greek god, dripped from head to toe in warm caramel, emerging from the open plains of Kansas.

She nodded in his direction. "It's nice to meet you both."

Evie and Grace walked over and joined them, with Grace's arm already slung around Evie's shoulder like they'd been buddies for years.

If Evie had been as struck by Tony's looks, she gave little indication. Well, little indication to everyone *but* Addie. Addie and Evie hadn't been friends more than a few years, but she could see when something interested her. From the pure twinkle in Evie's sparkling chocolate-brown eyes, Addie could tell that Tony interested her.

Evie flashed him a smile, reaching out with her other hand to shake his. "I'm Evie. Thanks for having us."

Tony slowly accepted the hand, his eyes on her in a way that already had Addie stifling a giggle. Evie was gorgeous by most standards. It wasn't the first time Addie had witnessed someone becoming mute at her appearance. How could they not? With her golden-brown skin and long, wavy black hair that most people could only dream of, she was an absolute knockout.

It was a damn shame that Evie preferred being behind a camera. She would have made one hell of a TV personality.

But if Tony's immediately shy disposition was any indicator, he wouldn't have the faintest clue that Evie watched him just as closely.

This was going to be interesting....

Grace nudged Ryan, who appeared confused by the greeting. "There was a last-minute change at the station. Sally couldn't come, so they sent us *the* Adelyn Walters and her camerawoman, Evie."

Ryan coughed a laugh. "Oh, no shit?!"

Addie threw her hands in the air. "Apparently, my reputation precedes me."

Evie nudged her from the other side. "I'm *definitely* gonna pry you for answers later. I gotta know what you did to that poor man that he's still talking about you years later."

Grace waved her off. "Nothing too bad, I can assure you. But it's nice to have some ladies on the team for a bit. It's been a bit of a sausage fest with these three," Grace said excitedly, earning a laugh from both her and Evie.

"Something about that metaphor makes me feel gross." Ryan grimaced. "Can you not use *us* and *sausage* in the same context, please?"

Grace batted her eyelashes at him. "Would you prefer it if I called you a bunch of weenies?"

Tony chuckled abruptly, broken from his trance-like state moments prior. "Why you insist on trying to fight with the person you shared a womb with, I'll never understand."

Ryan frowned. "She started it."

"Alright, Napoleon, chill out."

Addie was already starting to like this group, even if they probably thought she was some kind of snake lady from whatever the hell Ben had been feeding them.

Another member of the team appeared from the RV—a tall, slender man who was almost as tall as Ben but easily towered over both Addie and Ryan. The dark-black curls of his hair poked out from beneath a red baseball cap, complete with a little woodchuck mascot plastered on the front.

He had an easy, bright smile when he extended a hand out to Addie, the thick black mustache under his nose stretching out. "You must be the new girls. I'm Brody."

"Addie," she greeted as she shook his hand. "Nice to meet you."

Behind them, Ben appeared once more, clapping his hands and rubbing them together. "Alright, let's get down to business."

CHAPTER 3

Addie and Evie sat next to one another as the group gathered inside the RV, huddling close together. Ben hovered in front of the group next to a large whiteboard. Whatever had been written there before was long erased, the traces of the previous scribblings etched in faint black scratches along the surface. Ben rolled up his sleeves, exposing his forearms, grabbed a black marker from a nearby container, and began to write.

When he finished, he turned back to them. "Alright, with Addie and Evie on our team, I want everyone to get their phones out. Exchange numbers, all that jazz, and share your locations. Addie, Evie, please be sure to share yours as well."

Evie asked the question before Addie could open her mouth. "Why the location sharing?"

Tony cleared his throat next to her, his gaze flicking from her face to the floor, as if he couldn't quite keep her gaze. "It's in case we're separated during a chase. We use radios to keep in contact, but we use location sharing as a backup option."

Ben nodded. "Saved our asses on more occasions than I can count. Now, we need to discuss a game plan for this documentary and—"

Evie interrupted with a raise of her hand. "Isn't the game plan to film tornadoes?"

When he spoke again, there was an exasperated quality to his voice. "Yes, that is the plan, but it's not that simple. We're gonna have to film all throughout this season so that we can get as much footage as we can of this system. That means that we'll be together for a few months. We'll have to balance our time between getting shots for you, talking segments, and actually chasing these things—which is chaotic in and of itself, especially with newbies in tow."

Newbies?

Sure, Addie was likely rusty from sitting on the bench for a few years. It might take her a few minutes to get back into the groove, but a *newbie?*

She frowned, folding her arms across her chest. "I'm not a *newbie*, Ben."

Those amber eyes of his cut to her. "You're new to my team. You're new to the way we work and the way we operate. So, you're a newbie. Right?"

The frown set deeper into her cheeks. "I guess so, but—"

"Right, then let's all give a moment of silence to acknowledge Addie's in-field experience…." Ben lowered his head for about two seconds before clapping his hands together. "Okay, now that that's over, let's get this straight—*I'm* in charge. I don't joke around about safety out there with my team, and there certainly won't be any exception for you two. You are our *guests*, so your safety is under my care. This is a dangerous job. You have experience, Addie, but Evie doesn't. She's never been out on a tornado chase, right?"

Evie nodded, looking down at her feet. "Sorry."

"Everyone has to start somewhere," Tony offered her quietly, earning a small smile from Evie.

"Nothing to be sorry about. I'm a hard-ass because it's chaotic out there when shit hits the fan," Ben started, folding his arms across his chest as he planted his feet firmly on the ground in front of them. "The last thing we need, when every second counts, is for people to be running around like chickens with their heads cut off. Not to mention the fact that, documentary or not, this system is the first like it that we've seen in almost a decade. Every team out there is already frothing at the mouth over it, so we won't be the only ones running around."

That, they could agree on.

She'd been lucky back when she did this regularly, but she had heard the story or two of teams getting into sticky situations because of a lack of communication. Particularly between other teams when a bottleneck on the road would occur.

"Therefore," he continued when he seemed satisfied that Addie wouldn't comment, "you two are sitting out the first deployment."

"What?" Addie exclaimed, jumping up from her seat. "We can't just *sit* it out. That's what we're here for!"

As she stood, the weight almost went out from beneath Addie's feet, and she grabbed onto the counter for balance. Shit. Luckily, no one seemed to notice as she quickly righted herself—appearing more like she'd almost lost her footing than the fuzzy feeling in her head almost overtaking her. She quickly shook off the feeling and focused on the discussion.

Ben's eyes narrowed on her for a split second—a glimmer of something softer shining through before he blinked and it was gone. "I didn't say you weren't going with us, just that you are sitting it out. I'll explain our process to you both, but the best way of you getting used to things is to have a ... practice run, should I say? And we have to prep for that, so you both are aware of what's going on. I'm not just gonna throw you in and hope for the best."

"Do we need a *practice run*, though? We don't know how many tornadoes this thing is gonna churn out, so we have to use every single one we can. Both for deployment and for the documentary."

Ben glowered at her. "Look, I know you're eager to hit the ground running, but we have to calibrate our equipment, get proper readings, and make sure our predictions are accurate before we can continue. If we don't have accurate data to let us know what the system is doing, we'd just be wasting our time."

Addie rolled her eyes. "Fine, then let me go with the lead team on the chase. I won't do anything for the deployment, but at least I can acclimate to being back in the field more quickly."

"Absolutely not."

Addie balked. "Why the hell not?"

Ben placed his hands on his hips. "I need you to be in the RV. It's been a while since you worked with equipment last, so you need some practice. While we're deploying, you can get up to speed and can get practice being in the lead vehicle on the next one."

"I've used all of this before," she argued as she waved at the equipment around them for emphasis. "If you're looking for me to *practice*, then why wouldn't you want me in the field, setting up the collection equipment with you?"

Ben's eyebrows furrowed together. "Because we've had a few updates in technology since you were last out in the field."

Addie scoffed. "I've been out of the field three or four years, not a few *decades*, Ben."

"You need to learn how to use all of it again."

"And you need me to be doing that in the middle of a chase when I could be out helping? I can just practice with the equipment when we're camped out, if you think I need it so much," she said, trying to keep the frustration from seeping out in her words.

"You're not gonna be much help if you don't know how we operate, will you?" Ben said flatly. "Would you prefer being in the way and getting sucked up into a funnel? Because that can be arranged, with or without my team being involved."

Addie would have laughed if she weren't so worked up. Instead, she narrowed her eyes at him. "I'm not trying to hone in on your *territory*, Ben. You can relax your ego a bit. We're supposed to be a *team*, remember?"

"This is *my* team, Addie. What I say goes," he shot back, agitation curling at the edges of his voice. *Good.*

Addie crossed her arms over her chest. "Alright, *team lead*, would it be easier if you marked your territory? I can turn around if you need to take a piss around the perimeter?"

Ben muttered a curse under his breath and rubbed his chin. "You are just as stubborn as I remember."

"And I'm starting to remember why you pissed me off so much," she spat back.

"Do you think this is what they were like at school?" Grace asked as she leaned into Ryan's shoulder, looking between Addie and Ben.

Ryan shrugged. "Ben's like this all the time, but no one goes toe-to-toe with him like this."

"I haven't seen Addie this *spicy* before. I *love* it." Evie asked, "Do you think I'll have time to make popcorn?"

Brody cleared his throat. "Guys, not that my opinion matters, but I think Addie might *actually* have a bit of a point. Evie should be in the van with the equipment first since she knows the least about it. It'll be a good opportunity for her to get some establishing shots of the equipment before things get too crazy. And Addie can get back into the swing of things from the safety of the car, so she's out in the field ... right?"

Brody was officially Addie's new favorite team member.

"Uh, guys?" Grace said, her head focused on the screen behind them.

Ben clicked his teeth, his eyes cutting over to the group before turning back to Addie. "Fine. You can come on one condition—you sit your ass in the car the entire time. Take a step out of the car, and I will personally throw you back into it. Sound fair?"

Addie stuck her chin out. "Deal."

"*Guys*?" Grace repeated.

"What?" Addie and Ben both shouted at the same time.

Grace blinked a few times before nodding her head to the screen. "Unless you want to catch the next one, it looks like there's a possible tornado spinning up just south of us."

CHAPTER 4

Angry-looking clouds swirled violently in the sky up ahead—in the direction that the team was heading. They flew down the road at a near breakneck pace in hopes that they could get there before a funnel had the chance to descend.

The three vehicles that made up their team followed in a neat line down the narrow road. Ben's SUV led the charge at the front, Ryan and Tony followed immediately behind in a small blue sedan, and the RV camper held up the end of the line a bit further back.

Addie clutched onto the dashboard in Ben's SUV and listened to Grace shouting directions to them over the radio. She wrapped her hand firmly around the passenger handle, holding her securely in place with her eyes turned upward at the dark clouds.

A dark greenish hue overtook the sky and swallowed up the approaching wall of clouds. It wouldn't be long now for a funnel to develop. Addie noted the good conditions with an eagerness not completely unlike her first tornado.

Excitement and nerves swirled deep in her gut, knowing this was not only their first reading of the season but it would be the first time in three years she'd been alongside one of these monsters. She wondered if it would be more like trying to ride a bike again or getting thrown into shark-infested waters.

The sharks were the more likely comparison with how volatile some of the tornadoes she'd chased in her life had been.

It wasn't the nerves, though, that had her grip on the passenger handle slick with perspiration. Her life had taken a completely different trajectory than she'd imagined for herself, and while she couldn't regret the choices she'd made that put her there, she *did* miss this feeling more than words could ever fully express.

"Alright, practice run, you better explain how this process is gonna work quickly," she said, shoving the tremor of adrenaline from her voice. The last thing she needed right now was for Benjamin Borack to think that she was suffering from *any* kind of 'newbie' energy.

"Easy," Ben said without looking at her. "We're going to be deploying equipment, therefore we position ourselves ahead of it and—"

Addie rolled her eyes. "I know how to deploy equipment, Ben. I meant, who takes point? Where do the other two vehicles position themselves? Are you the only one who deploys, or does anyone come to help? How do I help you *keep* people from getting sucked up the funnel?"

Ben chuckled. "Touchy, aren't we?"

"You made a huge deal about me not knowing how you guys operate and needing to learn, so here I am trying to learn. I'm not sure what more you could ask for," she said as simply as she could muster, already feeling frustration curl in her stomach. "I'm not the one who made a big show out of being in charge and calling me a newbie."

Another chuckle. "Should've known that would've put a thorn up your ass."

She scowled but watched the clouds as they continued to darken. "I don't have a thorn up my ass."

Ben's amber eyes flashed in her direction for a beat. "You've had a thorn up your ass as long as I've known you. And you are bossy as hell," he stated matter-of-factly.

"Bossy?!"

Wind lashed at the side of the vehicle, whipping it from side to side. It nearly jostled Addie out of her seat, holding onto the dashboard as she turned back to Ben, who appeared cool as a cucumber.

This tornado was going to drop down at any second.

"Yes, bossy." He continued, "Who the hell meets a team they're just joining and starts making demands?"

"I did not ... I did not start making demands," Addie spluttered incredulously.

"You sure as shit did. You didn't like that I didn't immediately put you in the field, so you argued until you got your way."

"Until I *got my way*?" she practically shrieked back. The audacity of this man never ceased to amaze her. "I hardly call getting thrown on this documentary, literally at the last minute, and giving up several weeks of my life to be here with *you* as *getting my way*."

"Yes, but you get the pleasure of torturing me while you're here," Ben shot back, but with that shit-eating kind of grin he had when he was trying to tease her. It had been a staple of his in school. It irritated her then, and it doubly did so now.

Despite herself, she chuckled. "You know, there *are* some silver linings after all!"

"To answer your previous question, firecracker," Ben said loudly to be heard over the ever-increasing wind, "my car is the only one that can fit the equipment in it, but because I have to fold the seats down in the back to fit it, Tony and Ryan follow up behind in the other car. Usually, one of them comes with me, but because you *insisted* on being in the lead car, I'm stuck with *you*."

Absolutely unbelievable. Addie wanted to scream but squeezed the handle harder instead. "Look ... I'm not trying to be bossy or to take over or whatever else bullshit you come up with. I'm just ... I'm just trying to find my bearings a bit."

Ben grinned. "Apology accepted."

"You are fucking *impossible*, you—"

The wind howled louder, deafening in its intensity and nearly matching the scream that threatened to rip from Addie's lungs. Sirens joined the howling a second later, echoing around them from the nearby town, but all Addie could hear was the high-pitched whine that entered her ears.

Ben's eyes were focused on the road, but she could see the smirk as it appeared on his face. She was ready to throw him out of the car, and he had the audacity to look *amused*.

"Uh, guys," Grace's voice crackled through the speakers. "Do you wanna continue arguing, or do you want to deploy?"

Heat crept up Addie's neck as she slapped a hand over her mouth—she didn't realize the radio was live.

"Talk to me, Grace," Ben said, narrowly avoiding a pothole in the road.

"There are velocity couplets showing on Doppler another three miles ahead," Grace answered.

Ben glanced at his watch. "When was that reading?"

A pause before Grace's voice crackled through once more. "Five minutes ago."

On either side of the road, trees had sprouted forth to separate the plots of land. They swayed dramatically as the wind steadily began to rise in intensity. Their roots were nearly pulled from the ground in the opposite way that the SUV was traveling.

Cold realization froze the tendrils of embarrassment that had heated her face moments prior.

"Ben ... We need to go faster...."

Ben, to his credit, didn't start in on her with another barrage of sarcasm and instead glanced at her curiously. "Why? What are you seeing?"

Addie pointed to the trees just outside her window. "The roots, they're bending in the opposite direction we're going. The grass and wheat is going where we are, so I think we're just catching some of the down drafts and not the main storm."

"It's going to drop right behind us," he whispered.

Addie nodded. "If we're going to deploy, the camper needs to get the hell out of here, and we need to drop the equipment in that field over there before it hits." She pointed off to the left, toward the upcoming field.

"I think you might be right." Ben glanced up at the sky and grabbed the radio. "We need to set up in this field now. Grace, get off this heading and go—"

"We saw it on the Doppler, too," Brody cut in. "We're heading west to get out of the way."

"Good. Tony, how far behind us are you guys?"

"Quarter mile behind. I can see you guys ahead. Will we have time to set the equipment out?"

"If we hurry, we will," Ben said as he turned the car toward the field. "Grace, tell Brody to hang back. We're going to try to deploy."

"Aye aye, captain!" Grace called out on the other end. The radio clicked off as the SUV tore through the field, hitting just about every bump and rock it could find in the process. Addie clutched tighter onto the handle she was already white-knuckling, relieved that nausea wasn't finding purchase in her stomach.

Ben slammed on the brakes and threw the car into park. Addie went to undo her seatbelt, more out of habit than anything else but was surprised when he reached over to click it back into place.

"Sit your ass in the car, and tell me when it touches down!" he barked, slamming the car door shut before she could think up a response. Addie watched Ben rush to the trunk through the review view mirror, pulling and yanking equipment out as Tony and Ryan pulled up next to him.

Addie's attention returned to the sky, not having to wait long before the inevitable happened. Dust began to churn on the ground, kicking up dirt and stalks of wheat all around. A thin, delicate rope began to slowly extend down from the clouds. It danced above the field, teasing as it got lower and lower to the ground.

When the funnel planted onto the ground, a halo of dirt forming at the base, Addie slapped her hand on the dashboard. She rolled the window down, the air sucked through the opening as wind barreled into the car.

"Touch down!" she screamed, relieved when she could see Ben throwing a thumbs up in her direction as he and the other two worked.

The rest of the world blacked out around them, her vision tunneling to the vortex. All she could see was the wild will of nature as it swept across the field, a completely captive audience. A normal person would be afraid if they were in her shoes—sitting in front of the very thing most people ran away from.

But not Addie.

It was a spectacular sight of pure power and destruction.

This. This was where she really belonged.

Not in some stuffy studio set with camera lights melting swaths of makeup from her face.

Here. Where she could feel the wind caress her skin like a siren calling its lover out to sea, into the abyss. Where the force of nature could easily rob the air straight from her lungs without so much as lifting a finger. The ultimate game of chance.

Here, where she felt she could actually make a difference.

The familiar breathless sensation swept up her body as she watched it dance in the field. A twirling ballerina at the center of the ballet. Elegant. Graceful. Picturesque in the clean nature of the main vortex, like it came straight off the cover of *National Geographic*. Wisps of wind curled around the main vortex as the base began to thicken. The storm widened with each passing second as it practically sat in the middle of the adjacent field.

It practically sat…

Addie blinked away the dream-like state she'd been in.

Bushes on the far end of the field flew into the air. Ice froze in Addie's veins as she realized it hadn't grown. A commonly deceptive trick of the eye that made the storm expand and appear static in place. In actuality, its larger size only meant the storm was coming right at you. It reached the end of the field quicker than expected, which meant their time was up.

She glanced in the rearview mirror. They were much further away from the cars than she expected. Had they had issues setting up closer? Open fields like this could be an ideal spot for deployment *if* the ground was solid. Any uneven ground, any holes created by animals, any crops hidden beneath the soil, and it could cause the equipment to not be picked up correctly. Materials within the equipment could instead scatter across the ground and ruin data before it could begin to collect. She hadn't thought to watch what they were doing, so lost in the beauty of the storm that she hadn't paid attention.

They'd probably carried it further away to make sure it would hold up. Tony and Ryan had started to run back to their car, but the team lead remained, flipping switches to activate the data collection beacons. Ben wouldn't have nearly as much time to get back to the car as he thought he did.

Addie yanked her seat belt off and crawled across the console into the driver's side, instinct taking over. The car roared to life beneath her hands, the wheels spinning against the ruined crops.

She punched the car horn as she approached. Ben's attention shot to her, his expression unreadable with the wind swaying him from side to side. When she pulled up alongside him, she pointed to the tornado. "Time to go!"

Ben shielded his eyes from the wind. "I told you to—"

"I didn't get out of the car." She interrupted, waiting long enough for Ben to hop into the passenger seat and following after Tony and Ryan, who had managed to get to their own vehicle and were speeding back to the roadway.

The tornado roared behind them—a villain crying out in defeat as its prey slipped from its grasp.

Visibility became nearly impossible as dirt and dust churned up around them. Debris scattered across the road like missiles that she had to dodge. It took all of her focus to find the little dot on the horizon that was Tony's car.

"It picked our equipment up!" Grace yelled over the radio.

Ben whooped a cry, banging one hand against the dashboard as he ruffled Addie's hair with the other. Any other day and Addie would have been all over him touching her, but not now. Right now, she was going to celebrate that the deployment was successful. That she got to experience this feeling again after all these years.

"I'm gonna rip you a new asshole about that stunt you just pulled later," Ben called out. "But that can wait until we get back!"

Addie barely heard him over the adrenaline roaring in her veins.

Blood pulsing in her ears like the beat of a war drum preparing for battle.

The rush.

The excitement of the hunt, the chase.

How on earth could Addie go back after this? She'd had to rip herself away from it once before. It might kill her to have to do it again.

CHAPTER 5

It had been a long time since Addie had been camping. The last time it had been with her dad. She must've been about ... ten?

Most little girls would have balked at such an idea—having to sleep outside where there were *bugs*. But Addie and her dad were thick as thieves; what better way to have a quiet father-daughter bonding weekend than camping under the stars?

It was a lot easier distracting her with outdoor camping activities than trying to explain why her mom left without so much as a word.

The smell of burnt marshmallows tickled her nose from the memory, the nearby fire sputtering to life as Brody stoked it with a stick.

She'd certainly upgraded from that old dingy purple tent that her dad had once set up. Now she could enjoy an RV with more amenities than she knew what to do with. But with six people trampling in and out, Evie and Addie had been unceremoniously kicked out to hang out around the fire.

"Newbies get dish duty," Grace had informed them before closing the door.

All the better, honestly. It meant that she and Ben were separated for a bit.

Tensions had bubbled up after they'd wrapped up the chase. The rush of adrenaline and the high of a successful pick-up that had settled between them had almost as quickly vanished when Ben had whirled on her.

She replayed the conversation again in her head as she looked up into the twinkling night sky.

"Don't ever do that again," Ben hissed.

"Do what?"

Ben aimed a glare at her. *"You know what. You can't make decisions like that without telling me. It worked out in our favor this time—"*

"You're welcome," she snapped.

Ben clenched his eyes shut, taking a breath. *"Again, it worked out this time, but what if you'd been driving and visibility had been worse when I went looking for my car? I'd have been lost, you'd have been running around trying to search for me, Ryan and Tony would've circled back to try and collect me, and we all would've been screwed."*

She'd been right in her own way. Things could have been pretty dire if the tornado's winds had been any stronger or if it had continued creeping toward them like it had. Ben might not have made it back to the car in time, and both of them would have been in trouble.

On the other hand, he wasn't wrong either.

If she hadn't been so entranced by the storm, lost in her own little world, she would have noticed its trajectory much sooner. It was the only thing she could have done sitting there in the car—being the eyes and ears to warn them—but she hadn't paid enough attention.

Instead of honking to alert them sooner or contacting the rest of the team over the radio, she'd made a decision that could have endangered all of them. If the funnel had wrapped rain around it like a blanket, as a lot of them did, she'd have been blindly driving around in a field. Ben wouldn't have known where the vehicle had gone and could have been left out exposed.

She could've put them in a dangerous situation by changing the plan. Impulse had blinded her judgement. It worked out in their favor this time, but had circumstances been any different, they'd be mourning, not celebrating.

But she didn't think of that at the time. She got caught up in the thrill, the adrenaline.

Her first chase in years and she'd made the classic mistake of thinking that she knew best. A classic *rookie* move.

Evie came into view as she returned from the campground restroom. Her long, midnight-colored hair was almost lost to the shadows trailing behind her. Only the movement of the ponytail she'd tied it into betrayed it, swinging back and forth with each step.

Evie plopped down onto the bench next to Addie, letting out an exaggerated sigh. "What a fucking day."

Addie laughed. "What a fucking day indeed."

There hadn't been many opportunities to talk to her friend since they'd left the news station, so she was immensely appreciative of it now. After all, today had been Evie's first day chasing.

In fact, from the way their day had started to the way it ended … it *had* been a long fucking day.

"How can it be so clear?" Evie asked as she leaned back.

"Well, the system has moved northeast, so it's cleared up here," Addie replied quietly. As much as the science made sense to her, it *was* sort of an odd feeling staring up at a clear night's sky when they'd chased a tornado not a few hours prior. Stars twinkled overhead like nothing had ever happened. "Though, I do believe someone here has officially popped their chasing cherry."

"Yep, that was … that was very thrilling." Evie's usually confident smile faltered as she adjusted herself. Deceptively convincing if Addie didn't know Evie as well as she did.

"You alright?" she prodded. "I know you didn't exactly get a lot of time to think about what you'd gotten yourself into before you were thrown into the RV to chase one."

"It was a little scary at first," Evie admitted, lowering her voice, as if she were afraid the rest of the team would somehow hear, "but I have to admit, it was pretty exciting. I was at a relatively safe distance away with Grace and Brody, so *I* wasn't the one in any danger...."

"We were safe too."

"Ben didn't seem to think so."

"No, no, he didn't," Addie agreed, matching Evie's low volume. "And as much as I hate to admit it, he may be right."

Evie finally laughed, her normal smile sliding into place and replacing the fake one she'd plastered on. "I like him. I think I can honestly say that in all the time I've known you, I've *never* seen you light up the way you have today. I know I shouldn't say that, as your friend, but he seems like he genuinely cares about his team. And if he's the source that lights that spark again, I'm here for it."

It was tempting to lie, but it wouldn't work with Evie. As many late nights as they had spent hanging out in the weather room together because Addie was too consumed with work to go home and Evie too stubborn to leave her friend behind—they were familiar with each other well enough to know a blatant lie when they saw one.

And as much as it frustrated her ... Evie was right.

"Ben and I have a lot of weird history, so it's hard to forget sometimes how smart he is. I was right in a way, but he was too. I shouldn't have jumped in like that. I could've hurt someone," Addie said, ignoring the tingling in her tongue at admitting that—no matter how true it rang.

She'd have to apologize to Ben for her part, but she'd have to work up to that. Her pride needed to recover enough for something like that.

Evie nudged her. "How'd it feel being back in the field again?"

Addie chewed on her lip as she tried to think of a word for what she had felt. Exciting? Thrilling? How could she put it all into words when she wasn't sure why it felt so ... right?

"I haven't felt that alive in years," she finally relented.

An owl hooted from a nearby tree as they sat there in silence for a moment.

The taste of who she'd once been soaked her palate and soured in her stomach. The fact that she hadn't felt this alive in such a long time should have been a wake-up call long before now. Leaving her previous chase team had been the hardest decision she'd ever made, but her dad had needed her. What little time she'd gotten with him, to take care of him, had been worth it.

The campfire flickered in the distance. The occasional pops and cracks emanating from it were a comforting reminder of her earlier memories, making Addie's muscles slacken beneath her despite the conflicting emotions broiling just beneath the surface.

"I get that," Evie said finally. "I wasn't even there with you, and the adrenaline hit me like a fucking punch to the face."

Addie laughed. "Are you gonna be okay doing this for the next few weeks?"

Evie fiddled with her ponytail, trailing the raven locks through her fingers. "I think so. I'd like to get some of the longer-distance shots while I take a bit to get used to ... this...."

"That sounds more than reasonable. You didn't exactly get much of a choice on this either," Addie commented. As much as she'd been thrown into this situation, she knew Evie had it worse. Evie had a *life* outside of work. She spent a lot of time at the station with Addie, sure, but Evie had an entire social life that she got pulled from. All because she'd dared to be friends with Addie.

"Yeah, I'll be okay," Evie said clinically, her tone weighted like she was trying to convince herself more than Addie. "Besides, I've got you with me, so I'm not alone."

Addie chuckled. "You wouldn't be alone."

"You know what I mean," Evie said, nudging Addie with her elbow. "It's nice to have a friend with me."

Addie twirled a stray strand of her hair. "Well, I'm sorry being friends with me meant that you had to disrupt your life. If it hadn't been for that, they wouldn't have forced you to come."

"Hey," Evie snapped, jabbing a finger into Addie's shoulder. "Don't do that. That part isn't your fault. You and I both know this was John's doing. He *hates* me."

The sudden ferocity in Evie's tone, and in her eyes, made Addie flinch at its intensity. Evie had always been all sunshine and smiles, so to see the flash of anger was alarming. "H-he doesn't hate you—"

Evie scoffed. "Oh yes, he does. I called Frank out last month. Putting me on this with you is his way of punishing me."

Addie sat there mutely for a second. *Frank?* The name didn't confuse her—on the contrary, it contorted her face into a sneer with a wrinkle in her nose. She'd had the misfortune of bumping into Frank once or twice before, one of the longest tenured cameramen at the station. And none of those experiences had been particularly pleasant. Being John's brother-in-law certainly seemed to have its perks, otherwise the number of sexual harassment complaints that had been filed with HR would've kicked his ass out years ago.

When had Evie called Frank out? *Why* had she called him out? What had he ...

"What?!" Addie exclaimed, immediately recoiling at the volume of her voice and lowering it when she continued, "W-why didn't you tell me?!"

Evie rubbed the back of her neck. "I was embarrassed."

"What happened?"

Where the hell had she been that something like *this* had gone under the radar?

"Is it okay if I don't give the specifics?" Evie asked, more quietly than Addie had ever heard.

Addie scooted closer. "Of course, you don't have to talk about it if you don't want to."

"Anyway," Evie continued, "I got sick of him getting special treatment, so I called him out at a camera crew meeting. You can guess how John felt about that...."

Addie immediately took back every nice or understanding thought she'd ever aimed in John's direction. He was officially on her shit list. Frank had already been there, but now his name was at the very top, underlined in red.

"Evie, I'm ... I'm so sorry that I wasn't there for you."

She was officially the worst friend on the planet. After all the time she and Evie spent together, all those late night chats and gossip sessions... It had been just about the only thing that had kept her sane over the past few years.

And Evie hadn't felt comfortable enough to tell her.

Evie flicked a stray tear as it trickled from the corner of her eye. "Don't be sorry. You weren't there when we had that meeting. You're the only friend I had left there who didn't look at me differently. And it was ... It was nice. You know how most of the guys feel about Frank."

She did. Frank had a notorious reputation with the women at the station, but almost all of the guys loved him. Evie would've had a target on her back from the second she walked out of that meeting.

"So," Evie continued, "I really hate for you to think I'm *stuck* with *you*. Okay? John might think he was punishing me by banishing me from all the other projects I had lined up, but he actually gave me a huge gift. I get to hang out with one of my best friends, away from the station, for the next few months. This is gonna be a blast!"

Addie had certainly never thought being forced into this situation had been a gift, at first, but she was sure starting to warm up to the idea.

Instead, she leaned over to rest her head on Evie's shoulder. The two shared a few quiet moments together as they turned their gazes back to the dark night sky.

CHAPTER 6

"Alright, I've got one," Evie said as she leaned forward with her empty dinner plate precariously perched in her lap. "What's the *worst* chase you guys have been on? With this team or elsewhere."

It had been commented, more than once, that they hadn't had much of a chance earlier that day to get to know one another. So, a game of twenty questions had started after dinner. The team had easily settled into it, a lively and animated discussion erupting at nearly every question thrown out.

A good idea in concept, but Addie was a bit gun-shy at tossing out any questions. After what happened on the first chase—and the verbal dressing down she'd gotten—embarrassment oozed out of her in droves. So, instead, she opted to sit back and listen.

"Worst chase?" Ryan mused, leaning back on a log. "Definitely that one where the lead car got hammered with debris."

"Oh yeah, that was a bad one," Grace agreed, scrunching her face. The long blonde tresses of her hair were bundled into a haphazard bun, the sputtering fire catching a few golden highlights in the light.

"Well, would Brody telling that one tornado to *kiss his ass* count?"

Tony asked, scooting closer to Evie just enough that Addie caught his gaze and smiled. He grinned back sheepishly.

Addie's stomach rumbled, causing her to quickly clear her throat. The delicious scent of melted cheese from dinner lingered in the air, intermixed with the already prevalent aroma of fire and earth from the campfire nestled at the center of the group. But Addie had eaten the allotted amount of calories she could consume that day, meticulously noted on her phone. She'd even gone so far as to hand off the rest of her plate to Ryan to polish off the leftovers so that she wasn't tempted to eat more. All the while fighting the urge to lick her lips as she'd watched him finish it with ease.

She glanced at Ben across the campfire to distract herself, noting the change of clothes. The professional polo and long beige work pants were long gone. He instead sported a fresh black graphic tee, with some obscure band she'd never heard of, and light-blue jeans. His hair was ruffled loosely, looking more relaxed along with the rest of his ensemble. It suited him.

What the hell was wrong with her?

She hadn't dredged up the courage to apologize for her part just yet, and with the way he had avoided her most of the evening, she wasn't exactly raring for it. The last time she'd had to apologize to him was back in school after she'd thrown a book at his head during a presentation—and she'd had to grit her teeth through the experience.

He'd deserved it in that instance.

Not so much this time, but it was still *Ben*. After everything he'd put her through back in the day, she warred with herself to even apologize at all. Be the better person and admit her fault—like the more mature version of Addie that she'd become—or resort to the old version of herself that would've already thrown a plate of food at his head? Difficult choices indeed.

"No, that counts as the *funniest* one that we've chased," Brody corrected.

"But you only said that because it had changed paths," Ryan insisted. "And because *someone* had decided that morning to do some maintenance on the SUV, we had to scramble to get it out of the way."

Grace rolled her eyes, shoving a bite of food on her plate around with her fork. "You will never let me live that one down...."

"At least she didn't steal my car...." Ben quipped with a pointed gaze across the fire in Addie's direction.

Option two would be so much easier if she hadn't given Ryan her plate.

The light from the fire seemed to spark in Ben's eyes, pinning her to the spot. There was an intense, almost heated, look that he gave her that managed to prick goosebumps across her skin. Not angry, as she would have expected, but something else entirely that she couldn't quite put her finger on. One that made her fidget in her seat.

Shit, what the hell was wrong with her?

Those feelings had vacated the premises a lifetime ago.

She cleared her throat. "Okay.... I didn't *steal* your car. That's a bit dramatic."

Ben's lips quivered with effort. "We'll agree to disagree on that."

About ready to grab someone else's plate to launch at him, Evie mercifully saved her. "How, uh, how strong was the one we chased today?" she asked quickly.

"Hard to say," Brody said. "The NWC folks will have their official rating after they evaluate any damage."

Evie wrapped her arms around herself. "If you had to guess, then?"

"If I had to guess? Based on wind speeds and such, probably an EF0—maybe an EF1 at the most?"

"If the wind speeds had been higher, could it have picked you guys up?" she asked, her voice much quieter than before.

Addie changed her mind—the look on Evie's face was way worse than whatever tension there was in the air with Ben. The smile plastered to her olive-kissed face was as fake as she'd ever seen, and despite their previous conversation, it pained Addie to see her worry.

Ryan shrugged. "Potentially."

Ben scrunched his nose, his glasses scooting up the bridge of it. "Near misses like that happen all the time, regardless of circumstances. It's why I'm such a stickler for that kind of thing, even if it means not collecting data for the day. Both of you will be safe with us, I promise."

The smile on Evie's face turned real as the arms she'd wrapped around herself loosened. Addie didn't look in his direction, but she was grateful. He could be mad and ignore her all he wanted, so long as he continued treating her friend kindly.

"Alright," Grace exclaimed, turning to face Evie. "My turn to ask a question! How long have you been behind the camera?"

"Probably…" Evie pursed her lips as she looked up into the air. "I don't know, maybe ten years? I went to Wichita State University for my bachelor's in film production and managed to snag this job right after I graduated."

"Oh, a fellow WSU alumni!" Grace exclaimed, offering a high five.

"What about you, Addie?" Tony asked. "We know you went to grad school with Ben, but what about for your undergrad?"

"University of Kansas. Got a bachelor's in atmospheric sciences," she replied.

Brody leaned back and nodded at her. "What sent you all the way to Columbia University, then?"

She lifted a shoulder. "Always wanted to go. My dad thought it was the coolest thing in the world for his only daughter to get into an Ivy League."

Brody nudged Ben. "That's so funny. Ben's told me that his dad was the same way when he—"

"We get it," Ben interrupted. "We all know she and I went to grad school together. Next question please."

Grace raised an eyebrow in his direction, but he didn't meet her gaze.

"Alright, my turn," Addie said, attempting to keep the question game going. "Where do you send your data?"

"We partner with the National Weather Center," Ryan explained. "We collect data for them, and they use it for some of the initiatives we're working on to help build more advanced warning systems."

"Any initiative in particular that you guys are working to support?" she asked.

"Yeah, we're helping to—" Brody started before Ben clapped him on the back.

"Alright, I think it's time for newbies to pony up," Ben said as he stood. "Dish time."

Interesting. Yet another layer to the onion.

CHAPTER 7

*A*ddie groaned in frustration. It had gotten so easy to fall asleep in her little studio apartment. The cacophony of sounds that reverberated through the walls of it had started to feel like a lullaby. The lack of trains rattling down their tracks, the low hum of car engines, and police sirens whirring by now felt unnerving. An inescapable quiet void that threatened to swallow her alive.

She'd managed to catch a few minutes of sleep earlier, but the nightmare had been there to embrace her. The dredges of dark and murky water pulling her under, powerless to stop it. Her father's face in the distance, smiling sorrowfully at her as she sank beneath the surface. She hadn't woken up screaming as she normally did—thankfully, since there were two other people sleeping peacefully nearby—but since then, she'd merely stared up at the ceiling.

Despite the more-than-reasonably-comfortable accommodations, Addie had spent most of that time tossing and turning, too afraid to fall back asleep but too tired not to try.

Finally, she gave up the ruse and threw the blanket off.

Light snores echoed around her as she tried her best to stay quiet. The last thing she needed was to wake them up. She tiptoed around Evie, whose sleeping bag was situated between Addie and the door, pausing only once when Evie let out a light sleep-filled snort and turned over on her side.

The cool night air was exactly what her sweat-soaked skin begged for, both jarring from the warmth radiating off of her and comforting. She adjusted the old, dingy gray sweatshirt that she wore to let more air flow across her skin.

A shadow loomed ahead, only illuminated by the light of the campfire as it danced around their silhouette. It was hard to tell at this distance, and with the shadows lurking around them, but she was pretty sure she knew who it was. She paused, wondering if she should retreat back to the comfort of the camper.

Would he talk to her, or would he continue to pretend she didn't exist?

The old version of herself would stomp over and demand his attention. Inform him that he was going to accept her apology whether he liked it or not. But this version of her? This version hesitated—knowing she *should* be the bigger person but fearful that she would say the wrong thing and make it worse.

Well, if she wanted privacy to talk, what better time than now?

A twig cracked beneath her feet. Ben whirled in his seat, his eyes wide for a millisecond before he relaxed. "What are you doing up?"

Addie grimaced, lowering herself into the adjacent chair. "I couldn't sleep."

Ben hummed low. "Not too surprising, I guess. It's been a day."

"You could say that. I hope you don't mind too much if I join you for a bit?"

"Yeah, that's fine," Ben said, turning back to face the fire. Tension settled between them once more, thick enough that Addie wasn't sure she'd be able to cut it with a knife. A chainsaw, maybe.

She glanced in his direction, angling herself so it wasn't so obvious that she was watching him. In the dim firelight, Addie could make out some of his features. The laugh wrinkles that creased the corners of his eyes. The sharp edge of his jawline, only further highlighted in this lighting. The fullness of his lips…

Why did he have to be so damned handsome? She hated that he'd only gotten *more* handsome in their time apart. There had once been a time when she'd studied each and every feature of his. The sting of longing never truly died—despite the hurt that lingered. It frustrated her that after all these years, that sense of longing tingled at the edges of her nerve endings—threatening to resurface if she wasn't careful. But she'd learned her lesson there.

Addie adjusted herself in her seat, trying to distract herself for a moment to think—and not about *that*.

If they were going to survive the next few months together, she had to clear the air. The last thing either of them needed was to continue snapping at one another's throats. Addie's sanity wouldn't last otherwise.

"I'm sorry, Ben," she finally relented, her voice barely above a whisper as courage vanished.

Ben turned. "What?"

She sighed, turning her attention back to the fire before them. "You were right. I shouldn't have made a call like that out there, especially on my first day back in the field. So, I'm sorry."

Ben opened and closed his mouth a couple of times before leaning in while cupping his ear. "Can you repeat that?"

Of course he'd milk this.

"Oh, you asshole, you heard me plenty fine!" she snapped.

"No, I think," Ben started before dramatically shaking his ear and leaned closer. "I think I had something in my ear. What did you say?"

The one benefit from her time at the station? Patience prevented her from completely launching herself at him and tackling him to the ground. Grad school Addie wouldn't have given it so much as a second thought.

"I'm *sorry*," she huffed in his direction. "Need me to record it for you, so you can use it as your ringtone?"

Humor lit up Ben's eyes when he lowered his hand. "Just wanted to make sure I wasn't dreaming. I didn't think I'd *ever* hear those words leave your mouth."

"I can just go back to the RV if you're gonna—"

Ben held a hand up as he chuckled. "I'm teasing. I do appreciate it, though I feel like I should issue an apology of my own."

Addie scrunched her eyebrows together. "For what?"

"I shouldn't have yelled at you. Your heart was in the right place," he said. "It wasn't very *team lead* of me."

"You've always been an ass, so it didn't surprise me. But I don't blame you for it either, honestly. If our roles were reversed, I'd be upset too."

His smile widened, tucking into the subtle dimples into his cheeks. "Look at us, acting like adults."

Adults indeed. Considering she'd already had to restrain the urge to strangle him on several occasions, she wasn't sure if that fit.

"I know." She chuckled. "We might make it through this yet."

Ben winced. "I certainly hope so. I hope there's no bloodshed."

Addie held her hands up. "I promise I'll keep my claws retracted."

"And your mouth, too, please."

"That was *one* time!"

Ben laughed. "Twice, but who's counting?"

"I warned you. You shouldn't have stuck your fingers in my face," she mumbled, mostly to herself.

Turning further, Ben held out his hand. "A truce, then? As much as we can have one?"

The words rang through her entire body like a warning bell. Memories from years past, as fresh as if it had been yesterday. The looks and stares she'd gotten as she'd been marched to the Dean's office. The accusation. The confusion. The betrayal. The *anger*.

"Nice try," she practically spat. "The last time we tried that, I got called into the Dean's office."

A pained expression flashed in his eyes as his breath hitched. "Addie…"

Addie shook her head and shifted in her seat. "Just … forget it. We're fine for now."

"It was a mistake. Will you really never believe me?" he asked, a slight tremble in his voice.

A *mistake*?

"So, you admit that accusing me of plagiarizing your friend's paper was a mistake? Mighty big of you after all these years," she snapped.

"It was a *mistake*," Ben stated, "to believe that *you* were the one who had plagiarized anything. I trusted the wrong person."

She scoffed. "Yeah, no shit, you trusted the wrong person. Glad we can agree on that."

"I tried to tell you right after, but you wouldn't listen to me."

She tried not to let the years worth of anger come out through her voice, though a bit of it did arise. "You almost ruined my *life*, Ben. I would have been expelled, lost my scholarship, and would have been essentially blacklisted from applying to any other program with something like that on my record! All so you could be top of the class? Why the hell would I have listened to you?"

"I know…. I was stupid and immature, and he was one of my *only* friends at the time. The professor had already confronted him about it, and he said he needed my help proving he was innocent. What reason did I have not to believe him, to trust that he was telling me the truth?"

"You hated me enough not to care." She wrapped her arms around herself, trying to shield herself from the emotions slamming into her.

Ben reached out like he was trying to take her hand but stopped himself. His hand balled into a fist as he placed it in his lap instead. "Addie, I've *never* hated you. Never, not once. Annoyed and frustrated like fuck? Sure. Competitive with you, of course. But *never* that."

"He told me it was your idea after the meeting!"

Ben reeled back like she'd slapped him, shock interwoven in the furrow of his brow. "What?"

"Afterward, before he was escorted off campus, he told me that the whole thing was your idea…." she said, the words coming out more unsure than she'd ever felt as she saw the expression on his face. He looked outright horrified, and as much as she wanted to believe he was acting, she could tell he wasn't.

Addie's stomach coiled, feeling conflicted. She'd always thought he'd tricked her—to agree to put their silly little back and forth to a truce—only for that to happen the very next day. It had seemed too much of a coincidence. She'd hated him for so long after, outright convincing herself over time that he must've conspired with his friend over the whole affair.

"We'd only just agreed to a truce the day before...." she added, a sob lodging itself in her throat, but she refused to let it free.

Ben's hands balled into fists in his lap, his knuckles turning white from the pressure. "I'll promise on whoever's grave you want me to that I had *no* part in trying to set you up."

"How could I have believed that? You knew how *hard* I worked, and you knew how much he was barely skating by."

"I know."

"You believed him over me. I thought we might be friends, that we had turned over a new leaf, and you betrayed me," she spat, the past and present emotions swirling together until she felt like that same grad student. The one trying to prove to the world that she could do whatever she set her mind to. All almost completely flushed down the toilet because of a *mistake*.

"I wanted to keep the one friend I thought I had, and he was very convincing," he said slowly, finally unclenching a hand to rub the back of his neck. "He said he needed my help to back him up—like who would believe that one of the smartest girls in the class would steal from him?"

He'd chased her down for weeks trying to explain … but she wouldn't hear a word of it. She'd been too hurt. Too angry. He eventually gave up, and their rivalry had only worsened until the day they graduated. Then she left without a word, trying to forget him.

But she never really forgot, did she?

"I don't—I don't know what to say to that," she stammered.

"You don't have to accept my apology. I know that might take a while," he continued. "But if we're issuing apologies, I wanted you to know that I'm sorry for accusing you like I did, and I *promise* I had no part in it. You didn't deserve that. I realized too late what an awful mistake I'd made. You believe me when I tell you I'm genuinely sorry, true or false?"

Confusion struck through Addie as she blinked, only for the memory that statement brought on to slam into her. A technique they'd been forced to do in school, as suggested to them by one of their professors when their arguments had become too disruptive. When tensions grew high, they had to ask a simple question, followed by true or false. The other had to answer honestly and calmly, then follow up with evidence to support their response. It was supposed to make things more pragmatic and professional, scientific.

It kept the two civil enough to not kill one another.

"Are you really using that on me right now?" she asked.

Finally, he smiled—enough to light up the amber twinkle in his eyes. "If it worked back then, it should continue working now. So, true or false?"

She heaved a sigh. "Fine, true. You have provided adequate information to disprove that you had any malicious intent. Can I sit on it before I issue any truces? I'd like to digest this."

Ben visibly relaxed. "Of course."

The two turned back to the fire in silence. Addie had whiplash from their conversation and wasn't sure what to think. She'd gone in ready to apologize for the chase and had come out on the other end with an apology for something that had haunted her for years.

Life was funny that way.

"So... How long have you known Evie for?" Ben asked suddenly, dragging her back from her thoughts.

Addie raised an eyebrow. "You don't do silence much, do you?"

He flashed her a lopsided grin, showing off that dimple that always softened his face. "Guilty, sorry. I can stop if you'd prefer some peace and quiet."

"No, no, it's fine," she assured. "I've known her for a few years. We met a little while after I started working at the station."

"She's nice," Ben said. "I like that she's confident and sure of herself. Her experience in the field is lacking, but I think she'll be a quick study."

Addie smiled. Evie would *love* a compliment like that. "She is. She's incredibly smart, especially with people. What about your team? How long have you known them?"

"Varies. I met Brody first. We interned at the same meteorologic center, not long after we graduated. Grace and Ryan both came highly recommended by an old colleague of mine, so I brought them on when Brody and I decided to start chasing. Tony was on a different team for a while before he decided to join us."

"Does Brody prefer staying in the camper during chases?"

At that, Ben laughed more heartily. "Brody? Nah, not at all. He's just better at the equipment and readings than I am, so it makes more sense for him to hang back with Grace."

"Grace is the one who modified the camper, right?"

"Yeah, she's really good at that kind of thing. She's good at the mechanical side, so she sticks close in case it needs repairs."

"I like them so far," she said, darting a glance to see the warmth in his smile before quickly looking back.

There were times she missed the bond of a chase team like this had. They'd stayed connected for a while after she'd left, promising to keep in touch. But time and busy work schedules had lessened the phone calls and texts until they finally stopped altogether.

Whereas here, with this team, the dynamic felt different.

From what little she'd seen so far, she liked how close they were. Like one big family that didn't have any problem calling each other out when needed but watched out for one another at the same time. And they'd already made her laugh, *genuinely* laugh, more times that she could count already.

She looked forward to getting to know all of them more over the next few months.

"They're a good crew. By the time you and Evie pack up to head back at the end of all of this, you'll all be thick as thieves I'm sure."

"That'd be nice...." she mused, offering Ben a smile.

Ben narrowed his eyes momentarily before clicking his teeth. "You know ... Those green ones don't do you justice."

Addie blanched. "E-excuse me?"

"Do you wear colored contacts on set?"

"What the hell are—"

"Your eyes," Ben said as he pointed to his own eyes. "Your eyes are usually green when you're on TV."

"You've ... You've watched me on TV?"

"Of course. I had to do some re-con when I found out about this contract. I watched Sally to see how she operated, but I happened to catch a few of your reports. You're a natural in front of the camera."

She wasn't sure if it was supposed to be a compliment or an insult. Given how they had started this whole adventure, it could fall either way.

"Though, that pair of green contacts you wear always throws me off," he continued. "Makes you look ... I don't know, just off."

Definitely not a compliment, then.

"Great start to a truce," she grumbled. "What's wrong with the green pair?"

"They're just too light. They don't fit you."

Addie scoffed. "Not possible, have you *seen* my eyes? They're so dark they're almost black."

"I *have* seen them. They're unique," Ben said, a surprisingly gentle quality to his tone. "They're like this deep onyx color that I haven't seen before—like dark clouds in the sky just before a tornado touches down. I don't think I've seen many people with eyes quite like yours."

No one had ever described her eyes like that before, or in such detail. She tucked a loose piece of hair behind her ear. She shuffled her feet, looking down at them. "Some of the viewers, back when I first started, said that they're too spooky. Management forced me to wear them."

Ben frowned. "That's stupid."

Addie laughed for the first time that night. She'd thought the same thing when the producers had come to her about it, but she'd really needed her job. And ... she hadn't really looked at them the same since people started commenting. A feature that she'd always thought made her stand out, now only made her feel that much more self-conscious.

"What made you stop chasing?" Ben asked.

Addie blinked slowly at him. "Jesus, talk about a fucking whiplash, Ben."

"Figured I'd take advantage of the moment." He shrugged. "But what made you stop? You just ... I don't know, you just seemed really in your element. You were practically glowing."

Addie kicked up a bit of dirt. "I just ... I had to—"

A loud snore broke through, causing Addie to stop mid-sentence. She and Ben both looked over at the camper, quiet for another moment before another loud snore vibrated through the silence.

Humor bit into his voice. "That's Tony, most likely. Snores louder than my old college roommate ever did."

Addie chuckled, but she was glad for the interruption. She wasn't anywhere near ready to unpack all of *that* right now. She patted her legs with a finality of the conversation before grinning. "That's my cue to head back to bed. We have a long day tomorrow."

"Goodnight, Addie."

"Goodnight, Ben."

*A*ddie stumbled out into the early morning light, holding her hand up to shield her eyes from the assault of the sun. She hadn't managed to get much sleep after all.

Her second attempt had been for entirely different reasons than the brutal day.

Time faded a lot of the hurt and betrayal, but the flicker of it had roared to life last night. Back then, Ben had just been annoying. Constantly competing with her to be the best. Now, knowing that the only reason that she hated him for so long afterward had been a genuine misunderstanding? One that, despite the fact that she was on the receiving end, she could understand. Addie had more friends back then than she did now, so if one of her friends had accused Ben of something similar, she knew that she wouldn't have hesitated to do the exact same.

Still ... could this be just another ruse, like it had been back then? A pretty lie to lull her into another sense of false security before ripping the rug from beneath her? She wasn't sure what his motive would be now, other than placating her into an easy partnership. No. She was going to keep her guard up for the time being. Then she could protect herself from getting hurt. She wouldn't be unprepared this time.

It was the tantalizing smell of coffee, however, that ultimately forced her out of bed. The earthy smell felt like a siren's call, luring her out into the brisk morning air.

The campfire where she and Ben had their chat hours before had died down considerably, but Brody was stoking it.

"Good morning," she croaked, her voice rough.

Brody turned, giving her just as bright a smile as he did yesterday. "Well, good mornin', sleepy head. Sleep alright?"

She shuffled forward in search of the delicious smell. "Not really, but I haven't gotten much sleep lately, so I'm pretty sure my body doesn't know how to handle getting real sleep."

He laughed and grabbed a kettle from the campfire. The mesh baseball cap he had, different from the day before, was turned backward. Beneath it, a tangle of dark-black hair curled up from beneath. The same kind of haircut that Ben used to have when they were in school together, wild and untamed.

"Coffee?"

"Yes, please," she practically moaned, accepting the cup.

The cup warmed her chilled fingertips as she took the first generous sip. The sharp, bitter taste of it was entirely blissful compared to the shitty station coffee she'd been forced to grow accustomed to, and a contented sigh whisked out of her.

She hadn't realized how terrible it was until she was faced with *good* coffee.

"I take it I'm the first one up?" she asked.

Brody rocked on his heels. "Aside from me, you are. Won't be long before the others get up. We'll want to head northeast to see if the tail end of that storm from yesterday spits anything out for us."

She nursed the warm cup in her hands. "I hope I can be taken off the naughty list for this one."

Brody chuckled. "I don't know. You'll have to talk to numero uno for that one. He's a particular pain-in-the-ass about that kinda stuff, but I think you already know that."

The deep, chocolatey color of his eyes looked over the rim of his coffee mug at her in a way that initially read as playful, but Addie could tell that it could just as easily become deadly should the occasion call for it. Like a rattlesnake coiled and ready to strike the first person that fucked with one of his.

It was unmistakable because she *knew* that look. This team was his family, that much was obvious. But it was that protective glint in his eyes that she recognized.

Her dad had been infamous for them when he'd been alive.

She never thought a look like *that* would make her miss him more … but it did.

Addie grimaced as she rubbed her chest where it ached. "I talked to Ben last night, but I wanted to apologize for how I acted yesterday. I was entirely unprofessional."

Brody's expression softened, the playful and carefree edge to it returning. "Nah, you ain't gotta apologize to me—though I do appreciate a girl who can admit when she's wrong."

She'd been sure of it when she met him, but she liked him. He had this energy about him that made it easy to talk to him, like they'd already been friends before they'd met.

Addie turned to face the sunrise as it began to trickle over the horizon. How long had it been since she had last been able to stand out in the early morning sun just to watch it rise? And not because she was trying to get weather readings. The pinks and oranges stretched out across the sky as the last tendrils of night released them from the clouds dotting the horizon.

It was quiet. Peaceful.

A stark contrast to her life at the station, and for the first time in what felt like ages, Addie felt like she could take her first *real* breath.

"Just don't kill him. For me?" Brody said next to her. "I kinda need him around."

She raised her mug up. "I promise I'll do my best."

"If the people out there talking don't shut up and give me a coffee pronto," a male voice boomed from the nearby tent, followed by another two male-sounding groans. "I'm gonna start *screaming*."

Brody rubbed the back of his neck, an exasperated breath hissing from him. "Then again, if you want to start picking off some of the *other* ones, I can't say I'll protest too much."

Addie hid a giggle behind her coffee cup as the door to the camper slammed open. The suddenness of it almost caused her piping-hot coffee to slosh dangerously over the edge, so she danced around the motion of the liquid as Grace nearly tripped out of the camper, tugging on a pair of boots.

"Get up!" she called out loudly. "Everybody get up! We might have something!"

CHAPTER 8

*I*t had taken a few hours to get there in time, but it was worth the wait.

The storm was initially rain-wrapped when they first arrived on the scene, not atypical of large cells like the one they'd seen on radar. Now, as they got closer, the rain dispersed enough to reveal the cone within it. Narrow at the base, the funnel got wider and wider the more it reached up to the heavens—creating its namesake of a giant gray cone that practically glided across the open plains.

It was stunning to look at.

"What a beauty...." Ben whispered with awe.

"You can say that again," she agreed. "Look at how well defined it is...."

Addie replayed the plan in her head again—the one that they'd discussed on their way there. No data collection this time. Grace hadn't finished calibrating the new deployment equipment they'd had to run to pick up that morning, so this was purely for the documentary. Evie would film the best she could for some traveling establishment shots, as well as some interview shots with Grace and Brody while she had them, and the rest of the team would be tracking to make sure they were outside the damage path.

She should have gone with Evie and Grace to work on filming, but she hadn't been able to help herself. Without a second thought, she'd jumped into the passenger seat of Ben's SUV.

And unlike last time, he hadn't protested.

Hooray for progress.

Though, here she was, back out doing what she loved, with the guy she wasn't sure she was ready to forgive yet. And worse, why Ben Borack was suddenly distracting to look at was not something she wanted to figure out. But he was.

Maybe it was the scent of pine and citrus that filled the vehicle and wrapped around Addie's throat with a vice-like grip. Did he know that was her favorite scent? The scent itself wasn't overpowering—at least not in that '*Hey, buddy, lay off the aftershave*' sort of way. When the hell had that smell become so intoxicating? If anything about him remained the same over the years, it was his smell. Comforting and alluring all at once in a way that made her want to curl into it.

Or it could be …

Fuck, she was doing it again. Talk about complicated.

"How wide do you think that base is?" Ben asked.

Addie tried to calculate until she came up with a better idea. "Hold on. I need to get a better look."

The camera that Evie had was a hell of a lot better than her cellphone's camera, but getting some action shots from a different vantage point might be a nice touch. Addie pulled her phone from her pocket and rolled the window down. She zoomed in as closely to the base as she could, struggling to keep her phone in her hand from the sheer force of the wind rocking the vehicle from side to side.

"Maybe a few hundred yards?" she shouted out, the howling of the wind nearly drowning her out.

What a force of nature.

It was a murky, ruddy color but neat. The edges of it were straight as a pin as it extended up into the sky. Rain-wrapped tornadoes were notoriously harder to track visually because of the cloud coverage, so she could only tell it was moving because of the shades of color as it swirled—kicking up soil and dirt as it went. It wasn't nearly as whimsical in its movements as the rope tornado they'd seen the day before—instead more like that of a lumbering giant.

An angry giant at that. And dangerous.

A rush of wind suddenly lashed at her as three large SUVs whipped past them, nearly taking out the passenger-side mirror in the process. She shrieked and yanked her arm back into the car.

Ben cursed and attempted to keep the vehicle steady. The back tires kicked up dirt as he struggled to stay on the already narrow dirt road, the wind immediately sucking it into the funnel cloud in the distance.

"What the hell?!" She flexed her hand in her lap, rubbing it with the other to make sure all fingers were still attached. No injuries that she could see, but she felt the tingle of a close call. Luckily, her phone hadn't been knocked out of her hand, but it had come dangerously close to it.

"Are you okay?" Ben asked, his fingers flexing on her elbow, where they rested. When the hell had he grabbed onto her? His eyes were wild, flitting back and forth from the road to her.

She nodded after a moment. "Yeah, I'm okay...."

From her experience, there were two types of storm chasing groups.

There were the scientific groups, who typically had the hard-equipped machinery for data collection and deployments. They were easy enough to spot, including her own team, with the organized and practically militaristic progression of vehicles.

Then there were the ones who did this for fun. The ones who respected the power of nature and considered themselves lucky enough to witness it. No less informed than the former, they typically lacked the numbers that formal chasing teams did. More lone-wolf types on the road that were relatively easy to spot given the telltale sign most other cars raced in the opposite direction.

Then there was the secret *third* category. The adrenaline junkies. The super-small minority who had something to gain out of the experience. Whether it be popularity and fame, money, or sponsorships, the motives were always the same.

When Addie spotted the vehicle that almost took her arm off, two sets of fists pumping in the air out of the window—Addie had her answer as to which group this was.

"Fucking idiots," she whispered. "Friends of yours?"

Ben sneered. "Not in the fucking slightest. Looks like *Billy* and his team happened to be in the area and, as usual, decided to swoop in."

"Billy?" she asked.

"Yeah, Bill Witeman," Ben snorted. Something about the name flared recognition, though she couldn't quite put her finger on what exactly.

"Where have I heard that name before?" she asked.

"He runs that YouTube channel about him and his team chasing. Storm something or other."

She blinked. "Storm Stalkers?"

"Yeah, I think that's it. Heard of them?"

If he meant that she'd come across a few of their videos and showed them to Evie and Sally as examples of how *not* to chase a tornado, then yes, she'd heard of them.

Addie scoffed. "Who hasn't? They have … quite the reputation, though it seems to precede them. Doesn't he know basic chasing etiquette?"

When she looked over, Ben was smiling—that wide, amused kind that was frustratingly handsome. "Glad they've already left such a great impression on you."

Lightning flashed in the distance, and Addie counted in her head until she heard the crack of thunder. One. Two. *Boom.*

It wasn't the most reliable indicator of how far they were from the main storm, but it was close enough for her to know that those chasers were *way* too close. The funnel was neat right now, but that could change at a moment's notice. From where she could see, they were on a road so close to the funnel that the dirt kicked up by their vehicles was almost immediately sucked in.

"Are they nuts?!" Ryan squawked over the radio.

"You have *met* Billy before, right?" Brody scoffed.

Addie folded her arms. "I can't stand those adrenaline-junky types.

They make things dangerous for everyone else. And for what? So they can get a *cool shot*?"

Ben chuckled. "It's a complicated relationship. They're who we were up against for the documentary contract. He probably thinks his team deserved it more, so he's being more of a dick than usual."

Addie cringed. Getting stuck with some ego-maniac like the one she'd seen in those videos? No, thanks.

Ben let out a hearty laugh. "See? You could've had it worse than me and my team."

"It was never *your team* that I was worried about."

"Hey," Ben scolded lightly. "I thought we called a truce?"

She turned to hide a smile. "I didn't one hundred percent agree to that yet, if you recall. You're still on probation. And it doesn't mean I can't still give you shit every now and then. I'm adding that as a clause."

Smug satisfaction glowed within her when she noted that Ben's grin widened, but her stomach fluttered as it did, which annoyed her all over again. She really needed to get it together.

"Can we get some talking shots, Addie?" Evie's voice boomed from the radio, and—even over the roar of the wind around them—Addie winced. "Sorry, was that too loud?"

Only if hearing was required.

"No, that's a good idea," Ryan called out. "There's a small town near the path of this, so Tony and I can go check to see if anyone needs anything and will report back."

"Sounds good. Just be safe, guys. Let us know if there's anyone there who needs anything. Otherwise, we'll plan to set up in the field for Evie and Addie to get their shots," Ben said.

CHAPTER 9

"Alright, we don't want to be here too long in case it turns," Ben instructed as Evie began to set up her camera. "You're gonna want to make this short, sweet, and to the point."

Addie was only vaguely listening to him.

Brody and Grace helped Evie set up the camera. It took both of them just to keep it steady where it stood perched in the field. Where they were now, several miles ahead of the storm, the wind was still strong enough to make filming difficult.

Addie secretly crossed her fingers behind her back, hoping that it was difficult *enough* that she wouldn't have to be on camera for long, if at all. There was no script for these segments, but she didn't need one. She already had an idea of what she wanted to say, what she wanted to point out, all while making it short and sweet. As much as she hated being on camera, figuring out what to say had never been a problem.

The *problem* was the storm approaching.

In this part of Oklahoma, people were few and far in between. Most towns had a population that barely reached double digits. It was mostly open fields of varying crops spreading out across the horizon.

That said, the well-defined cone quickly morphed into a large, messy monstrosity. It was as deadly as it was beautiful.

"Almost ready!" Evie called out, bringing her back to reality.

Addie never imagined herself being the one in front of a camera like this—always more comfortable behind the scenes. Doing deployment drops in the field. Driving the RV at the back of the pack to keep a lookout. She'd even put some of the skills her dad had taught her growing up to good use with any electrical and plumbing issues. Anywhere and everywhere she was needed, she slotted herself as seamlessly as she could.

But this? This had been *well* outside of her comfort zone. If she hadn't had to return home to help her dad, she wouldn't have considered it.

She hadn't expected the influx of commentary on her body and appearance that often flooded the station's inbox. Notoriously scathing, mostly for any woman who dared to be on camera, Addie hadn't yet learned the golden *'Don't read the comments'* rule until after she'd spent more than one occasion crying in the bathroom.

But ... a job was a job—or that's what she rationalized when she'd accepted it.

That and she desperately needed a steady paycheck when the debt collectors started calling.

This was different from being on live TV, where a perfect appearance was standard, *expected*. Now she was actively chasing tornadoes with a crew. There wasn't time for makeup, a fancy hairdo, or camera-ready wardrobes.

Her hair tangled around her when the wind shifted, forcing her to pull her long, brunette locks up. She picked and pulled at a few strands until she thought it would look halfway decent.

She'd managed to slide the colored contacts into place, but she also had to be prepared to chase at a moment's notice. Her current appearance would be much rougher on camera than it would under the hot studio lights.

That also meant that every little blemish, every speck of dirt and grime, would be visible for all to see. Would the angle and lighting flatter her figure this time, or would it betray her? Or would it showcase some *other* part that she'd need to shave calories off for? It had only been a few days, but the slightest fluctuation of her weight could be seen. Or so she was told. Management was a stickler for appearances.

A familiar pang rang through her gut, cramping uncomfortably as it clenched on nothing. It wasn't unfamiliar, just inconvenient at this point as she didn't have a protein bar to shove down to satiate the ache. The little voice that had grown over the past few years whispered past comments into her ear. *Cow. Pig.*

Where had that ringing sound come from?

Addie's heart pounded in her chest. The lens pointed in her direction felt more like a microscope, aimed to point out her every flaw, every imperfection.

"Addie," Ben repeated forcefully, ripping her from her thoughts.

Shit. This was the last thing she needed to be doing at the moment. Film this segment, get it over with, and get out. Then she could fret over the rest.

"Sorry—was just thinking about what to say," she lied. "What's up?"

Ben frowned, his eyes lingering on her. "Not exactly a great time to daydream there, huh, firecracker?"

It was Addie's turn to frown. She wasn't sure how she felt about the nickname but didn't have time to comment as Evie waved over Ben's shoulder. "We're just about ready!"

"Yeah, yeah," Addie assured him as she pushed him out of frame. "Short and sweet, I got it."

She primped herself a bit as she stepped toward the spot Evie had pointed her to earlier. A few deep breaths as Evie started to count down with her fingers and she was able to shove the feeling to the side for the time being.

The words were already ready to tumble out of her in excitement, so she quickly plastered her signature smile on and began. "As some of you may already be aware, we have been following this supercell for a while," Addie said as clearly as she could, though the wind was making it difficult.

"If you look there," Addie continued as she pointed to the base of the funnel behind them, "you can see the rotation at the base. We can see clear evidence of strong inflow winds feeding directly into the vortex, meaning that it is likely to continue to grow in intensity."

She stepped to the side, changing the angle of the shot to allow Evie a wider view of the storm. As she did, the wind knocking the group about kicked harder against her, nearly taking her off her feet. "We are trying to keep a safe distance, but as you can tell, the wind is pretty intense."

In her periphery, Ben hovered just off camera. His arms were folded, but he swayed back and forth on his feet as if he were ready to pounce at a moment's notice. She wasn't sure whether that made her feel better.

The nearly-neat column had long grown messy, wisps of wind extending from the main vortex like tendrils reaching out to latch onto whatever was in its path and hurl it aside.

"Addie!"

Addie had about a millisecond before she was knocked to the ground. The sudden force of it knocked the air from her lungs, unsure which way was up. Gravity took over, slamming her onto her back with a definite thud that she felt down in her bones. Her stomach lurched as she lost all sense of direction.

The wind howled—loud enough that she could barely hear anything aside from the beast tearing through the plains. Oxygen returned in a ragged cough that shook her lungs. A scream ripped from her—but that was sucked away too.

Had she been tackled? Addie turned her head, pain throbbing from the back as grass tickled her cheek. She tried to look, to see what was happening, but couldn't. Her eyes physically wouldn't open as a gritty texture glued them shut. Tears pooled behind her eyelids, and panic seized her. What the hell was in her eyes? Was it dirt? Debris? Glass?

The insatiable urge to rub at them gnawed at her. If her arms weren't pinned at her sides, she would. A new panic seized her at that realization—something hit her. Was she trapped? Was that why she couldn't move her arms? Where had the rest of the team gone? Where had—

"Stay down," a familiar voice yelled above her, the sound almost completely drowned out by the wind. "Debris!"

Ben?

Tears and dirt blinded her, but she felt him now. The heat of his skin. The tickle of his hair against her neck. The strain in his arms as he hovered over her.

"I think we're clear now!" Brody called out from nearby when the wind finally managed to calm.

Addie managed to wrangle her arms free and rubbed at her eyes, feeling the last of the grit trickling down her cheeks with her tears. It was blurry, but her sight started to clear enough to see Ben's face over hers.

His eyebrows were drawn together in unmistakable concern. As if he were afraid that if he looked away, she'd disappear with the wind. He was panting, his rough breath wafting against her skin like butterfly kisses—as if the effect took every ounce of his strength to keep them both on the ground.

She rubbed her eyes again, her vision clearing with each blink as she wiggled her fingers, then her toes. Still functional. Words were a commodity as Addie's throat clenched with a new set of tears that trickled down her cheeks.

They were okay.

What the hell happened?

That's when she spotted it. A large, mangled, piece of tractor lodged into the earth—right where she'd been standing moments before. The telltale bright-green paint on the structural beam, her only indicator as to what it had once been—now distorted and smudged with muck.

Her focus shifted back to Ben, still straddling her on trembling arms. Rooted in place, as if he were afraid they'd be swept away. The cramped space between them felt suffocating, and she was dying to shove him off. Her mouth opened to bark out an order, but the words died somewhere in her throat. There was something in his eyes that gave her pause. Genuine fear, concern even.

He'd *never* looked at her like that before.

"Oh my God, is everyone okay?!" Evie shouted somewhere nearby.

Ben finally appeared to come to his senses and flinched, like hearing the others woke him up. "You alright?"

Addie simply nodded, unsure of what else to say. She still had no idea what happened, though she was starting to get a better picture when Ben pulled back to stand and offered her a hand.

"What the hell was that?!" Evie yelled, where Addie could now see was hunched behind the RV with Brody.

"Backdrafts kicked debris our way," Ben answered gruffly, his voice hoarse. "We should wrap up and check in with Ryan and Tony to see where they are."

The gritty texture resurfaced again to bother her eyes, making her unable to see clearly for a few moments before she decided to toss the colored contacts out to alleviate the uncomfortable sensation. She swiped the lenses out, flicking them off into the distance without a care. The relief was instant as more tears rolled down her cheeks.

Another few blinks and Addie looked up to see Ben watching her. "Good riddance to them if you ask me."

"Oh my god, Ben!" Addie shrieked as she noticed the slow trickle of blood extending from a cut just below his right eye, behind his lopsided glasses. She placed a hand over the cut to try to stop the bleeding. "Do we have any bandages?"

"I'll grab them!" Grace shouted as she began running toward the RV.

Ben tried to push her away gently. "I'm fine, Addie. It's just a little cut."

Addie stood rooted in place, shoving his hand away with her elbow. "Shut up and hold still, then. I'm just trying to stop the bleeding."

"It's not a big deal. Just—"

"I said shut up," she barked. Where the hell were the bandages? "You're hurt. Just hold fucking still."

Grace handed some bandages to Addie before rushing over to

check on Evie and Brody. Addie ripped the package open with her teeth and lifted Ben's glasses, which were miraculously still intact, to get a better view of the cut.

Blood trickled down his cheek when her hand pulled away, but it didn't appear to be a very deep cut.

Ben went to grab the bandage from her. "I can do it, Addie. I'm alright."

She yanked it from his reach and pulled his face down so that it was level with hers. "I said shut up. Now, hold still."

"Addie—"

"Thank you..." she whispered, interrupting him. What else could she say to someone who'd just saved her life? Someone that up until last night, she'd thought the worst of? She wasn't sure what else to say, especially to get him to stop wriggling about, but that seemed to do the trick as he froze in front of her.

"Don't mention it," Ben replied, a soft and gentle tone in his voice that prickled goosebumps across her skin.

He cleared his throat and broke eye contact to glance over at Brody and Grace. "I think that's enough excitement for one day. Let's pack up and head to the motel for the night. I think we could all use some rest."

CHAPTER 10

*A*ddie pulled herself up in her seat, rubbing the back of her head. A noticeable lump had formed there, dully throbbing like it had a heartbeat of its own.

How had she not seen that coming? Addie had always been careful and alert when chasing—so how could she have missed a giant piece of farm equipment sailing at her head?

Better yet, why on earth would Ben risk his own life to save hers? He'd not only thrown himself onto her to get her out of the way but stayed there to shield her. Granted, yes, it would be highly frowned upon if his weatherwoman had her head chopped off on the second day. And, yes, it would be an asshole move not to help in a situation like that. Haunting him would've been a genuine pleasure afterward if it had gone the other way.

She knew all of that.

But ... the way he'd looked at her after, the genuine fear and concern swimming in those pools of amber. That was real. That was *more* than just doing what he had to do. And *that* is what made Addie's chest buzz like TV static, her hands fidgeting in her lap repeatedly.

"Thank you," she said without turning.

Ben chuckled. "You know that you don't have to keep thanking me, right? It gives me too much power to lord over you."

"I don't like you *having* that power over me, hence the thanking. Maybe if I thank you enough, I'll pay my debt."

She did glance at him then, expecting a smug look that would tell her that she was thinking *way* too hard about all of this. Something to let her know he'd hold this over her head for the rest of this trip.

Instead, he looked almost ... sad?

"Saving you from getting your head cut off by debris isn't a *debt*, Addie," he said quietly. "And you saying that makes me think you didn't realize I was *joking*. I know we don't exactly have the best track record, but jeez, do you really think that little of me?"

Her answer before his apology would've been an outright yes. But now?

Addie ran a hand through her hair. "I'm sorry. I wasn't trying to make you feel bad. I'm just ... I don't know. I've just been questioning how good at this I am."

"What do you mean?"

She shrugged. "I used to think I was *good* at storm chasing, but now I'm not so sure. I made a dumb call on our first chase, and now this...."

"Let me stop you there," he interrupted. "You are doing *just fine*. You can't immediately be back on top of your game after sitting out for a few years. Give yourself some grace. Plus, that thing was coming at you at Mach 9 speed. If you had been able to catch that while also trying to focus for the camera, I'd be calling you Superwoman."

Addie chuckled. "I guess ... I think I've also been trying to figure out whether I forgive you or not after our talk. And my feelings are a bit all over the place."

The smirk he threw at her was encouraging. "I suppose helping you keep your head attached would do that."

"Exactly," she said, ignoring the lump that settled in her throat at the thought of Ben being more heavily injured than he was. "So, let's just call us even and start fresh?"

"Sounds fair enough—it'd be great to look at you and not wonder if you're stabbing me in your imagination."

She laughed. "Who said that was gonna stop now? It wouldn't be the first time I've imagined what I'd do to you after you've pissed me off. Stabbing is only *one* option."

Ben quirked an eyebrow. "Careful, or I'll think you're flirting with me."

She rubbed her face as heat crept up her neck. "You *wish* I was flirting with you."

"You have no idea," he said quietly, the sound of his voice nearly drowned out by the hum of their vehicle. She opened her mouth to ask what he meant when he cleared his throat and continued, pointing ahead to the gas station coming up on their right. "Gonna have to pull over up there. Need to fill up. The RV's gotta be pretty low by now."

When the car came to a stop at the pump, Addie opened the door and stretched. Her white tank top raised up as she did, exposing a bit of her stomach. Tugging it down, she internally groaned at her lack of clothing options. When she'd thrown things into her bag for this trip, she'd grabbed everything she had that was conducive to chasing—which wasn't very much.

Back when she'd chased regularly, her wardrobe had been specifically curated for that exact purpose. Loose and comfortable all the way. They had to be practical, not fashionable.

Her wardrobe now was vastly different. Tight-fitting and restrictive to the point that walking around the studio proved challenging at times—especially in those godforsaken stilettos they put her in. If she never saw a stiletto again, she'd be thrilled. Not that she didn't appreciate the beauty of the designer pieces she was always shoved into. What girl didn't dream of wearing stuff like that? But at the same time, it only enhanced that impostor syndrome always simmering in her veins.

Addie still had most of her old clothes from back then, but they now hung loosely on her frame. She'd still grabbed some of them, hoping to make it work somehow. The tank top was the only casual item she still had on standby, using variations of it for layering, which was now a blessing. Even the pair of long khaki pants she had on was tied tightly with a black belt.

Maybe she and Evie could convince the group to sneak in a quick shopping trip? Otherwise, she'd need to be extremely strategic.

More importantly, however, was the grumble that permeated through her body. She couldn't remember the last time she'd had anything to eat. Crap. The last thing any of them needed was for her to pass out because she'd missed her alarm. A quick run inside to grab a few protein bars to keep on hand might be a good idea.

She took a step in the direction of the main building when an idea struck, and she paused. From her experience, nothing spoke better for good camaraderie than acquiring the junk food for the road. Her old lead, Chris, had been partial to those little gummy fish and had been cranky on more than one occasion whenever his stock of them ran out. If she wanted to integrate herself and Evie better into the team, what better way than through their stomachs?

"I'm gonna go in and get some snacks for the road," she called out, a few heads swiveling in her direction. "What do you guys want? My treat!"

Ryan's hand shot in the air. "Jerky!"

"Chips!" Tony yelled from the gas pump by the RV.

"Gummy worms!" Grace shouted, clapping her hands excitedly.

Ben leaned back against the car, giving her a smile that was aggravating in how charming it was. "Thanks, Addie."

Dammit, now his *smile* made her insides turn all gooey? Those old feelings she'd kept bottled up were starting to prick back to the surface, one by one. It was quickly becoming a problem. Definitely something she'd need to keep under lock and key.

Addie returned his smile as casually as possible and waved. "No problem. I'll be right back."

Evie ran over from the RV and looped their arms together. "I'll go with you. I could use a bathroom break, anyway."

"Doesn't the RV have a bathroom?"

"It does," Evie started before lowering her voice as they entered the snack aisle, "but I think I'm gonna have to work up to it."

Addie, unable to help herself, laughed. "You'll have to *work* up to it?"

"Don't make fun of me!" Evie scolded and gently slapped Addie's shoulder. "Anyway, I also wanted to check to make sure you were actually okay. That whole thing was pretty ... spooky."

Spooky was an understatement. "Spooked me since I didn't see it coming, but yeah, I'm okay. Are you? I'm sure that must've been scary."

Evie shrugged, though she averted her gaze as she spoke. "It's just something I'm gonna have to get over since we're gonna be doing this for these next few months. But I'd be pretty fucking bummed if my best friend got wiped out so early on our adventure."

"Ill try not to let that happen again," Addie laughed as she spotted the jerky and grabbed a few options. "I just feel so rusty."

"Why?"

"Because I didn't see it coming? It's literally what I did for a living for years. I *loved* being in the field, and I used to think I was good at it, but now I feel like a duck out of water."

"How the hell could you have seen that coming? Hell, I don't think any of us did except Ben. And for that, I think I'm gonna have to give him a hug later. He saved my best friend," Evie added, untangling her arm from Addie's as she followed her into the next aisle.

"Ben getting hugged by a knockout like you? He'll only be so lucky."

"It's not my hug I think he's looking for...." Evie tutted as she handed Addie a red grocery basket. "But I'll be right back. I really do need to use the bathroom. I've been holding it most of the day since I've never had to pee on a moving object before."

"You know the toilet doesn't move, right?" Addie teased, bumping her hip into Evie's.

"I'm aware, but the *RV* is moving. Look, I'm just gonna use the bathroom. I'll be back in a minute," Evie grumbled, stomping in the direction of the restrooms.

Addie laughed as she tossed the jerky into the basket and began to search for the other requested snacks. The bag of cheesy popcorn to her right practically called her name, whispering sweet nothings into her ear. God, she fucking missed cheesy popcorn. It had always been her guilty pleasure. She forced one foot in front of another to pass through the popcorn section and enter the chip aisle.

Instead of thinking about the food right at her fingertips, her mind wandered to the documentary. If there was any upside they'd been given, it was creative control. Of course, that had been initially meant for Sally and whoever she'd been originally paired with, but Addie wasn't going to complain. It meant that she could be more herself and focus on the facts instead of the small-talk-esque chatter the writers usually forced her to say.

They'd need to film a few introductory pieces to start the documentary with, so as she perused the aisle, she started brainstorming. They'd need to get that done within the next few days, so they didn't get too far into the season and completely forget about it.

As she thought of everything she'd want to include, she was startled back to reality when a figure entered her periphery.

"Well, I'll be. You're Adelyn Walters!"

She turned, craning her neck to look up at the man standing next to her. Instant recognition flickered, and Addie bit back a groan. "Bill Witeman."

He looked almost identical to what she remembered from his YouTube channel—long, messy blond hair that was tied back into a knot, a full, thick beard that looked as meticulously groomed as his near-flawless complexion, and tattoos that poked out from just about every opening to his white shirt. In other words, he looked like just about every hipster guy she'd ever met in the city. The ones that tried *just* the right amount to appear more woodsy and *manly* but not enough for the effort it took to not catch her attention.

Addie would've drooled over a guy like him when she was younger. He had *'bad boy'* practically stamped onto his forehead, and that would've been like catnip to her teenage self.

"In the flesh, but you can call me Billy," he replied as amber eyes roved up and down her body, resting on her chest for a beat longer than socially appropriate, before raising them back to her face. "You're a hell of a lot prettier in person than I thought."

Charming.

Addie knew his type—and avoided it like the plague. Billy was clearly the kind of guy who thought he was God's gift to women and was more than confident that she'd swoon at him with the first wink of his eye. It made for the perfect kind of confidence for his live-streams, but it was the same kind of confidence that only soured Addie's appetite.

"You thought I'd look ugly in person?" she commented, turning back to the snacks in front of her in hopes that he would leave.

He didn't.

"You just looked a bit more … I don't know, like you had a stick shoved up your ass?"

Addie turned back. "Do you talk to all women like that, or am I just special?"

His grin widened, flashing the set of pearly white teeth. "If I said it was because you're special, would you let me show you a good time?"

Addie shrugged, trying to appear indifferent, but really just wishing he would go away. *Where the hell had Evie gotten to?* "Not likely. Not my type, sorry."

"You're a little firecracker, aren't ya?" he practically purred, raising an arm, placing it on the shelf above her, and caging her against him.

That was the second time someone had called her that recently. For reasons she still wasn't prepared to deal with, she hadn't minded it so much coming from Ben. And, granted, he actually had a reason to call her that with how explosive their fighting could get. But coming from Billy? It felt borderline dirty, especially paired with the look he was giving her.

She met his gaze, jutting her chin out. *Fight fire with fire, right?* "If I'm the firecracker, are you the lit match?"

"Does that mean I turn you on?" Billy asked, his tongue running over his teeth. Addie tried not to cringe, instead feeling like her skin was crawling. Did that really work on other women? She hoped not, for their sakes more than anything.

"No," she replied with a grin before quickly ducking under his arm and moving away. "It means you're trying way too hard to create a spark that just isn't *fucking* there."

Billy chuckled, folding his arms across his well-toned chest. "What can I say? I do like a challenge."

"No, thank you. I'm a person, not a challenge. Now, if you'll excuse me, I need to get back to my team," she started before Billy stepped in her path again.

He grinned down at her. "Your team, huh? You mean Ben and those boring-ass pencil pushers?"

That caught her attention. Ben mentioned that they were familiar with one another, but she now wondered exactly what that dynamic was.

"You should change teams and come work for me. I'm sure I'd make for a hell of a better time than that," Billy continued.

"Don't you have better things to do, Billy?" Ben chuckled as he suddenly appeared next to her, taking a step just in front of her. Addie wasn't sure why he'd come into the store, but she couldn't deny the relief she felt at not being alone with this guy.

Billy's grin grew, though it lost its leering quality as it turned to Ben. "Oh, come on, Ben. You think your crew is up to snuff to make an entire documentary like this?"

Ben didn't answer for a moment. Instead, he glared at Billy with his jaw set. What the hell was that? Ben always had some smart-ass thing to say—especially to her. She'd *never* seen him look like *this* before. Mad, sure. And usually aimed in her direction.

"Not everyone needs an entire spectacle," Ben finally said as he lifted a shoulder, the movement appearing forced since she could see his muscles bunched in his back. "Though, your viewers don't seem to fit into the category a documentary like this would be aimed for."

Billy's eyes gleamed. "It's possible. But I'm more surprised that you *won*. Makes my job that much easier. Won't take much convincing at all to get Miss Walters to change teams."

Addie knew little of Billy outside of what she'd seen, but she already despised this guy.

"You won't, for the record," Addie said firmly. "And it's not like I can just hop from team to team. Ben's team won the contract, so it's theirs."

Billy folded his arms across his chest and chuckled. "We'll see about that, doll. My team is waiting on me, so if you two will excuse me, I'll have to try and sweep you off your feet another time. Ben … a *pleasure*, as always."

Pure venom reflected at Ben from Billy's eyes. It was tucked away in the little golden flecks of his amber irises, but she could see it there as if he had it stamped on his forehead. It was enough to take her aback, though Ben appeared almost accustomed to it as Billy turned and walked away.

"Thanks," she offered. "I didn't think I'd ever get him to leave."

Ben cleared his throat, giving her a once-over before offering a small smile. "No problem. You alright?"

"I've dealt with worse than him before."

He frowned. "Somehow, that doesn't comfort me in the slightest."

"Is he always such an asshole?" she prodded.

Ben snorted, some of the warmth in his tone returning. "Unfortunately."

CHAPTER 11

"What do you mean it was *cut*?" Ben demanded, one hand on his hip with the other applying pressure to the bridge of his nose. The rumble of passing cars rocked their little convoy from where they pulled over on the side of the road, but everyone's attention was on Grace as she stood on top of the RV.

Grace lifted her hands defeatedly. "Again, I didn't say it was *necessarily* cut. I said it *looks* like it's been cut, but that could very easily be explained by the debris we dealt with the other day—something could've easily sliced through. It's the only explanation that I have."

"Wouldn't we have known that the Doppler's wires had been cut beforehand, though?" Tony asked, standing on the other side of Evie. Midway through traveling to their next potential storm, the Doppler had stopped functioning, with the corresponding screen inside the RV going completely dark.

"More than likely, yeah," Grace replied. "It was working when we left, but if the wire had only been damaged and not fully severed yet, it could've finally snapped off from the bumpy roads?"

Brody shrugged. "It's possible."

"Is it something we can fix?" Ryan asked.

Grace thumbed behind her in the direction of the RV. "I have some spare parts and wires that I save off to the side for cases like this. It'll work in a pinch. It'll just take me a bit to get it up and running again."

"How long do you think?" Brody asked.

"Could be a few minutes," Grace mused with her lips pursed, the strands of her golden hair wisping from the confines of her bun. "Could be a few hours, depending on how complicated the wiring is and exactly which of the wires was cut. If it's just the connection to the monitor, easy fix. If it's something that deals with the mechanics of how it functions, that'll be more complicated. I've only messed with it once, years ago. So, I don't know how finicky a temporary fix like this would be."

"Is there a chance you won't be able to fix it?" Ben asked.

Grace's shadow loomed over the group as she placed her hands on her hips. "You doubting my skills there, O fearless leader?"

Ben chuckled. "Not in a million years—just need to know exactly what our options are."

"Again, depends on how complicated the cut wiring was. Optimistically, I think I can figure it out and get us up and running. Pessimistically, I might not, and we'll have to go somewhere where they can fix it, which will mean more time out of action."

"So, we're fucked," Ryan muttered.

"Unless you'd like to crawl up here and try to figure it out, smart-ass?" Grace snapped at her brother. The two quickly devolved into a series of obscene gestures thrown at one another as Addie chewed on her lower lip.

It had been a long time, and she was nowhere near the same experience level that Grace clearly was, but Addie still remembered her old team's Doppler. It had been finicky so she'd gotten decently familiar with how it functioned. But she'd messed up once before. What if she only made it worse?

"What are you thinking?" Ben asked, looking directly at her as if he'd heard what she was thinking.

She didn't feel confident that she'd actually be of any help but decided to offer anyway. "I could take a look? I used to help with my old team's Doppler maintenance. It was an older model, so it was known to be difficult—but I don't want to undermine your expertise, Grace, if you—"

"No, not at all," Grace interrupted. "I'd be happy for the second opinion, especially if you're familiar with this wiring."

Ben turned to Brody, the two exchanging a series of hand gestures. They were purposeful motions, concentrated and deliberate, which took Addie aback.

"Are they ... Are they using sign language?" she asked as she looked up at Grace.

Grace rolled her eyes. "Yeah, they do that occasionally when they want to talk but don't want us to know what they're saying. Cheap bastards."

How had she never known that Ben knew sign language? Granted, there had never really been an occasion back in school when he'd needed to use it, but it felt like yet another layer to the onion that he was. One more layer peeled back that she didn't know about before.

Addie watched, mystified, at the exchange until Brody placed his hands on his hips. "I don't want us sitting here out in the open on the side of the road with all these cars."

"Agreed," Ben hummed. "Let's pull off at the next rest station and see what needs to happen with the Doppler."

*T*wenty minutes later, Addie tugged herself up the ladder onto the roof of the RV.

"Alright," Grace said as she wiped away beads of sweat from her forehead. "I've opened the panel beneath it, so we can take a closer look at all the wiring. How much do you know about it?"

"I'm far from an expert," Addie explained. "But I was a quick study when my dad taught me."

Her dad had been an electrician most of his life, so if there were any skills that Addie was most grateful for her dad teaching her, electrical and plumbing would likely be at the top of the list. At the time, as a young girl with a single dad, she didn't understand why he would be so insistent that they spent time together, learning those kinds of things. Addie loved to learn, but the meticulous nature of both crafts hadn't always been her favorite bonding activity.

As an adult, however, she was eternally grateful.

Both had saved her ass on more than one occasion, and knowing how to deal with electrical wires had been a skill her old team lead had been a particular fan of.

"Fair enough. I'll take it."

Sun sank into Addie's skin, the afternoon heat rolling across the plains with the approaching storms. Even tying her hair up into a ponytail didn't seem to alleviate the heat, but as she lowered herself onto the roof and pulled herself beneath the Doppler, it provided enough shade to elicit a contented sigh.

"I know I'm not as good at this stuff as you are. I promise if I'm not useful, I'll—"

Grace laughed. "Are you kidding? I'll take any help that's offered. None of these bozos know anything about this stuff, so if you take a look and that's it, it's still a hell of a lot more than any of them could do."

Addie giggled. "You fit in well with them, though."

"Shit, I hope so. It's not always easy being the only woman on the team, especially with my brother here, too, but I like it. No one here questions me on whether I actually know what I'm doing."

"I get that," Addie said, knowing damn well that exact feeling. "I've sort of wondered this for a bit, but … why *do* you and Ryan work on the same team? I mean, it sounds nice to have family close by, but it seems like you two…"

"We bicker like children?"

"Yeah, that's it."

Grace laughed. "Our parents died when we were young, so we've been relying on each other for so long that it almost feels weird *not* working together. Does that make sense?"

"It does. I'm an only child, though, so if I'm honest, I'm a bit jealous," Addie admitted.

"Jealous?" Grace coughed. "Hell, you want him? I'll happily lend him to you whenever you need that brotherly *'I'm going to make it my mission to piss you off'* vibe."

Addie had to fight herself from doubling with laughter, not wanting to slam her head on the bottom of the Doppler, but she relented to let the laugh itself bubble out of her.

Ah, there was the latch she was looking for. She dragged it into view. Snapping it open, she barely managed to hold back the compendium of wires as they spilled out onto her.

It had been a while, but it was starting to come back to her as she thumbed through all of the different cords and wires. Some of them went to the Doppler, but several went in through the hole to the interior of the camper, so Addie tried her best to separate them out.

"If we're asking questions, though," Grace continued beside her, "what's it like being on TV? I've always wondered what it would be like."

Awful. "It has its moments."

"Yeah?"

"I like being able to help people, even if it's just through a weather report. The more information I can give them, the safer they can be."

"...But?" Grace prompted when Addie didn't continue.

"*But* ... if I didn't have to be on camera, I wouldn't. It's made me a lot more self-conscious than I used to be," she admitted as she wrapped her hand around the wire in question.

Grace huffed. "That makes sense, I guess. From the way Ben was always glued to the TV when he was doing *research* for the documentary, he certainly didn't seem to have any complaints whenever you came on the screen."

Addie muttered a curse when she involuntarily leaned forward and bonked her head on the metallic surface above her. Shit. Ben said before that he'd watched her on screen. After all, it was how he'd known about those awful colored contacts. Had he watched her more than just once? Why? They only recently hashed things out, so why would he want to sit and watch? It didn't make any sense.

"He was probably eating popcorn and commentating," she said. "Pointing and laughing."

"I don't think that was it," Grace mused, her tone curious. "Speaking of Ben, though, what is the deal with you two? Am I gonna have to keep a tape measurer on me to keep you apart at all times?"

Heat crept up her neck for an entirely different reason as Addie cleared her throat. "No, we hashed things out."

"That's good! You two are cute together, so it would be a shame if you tried to kill each other every second of the day."

The wire Addie had in her hand slipped through her fingers. "I, uh, I don't know what you mean?"

"Oh, come on. Give me something to work off of here. I'm *begging* for some girl talk. Do you know how starved I've been for the past few years with this pack of chuckle fucks?"

"What are you two talking about up there?" Ben called up, the suddenness and proximity to this conversation causing Addie to almost hit her head on the underside of the equipment. Again.

She caught a glimpse of Grace's shoes walking to the edge of the RV. "Don't you have some, like, team lead things you could be doing?"

"Not a whole lot for us to do while we're waiting."

"Well, go check footage or something. Evie?"

"Yeah?" Evie answered.

"Help us girls out?"

"Aye aye, captain!" Evie called back, forcing a smile to Addie's face.

When the RV door clicked shut, Addie released a sigh. She'd barely *looked* at the wiring when Grace had started talking. "I'm sorry. I'm still looking."

Grace laughed, gently tapping Addie's foot with her own. "No need to rush. It's nice to have a few minutes alone while they entertain themselves for a change. But don't change the subject on me!"

"Really … it's nothing. We've had a talk about some of our time back when we were in school and cleared things up."

"That's good! You seem a lot more at ease around him than you were when you first joined."

"You think so?"

"I do—and just for the record, I have known Ben for a few years now. I feel like this whole team is just a bunch of additional brothers that got lost out in a cornfield somewhere," Grace said with a laugh. "But I have *never* seen Ben look at anyone the way he looks at you."

"Because I annoy the shit out of him?"

"Maybe a little, but I think he respects you more than you give yourself credit for. I think he referred to you as *a force to be reckoned with* on more than one occasion."

After all the drama between them, it touched her that Ben thought of her that way. But another part of that deeply saddened her.

What *happened* to that version of her?

"I barely even remember that person," she said quietly.

"I mean, if that version of you was a fraction of what you are now, I can only imagine."

Addie blinked. "Of me … now?"

"Well, yeah," Grace said, like it was the most obvious thing in the world. "You're really cool. Do you not know that?"

Now Addie was starting to wonder if Grace had spent a little *too* much time out in the sun. Not a single person she'd ever known had ever used Addie and *'cool'* in the same sentence.

If anything, Addie felt like a complete sore thumb in this group.

Evie blended in so seamlessly with her sunshiney personality and her ability to talk to just about anyone. Grace was an absolute bombshell and smart as a whip about machinery. Tony, though much shier and quieter than the rest, was no less intelligent and looked like he'd been carved out of marble. Ryan was hilarious and could easily charm the pants off any woman he met with his boyish charm. Brody was like the witty older brother Addie always wished she had.

And Ben … Well, Ben was another story entirely.

Her, on the other hand? The phrase 'stick in the mud' still rang true, even if Evie claimed she didn't mean it. Addie *felt* it. She'd been asked to leave on this assignment for several months, and aside from Evie, who was *with her*, there wasn't a single person at home to miss her. Not a single one. Not to mention that, compared to these absolute knockouts that she was working with, she couldn't speak much on her own appearance. Brown hair, pale skin that looked like she hadn't seen sunlight in quite a while, and black eyes that spooked people enough for them to complain.

Sort of the opposite of what she would consider cool.

"I'm not cool," she protested, trying to sound casual, but she was betrayed by the slight quiver in her voice anyway. Dammit.

"What the fuck. Why *not*?" Grace snapped while tapping Addie's leg again. "You're on TV! When this documentary comes out, it's you that's going to be the star of it, and people will want to watch it because your name is attached to it. Do you know how cool that is?"

No, Addie really didn't. She'd never thought of it that way. It had always been the other way around, where she felt this sense of duty and obligation. With the documentary, she didn't truly think of it as *her* project to boast about. She was covering for the person who was actually meant to be here.

"I-I wasn't supposed to be here until the very last minute. I think people will be disappointed that it's not Sally."

Grace groaned. "Girl, I'm gonna have to tag team with Evie about your self-esteem. It could use some work."

Addie finally made it to the far end of the wire to find exactly where it extended down through the panel.

"You might be right," Addie admitted, skating over Grace's comment. "I think this is just the wiring for the monitor in the RV. All the other wires are intact as far as I can see except for this one."

Addie inspected the wire between her fingers. The edges weren't frayed like she would expect from something that had been torn apart. It was cleanly cut, the edges smooth and distinct—almost like it'd been sheared in half. But that couldn't be right, could it? It was likely just some of the debris they'd had thrown at them.

Yet something about it sat wrong with her. The wires were *beneath* the Doppler. It would take some very specific maneuvering for debris to have sliced through it. She chewed on her lower lip as something akin to doubt poked at her.

It was just a coincidence. And if it was the same equipment that

Ben had tackled her out of the way of, there *was* a possibility that it hit the Doppler and snagged a wire in the process. But she wasn't confident enough to voice that opinion. After all, how *else* could it have happened if not purely by accident?

"I think I can fix it real quick while I'm here—just need to strip the insulation from the two ends and tape them back together since I doubt we have anything to solder them?"

"Not with us, no. Need my tools?" Grace asked, her footsteps traipsing to the ladder.

"If you don't mind sharing your pliers?"

The RV door clicked open beneath them as Ben's laugh drifted to the roof. "Having a hard time up there, Addie?"

Addie frowned as she turned her head. "If I wanted your opinion, I'd ask!"

"Addie's fixing the wire, so it should be a quick fix for now," Grace said, a barely repressed giggle squeaking through. "We'll need to get it looked at professionally soon, but I think it should hold. We can just head directly to the motel for the night."

"I'm starving," Ryan whined. "Can we get something to eat first?"

CHAPTER 12

"This is, by far, the best country-fried steak I've ever had," Ryan moaned around the forkful of meat.

Brody reached around Tony to smack the back of Ryan's head. "Don't talk with your mouth full. Didn't y'all's mother teach you any fucking manners?"

Grace grinned. "Apparently only one of us."

"How many manners do we need at a roadside diner?" Ryan protested after swallowing.

Despite the happy chatter going on among the group, Addie's mind was somewhere else entirely. Her stomach rumbled as she looked down at her plate. She hadn't realized how hungry she was until the waitress placed the burger she'd ordered in front of her.

She couldn't remember the last time she'd eaten something that hadn't been counted, logged, and tracked. All to make sure she stayed within her 'allotted calorie budget' for the day.

The email warning she'd gotten months prior flashed in her mind.

You look like you've gained some weight on camera—better start working that off, or viewers might start complaining again.

White-hot rage simmered deep in her gut.

Addie had been petite growing up and continued to be even now.

But nothing ever felt good enough. Thin enough, lean enough, strong enough.

Nothing was ever enough for them.

But now, with no one watching, with this group of people who had been nothing but kind to her—she felt like she could let herself enjoy this small luxury. It felt like a small act of defiance, as odd as that might be to the others. Far more freeing than she ever thought it would be.

God, how she missed the smell of a good, juicy burger.

The scent of salt and charbroiled meat tickled her nostrils and caused her mouth to water. When she finally relented to having that first bite, she savored it. Eyes closed, she fought the hum of pleasure that raced up her throat and threatened to burst from the deepest parts of her soul.

It didn't matter that the burger was just average on a good estimate. To her, it felt like having the finest of caviars. A wagyu-level entree—as far as she was concerned—for the low price of $5.99. Complete with a side of crispy, golden fries and a small Diet Coke.

The only disturbance to her little moment of peace was the pair of eyes studying her from across the table. Ben watched her, a smile playing across his features. Why he was watching her, she had no clue. Feeling so open and vulnerable wasn't something she particularly liked, and right now, she felt exposed. Like a frog in a high school biology classroom—the scalpel inching closer and closer with everyone able to look in and dissect every piece of her.

"I'm only mad I didn't get to experience him," Evie said, drawing Addie's attention to the conversation. "Addie gave me the SparkNotes version when we dropped our stuff off in our room, but he sounds like the kind of guy I'd *love* to knock down a few pegs."

"I would pay money to watch that." Tony sighed appreciatively, a rosy quality to his cheeks as he looked at Evie.

"Are we talking about Billy?" Addie asked as she pushed her plate away, the remainder of her burger and fries left untouched.

"I'm so sorry you had to experience him," Grace said, the apologetic tone to her voice causing Addie to laugh.

"Good to know his reputation does indeed match what he seemed like in his videos."

Brody laughed, too. "He's actually worse in person."

"No, I can imagine," she agreed. "What's the story between you guys?"

Brody glanced in Ben's direction, who had noticeably started to push the last few bites of food around on his plate. Pretending like he wasn't listening when Addie could see the set frown shoved into his dimples.

Interesting....

"I mean, you've met the guy," Brody offered instead. "He doesn't exactly give storm chasers a good name."

Ryan scoffed. "That's an understatement. A few months ago, we stopped in this dinky little town further south to grab lunch, and we were basically chased out by the owner."

"Why?" Evie asked.

"Billy and his team had been there for breakfast a few hours prior and treated everyone like dirt," Tony answered. "Owner thought we were from the same team and wanted nothing to do with us."

Addie grimaced. "Based on how he acted earlier, that doesn't really surprise me."

"The rest of his team isn't much better," Grace added. "Bunch of ego-chasing adrenaline junkies who have only managed to skate by without killing anyone simply because they follow other teams to get a gauge on where to go. Then they bully them out of the way, so they can get their *shots*."

"They've run people off the road before?" Evie asked gruffly.

"Yep. They've run *us* off the road before," Grace grunted.

"If I got hold of Billy in person, I'd—" Ryan started before Grace bumped his shoulder with hers.

"You'd what?" she asked. "Lose yet another arm-wrestling match against them?"

"That was *one* time, and you saw their camera guy!" Ryan protested as he slammed his fist on the table. "Dude looks like he chugs protein powder like his life depends on it!"

The discussion settled into a debate on *exactly* which members of Billy's team Ryan felt he could take in a fight. Then the waitress swept by and began collecting the empty plates off of the table as the conversation continued.

Addie sat back as she vaguely followed the conversation, exhaustion sweeping over her like a tidal wave. They'd gotten some amazing footage, so it was well-earned exhaustion. Things might finally start looking up. If the producers liked the footage as much as she and Evie did, she'd be able to keep her job. They'd threatened to fire her so much over the years over every minor issue that imperfection simply couldn't be tolerated. And, after all, there was only one major bill left over for her to work through. The amount was still pretty high, but at least it was just the *one* left.

She pushed food on her plate around with her fork, glancing over to watch Evie and Tony across the way. She could tell they were starting to get on really well—if the bright smile on Evie's face was any indication. Tony was a relatively quiet kind of guy, hardly interjecting and often opting to be the silent observer of most conversations. So, it was nice to see how much he lit up around Evie. Addie already knew how easy it was to talk to Evie, but it appeared Tony felt the same. It was fascinating watching the little spark between them from afar—especially after everything Evie had been through recently.

It amazed Addie just how easy Evie made things look. Everything rolled off of her like water across a duck's back. She took things in stride and never let anyone dull her shine, especially assholes like Frank.

Meanwhile, she could only ever dream of being like that.

Despite how hard she pretended that it didn't, every snide remark, every comment flooding her inbox, felt like a bullet. She started losing pieces of herself along the way, as each bullet took something from her that she didn't know she had. She barely recognized herself.

Where was that wild and free girl who fought like hell for what she wanted? The one who didn't take shit from anyone and wasn't afraid of her own body.

She was gone, long lost with time and loss. Now that same girl pushed fries across her plate like they were public enemy number one.

The waitress appeared next to her and went to grab Addie's abandoned plate when Ben held his hand over it. The waitress simply shrugged as she continued on, despite Addie suddenly gaping in confusion between the two.

"Eat," Ben instructed gently when she shot him a confused look. "You haven't had much today. Don't need you passing out in front of a tornado."

She didn't need to ask what he meant, a frustrated and indignant sound rumbling from her as she snatched the burger from the plate and took a massive bite, purely out of spite. It felt a bit like getting her hand caught in the cookie jar but in reverse.

"Why are you watching what I eat?" Addie snapped quietly to avoid the others hearing her.

"The contacts were easy for me to see. *This* took me a bit longer." The crease between Ben's eyebrows crinkled as he frowned. "I'm worried about you."

Might as well have had it stamped on her forehead as Addie's entire body flushed under the attention. Bad enough that he'd saved her life earlier, but now *this*? She fought aggravated tears as she chewed.

"I'm fine," she mumbled. She wasn't, but she didn't want anyone to know that. The fact that Ben could see it was bad enough.

Especially because it was Ben.

Ben offered her this soft smile that softened the prickled edges around her. "I know."

"Don't patronize me," she practically hissed, though there was a notable lack of venom in her tone. She was still hungry enough to not fight him. The flavor burst across her tongue once more, drowning out any frustration she might have.

The left side of his lips quirked up. "Wouldn't dream of it. Just want to protect that nice ass of yours. Would be a crime for it to shrink."

She paused mid-bite, narrowing her eyes. "You've been staring at my ass?"

The bite of humor laced into the sound of his laugh. "Maybe."

She *should* be offended by that because, after all, it was Ben. Regardless of the recent developments in their relationship, he was still a massive pain. He goaded her just about every chance he got and took immense pleasure from it. But she couldn't deny that tiny little voice in the back of her mind that liked it *because* it was Ben. Fuck, she was screwed.

"I should slap you for that."

"Yeah, you probably should."

Before she could respond, Brody's voice broke the tension between them. "I've paid. Should we head out now?"

Ben cleared his throat and nodded. "Yeah, we can go. It's been a long day for everyone, so we should all be sure to get some sleep tonight. We'll sync back up tomorrow morning in the motel lobby at seven. We don't want the system to get too far ahead of us, so we'll want to be awake bright and early to find a good location."

CHAPTER 13

Thick, murky black water. A deep, dark pit as Addie sank inch by painstaking inch beneath the surface. Her father's smiling face, waving before turning to walk in the other direction. She screamed for him, like she always did. Begging him to come back, to fight for him, to fight for her. Don't go.

Don't leave me here alone.

Addie woke with a start, clutching her throat as she sprang up in bed. A scream rose on the tip of her tongue. The same familiar nightmare, consuming her until she finally managed to breathe through the panic.

She ripped the blanket off of her as if she were on fire, her skin practically sizzling with steam.

The nightmare always ended the same. He was gone. Death had come for him and left her with these awful nightmares.

Her black tank top was nearly soaked through with sweat, sticking to her like a second skin. Oxygen raced into her lungs with a long pull, forcing the air to sit there until she was ready to let it go.

Not choking. Not drowning. Just a nightmare.

She reached blindly for her phone on the nightstand—careful to shield the bright light so as to not wake Evie. Three in the morning, and there would be no way in hell she would be able to get any sleep. She needed to calm herself, get some air to clear her mind. It felt too vivid, too raw, for her to attempt to sleep again.

She crept out of bed and yanked on the only pair of flip flops she'd brought with her, still a bit damp from her shower.

If her previous chase team had taught her anything, it was to *always* bring a pair of shower flip flops. Motel showers could never be fully trusted. Camping in the woods was great, but with the size of their group—showering was a bit of a hot commodity, so a hot motel shower felt like a luxury.

She hadn't truly had a moment to herself in the past few days, so it was now or never. There was a motel pool downstairs near the check-in office that she remembered passing on the way in. So, remembering to tuck her room key into the pocket of her pajama shorts, she closed the door behind her.

A bit of fresh air would do her some good.

Addie followed the signs until she was able to clearly see the white metallic fence encasing the pool area. A large sign on the gateway meant to deter others from late-night dips did the opposite as she pushed her way inside. No lifeguard on duty? No problem. The last thing she wanted was to get into the water after the nightmare she'd had. Although she was a good swimmer, the thought of submerging herself made her nauseous. But putting her feet into the water and letting it cool her legs down? *That* she could sign up for.

The cold concrete felt good against her heated skin, and a delightful shiver raced up her legs as she carefully lowered one foot at a time into the crystal-clear water. The pool lights flickered from the movement of her feet, spreading out and distorting them as she looked down into the depths.

Her thundering heartbeat had calmed down considerably. What set the dream off in the first place, Addie hadn't the faintest idea. It always appeared at the most inconvenient times, but she didn't want to ponder that for long. It never ended well when she did.

Her thoughts began to drift as she swished her feet.

For some reason, the memory of Ben hovering over her in that field, right there on top of her, trickled in. His eyes had crinkled in worry like he actually *cared* that something might've happened to her. Shielding her from the wind and debris with his body covering hers...

Why was she so worked up about that? It was nothing. He'd seen something about to hit her and stepped in to help; that was it. She'd have done the same if she'd been in his shoes.

Then why did she feel like this?

It had taken a *lot* of work for her to try and forget him. It was easier dredging up the resentment, the anger about what had happened. Hell, it had been easy just focusing on how much they bickered in school so that she often forgot how much she'd *liked* arguing with him. She had never admitted it aloud to anyone, but she *liked* having someone that challenged her.

Ever since that first tornado she'd seen as a kid, watching as it swept across the horizon—everything was clear as a bell. It had been like a message delivered straight from the heavens into her eager hands. Every free moment of her time was spent studying. Working. And when she'd finally walked through the doors to start her first day at graduate school, she'd thought the hard part was over with. That she'd be able to coast her way through the program without issue.

Then she'd met Ben.

He didn't hand over victory easily; he taught her to fight for what she wanted. To be smarter, more thoughtful. Quicker on her feet. She'd been brash back then, more prone to letting her temper take over. Even that stupid true or false thing they'd been forced to do, it had made her stop and think before reacting wildly to whatever was thrown at her.

Not that she'd ever tell *him* that.

And she would *never* tell him about the crush she'd had on him back then....

It was in that sort of school-girl-ish way that a guy tugging on a girl's braids on the playground meant that he had a crush on her.... But she liked his intelligence. How hard he, himself, worked and didn't back down just because she was a woman.

She'd even liked his wild hairstyle and thick-rimmed glasses. They'd made his more wiry build look academic. And though she *absolutely* would never admit it, she'd often fantasize about him throwing her onto one of the desks in the library after a fight....

No! Addie shook herself, hoping the movement would shake the thoughts straight out of her head. It had to be her lack of any romance the past couple of years that was catching up with her if she was starting to look at Ben ... well ... like *that* again.

A voice echoed across the pavement nearby, the suddenness of it causing her to almost jump right into the pool.

"I already told you, the answer is no."

She was about to turn her attention back to kicking at the water, to give whoever it was their privacy, but the familiarity of the voice gave her pause.

"No. More money isn't going to change my mind."

Ben? With the deep timbre of the voice, there was no doubt in her mind. She remained frozen in place, her senses piqued and honed on the words reverberating to her, though she knew she shouldn't.

"I'm hanging up now."

Footsteps tapped along the pavement, heading in her direction, and for a moment, Addie panicked. Should she hide? Should she pretend she hadn't been listening? Should she—

"Hey there, stranger."

She pretended that she hadn't been listening and had only now noticed him, looking up with fake-surprise to see Ben standing a few paces away. Darkness swallowed the area, but with the aid of the lights around the pool, she could make him out clearly.

His glasses reflected against the pool lights as he lifted a hand to push them further up the bridge of his nose. His hair was messy, like he himself had been tossing and turning. Frustratingly, it only made him look adorably rustled. The gray T-shirt he had on hung loosely over a pair of black gym shorts, a look that once might have made him look long and lanky but now only showed off his lean muscles.

She cleared her throat as he lowered himself onto the concrete next to her, distracting herself from the sudden heat creeping up her neck.

What the hell was wrong with her?

"Is this gonna be a pattern for us?" Ben asked, a soft chuckle escaping him. "Sneaking out because we couldn't sleep?"

"Hopefully not, for our sanity," she said, as she turned to offer a smile, pausing when the light caught the edge of his bandage. "How's your eye?"

"It's fine. You and Grace made a bigger deal out of it than it was."

"You were *bleeding*, Ben."

"Better that than you getting decapitated."

Addie winced at the recollection, and her hand rubbed her throat thoughtfully. "I *did* thank you for that, right?"

"You did, but it sounds nice coming from you, so feel free to say it again, firecracker," Ben teased, throwing her a wink and nudging her playfully with his shoulder.

She nudged him back, fighting a grin. "You know, you're not *such* an asshole when you try—"

"The highest compliment, coming from you."

"—But you've *gotta* stop calling me firecracker."

Ben cocked his head to the side, jutting his chin out. "If it ever stops suiting you so much."

"How the hell does it suit me?"

"It just does. You're passionate, explosive, and most likely deadly for me."

"Keep calling me that, then, and you might just be right," she spat. "You've gotta come up with something else."

"I'll consider it."

She pouted. "Well, that's not fair. I don't have anything to call you."

"Pretty sure *asshole* has left your mouth in reference to me more than once," he teased, kicking water at her legs.

Addie released the giggle that had been trapped behind her lips, sloshing water back at him. "Unless you *like* me calling you that, I need a new one."

He laughed. "It defeats the purpose if I *tell* you what to call me. You've gotta come up with one on your own if you want one."

Addie frowned, but she conceded. "Fine. But it's gonna be a really embarrassing one."

"I look forward to hearing it, then." He sat back, the pool light striking his eyes in a way that made them almost sparkle with amusement. It felt alarming, as Addie had never really *looked* into someone else's eyes before. She'd become so paranoid of her own over the years, with the comments about how spooky they were, that she never paid anyone else's much attention. But now she noticed Ben's—taking note of the little flecks of gold there, encased in a shell of amber.

It took her a moment to realize that he was studying her just as intensely. What was he thinking? Amusement crinkled the corner of his eyes, a softness in them that matched his gaze.

"How long have you known sign language?" she asked, needing to break the tension there.

Ben lifted a shoulder. "My whole life?"

"How could I not have known that about you?"

"I didn't need to use it much then. I used it at home mostly," Ben said, kicking at the water and continuing before she could think to ask anything further on the topic. "Can I ask you something?"

"Hm?"

"You avoided my question last time, but I'm curious," he said, leaning back to rest on his elbows next to her. "Why'd you stop?"

She knew what he meant; she didn't need him to clarify. He was asking why she quit chasing again.

Her mouth opened to divert the question away from the topic once more, but that wasn't what ended up tumbling out.

"You know," she started, kicking her foot out and letting the water splash against it, "I woke up a bit ago because I had a nightmare. The same one I've had for about a year now. I thought it'd gone away, but it once again decided to show up."

Ben quirked an eyebrow at her. "Yeah?"

"Yeah. I dreamed that I was drowning.... Sinking further and further into this thick, murky liquid that keeps swallowing me up, no matter how hard I fight against it. Then I wake up."

She half expected him to make fun of her. Instead, he simply hummed low in his throat. "Sounds pretty scary."

"I wonder if that's how my dad felt..." she mused, fighting the lump forming in her throat. "... right before he died."

She felt Ben's eyes, but she couldn't look at him. He'd see the tears already welling up if she did, and she wasn't sure she could handle that at the moment.

"Is that what happened to him?"

She shrugged. "In a way. Pulmonary edema in reality."

"That's—"

"You asked why I quit chasing," she interrupted. "That was it. I found out my dad had late-stage cancer and had no one there to take care of him. He hid it from me for a while, but I found out eventually. I needed to be there for him, and I couldn't do that if I was constantly on the road. I didn't know how long I'd have with him. So, I quit. We only got a few months together, but I wouldn't take that time back for anything in the world."

He'd been far too weak to do all the things she knew he would've wanted to do, but she'd tried her best. They'd gone to the movies together, yelled in the stands for his favorite baseball team—hell, she'd tried to surprise him with a trip down to the zoo, so they could get a picture together at the giraffe enclosure. Like the one they'd taken when she was little.

The picture she'd set as her phone background the day after his funeral—and still had now.

"You have these nightmares about drowning because of him?"

She tried to discreetly flick a loose tear away from her cheek. "I know he didn't drown in the traditional sense, but that was basically what got him. The nightmares started a week or so after the funeral. It's how I ended up at the news station. His treatments were really expensive. I was drowning in debt, no pun intended. So, when I was offered a spot at the station, I took it. Not exactly my dream job, since I quite honestly *hate* being on camera, but I can't afford to lose it either."

"That's ... That's really rough. I'm sorry."

She tried to laugh, but it came out sounding wet. "Wasn't the sort of light-hearted answer you were expecting, huh?"

"No, but thank you for telling me anyway," Ben said, surprising her when he lifted a hand to wipe one of her tears away with his thumb. "I know our ... *friendship* hasn't exactly been the smoothest, but I'm glad that you felt comfortable enough to tell me that."

It surprised her, too, if she were honest. She hadn't planned on telling him anything—it just ... spilled out.

When they weren't arguing, he *was* surprisingly easy to talk to.

"About the truce," she said quietly as his breath tickled her face. He was so close. "Do you actually mean it?"

He smiled, that warm one she'd only seen a handful of times now. "Yes, I actually mean it."

"Is that what we are, then? Friends?"

Ben chuckled. "Yeah, I think we can be friends at the very least, right?"

She nudged him again, enjoying the warmth radiating from him and not bothering to scoot away. "*At the very least*, huh?"

"Yes, at the very least. We're both mature adults, I think we can handle that," Ben defended as he leaned over to quickly tuck a stray lock of her hair behind her ear. It was such a simple act, but the way he immediately froze after doing it, the way his breath hitched, she realized that he *had* done it unconsciously. But he also didn't move away —instead remaining there, his face hovering mere inches from hers.

There was an unwavering sort of question that lingered in the air between them that she wasn't exactly sure what it meant.

More alarmingly, however, was the fact that she wasn't pushing him away. She didn't *want* to push him away. What she wanted was to melt into this heat sizzling between them.

"You're not going to betray me again, right?" she whispered. "True or False?"

"True," Ben replied quietly, not breaching the space between them —nor pulling back. "The last thing I want is to hurt you, Addie."

It felt intimate, the way he looked at her. There was a hazy quality to it, a hooded gaze that rooted her where she sat. Their eyes remained locked, a question she wasn't sure how to word floating in that space. But when his eyes lowered to her lips, his pupils dilating ever-so-slightly before meeting her eyes once again, Addie's entire body ignited.

But just as quickly as the moment started, it came to a crashing halt. Her eyes widened as Ben suddenly stopped and snatched his hand back to his side.

"Sorry, you, uh—you had something in your hair," Ben stammered out quickly before clearing his throat. "Come on. We should try to get a few minutes of sleep. We've got a long day tomorrow."

He leapt to his feet, offering her a hand to help her stand. They parted ways just as abruptly with a hasty *goodnight* before Addie practically sprinted back to her room and shut the door behind her.

What the hell was that? What the hell just happened?

Did she just ... Did she just almost *kiss* Ben?

And worse... why was she disappointed that she didn't?

CHAPTER 14

The cool morning air prickled against Addie's skin. She rubbed her groggy eyes once more and shuffled across the motel parking toward the lobby. Evie did the same next to her, groaning about her significant lack of caffeine. Every room had a small coffee pot, though functionality seemed to be optional as they discovered. It was, in part, why the two of them were likely the last ones to show up to meet the group in the lobby.

Evie looped an arm with Addie's in an effort to keep each other upright in their sleepy state. The strands of her long, silky black hair were braided off to the side, but they still managed to tickle Addie's arm.

Early morning light poked out through the nearby trees to kiss the warmth of Evie's brown skin. The soft glow from the sun brought out the subtle undertones of amber and earth in it. She was ethereally gorgeous, and considering how effortless it had been for her to look like she'd walked off a set as opposed to just rolling out of bed, Addie couldn't help the flare of jealousy.

Lucky.

When she'd been getting ready, panic had swelled in her chest. She hadn't been able to find her colored contacts. It had taken overturned bags and flipped furniture before she remembered they were long gone. She'd flicked them away when the dirt had gotten into her eyes, after Ben had tackled her. Honestly, good riddance to them.

She could look at it as another small victory for herself, to record the rest of this documentary without them. Purely as *herself*. Or she could look at it as something *else* for the team back at the station to criticize later. She'd mulled it over the entire time she got ready then finally decided on the former. It felt like taking a little piece of herself back, no matter how small and insignificant it might seem to anyone else.

Besides, thinking about *that* was much easier to focus on than the other thing her thoughts kept drifting back to.

She'd almost kissed Ben.

Worse? She'd wanted to.

When she'd talked about her dad, Ben had listened—*genuinely* listened. He was the first person she'd ever told about the nightmares. Not even Evie knew about those. She hadn't expected for the words to tumble out of her like they had, but she didn't regret it either. He'd just listened, offering her a few words of comfort when needed.

And then he'd pulled back. All of the hurt—the humiliation—that she'd felt all those years ago came rushing back. But then again, he'd literally thrown himself on top of her to shield her from debris. That had to count for something, right?

Frustration pulsed in her temples. Sure, she'd already come around, forgiving him in her own way, but that didn't mean she had to tell him that she was in…

She nearly tripped over herself. No, no, no! She'd gotten rid of those feelings a long time ago. Tucked away in some Pandora's box she refused to touch all these years later. But … alarmingly … she feared that might not be the case.

Shit.

She cursed her foolish thoughts. That should be the *last* thing on her mind. Not mentioning that their history together was … complicated … but he was also her team lead for the next few months. He was her *boss* right now, so getting tangled up in all of that just spelled disaster.

Evie yawned. "What are you so lost in thought about?"

"Nothing. Just tired still, I think."

"I bet. I'd be tired, too, if I snuck off in the middle of the night."

Addie paused, whipping her head in Evie's direction. "How do you know that?"

"Girl, you are *not* as quiet as you think you are," her friend teased. "You just about slammed the door shut when you got back to the room."

Addie cringed. "Sorry. I promise I was trying to be quiet."

"I know. So, where'd you go?" Evie asked as she pulled Addie closer and slung her arm over her shoulders.

"Just went to sit by the pool to dip my feet in. Nothing crazy."

Nothing special—she only almost kissed their team lead and might possibly be developing feelings for him again.

"Run into anybody?" Evie asked, waggling her eyebrows suggestively.

Addie stopped and turned to look at her friend. "Now, how on earth could you possibly know that?"

"I don't, but there's only one person that would make you slam the door like that."

Dammit. She had a point. She could act like it was another fight if she played her cards right. She wasn't sure if she was ready to hash out these complicated emotions swirling in her gut until she'd sat on them longer.

"Oh, yeah, I ran into him on the way back. Another disagreement."

Evie eyed her, a suspicious glint aimed in her direction. It felt a bit like a child holding a magnifying glass over an ant in the hot summer sun—searing straight into her.

"Yeah? What'd you argue about this time?"

Addie kept her gaze straight. "How we would approach chasing today. The usual."

"Somehow, I don't believe you...."

Addie huffed out a sigh. "Seriously, it was nothing."

Evie excitedly tapped Addie's shoulder. "Oh, absolutely not. If only you could see how red your face is right now, you wouldn't argue with me. Spill the beans. *Something* had to have happened!"

Shit. Addie rubbed the back of her neck to hide the embarrassment flooding her senses. "Don't put words in my mouth. There's nothing to spill! Just drop it, please?"

"Come *on*. You have to tell me!" Evie whined, pushing and pulling Addie as if trying to shake some sense into her. Maybe she was. From the hard, determined line of Evie's eyebrows, Addie was starting to suspect that she had more of an opinion on the topic than she was letting on.

"Fine," Addie huffed. "But you have to swear to secrecy because I'm still not sure what happened and if I'm making a big thing out of nothing and—"

"Oh my God, Addie," Evie gushed, her hushed tone frayed at the edges with excitement. "I *knew* all that arguing you've been doing was just y'all flirting!"

Addie blanched. "W-what? I didn't say anything yet!"

"You didn't have to! Did you guys have a romantic walk in the moonlight?"

"Ugh," Addie groaned as she rolled her eyes and tried to stomp away. "You suck. Though, you're one to talk. I'm not the one making *googly eyes* at someone!"

It pleased Addie immensely when Evie looked away with her lips pursed into a pout. "I don't know what you're talking about. I'm not making googly eyes at anyone!"

"Uh-huh. Then you have no thoughts on what *Tony* is up to this morning? Maybe I should go ask him—" she teased as she quickened her pace, erupting into laughter when Evie leapt ahead to try and tackle her.

She dodged her once, and as Evie rushed to catch up with her, something else managed to catch their attention. Excited shouting and clapping reverberated across the parking lot from a small crowd gathered ahead—right where they'd been heading.

"What the hell is going on over there?" Addie asked.

Evie shrugged. "I don't know. Let's go find out."

Ear-piercing squeals and clapping got louder with each step and felt like a hammer beating Addie's brain. Then again, that could be her distinct lack of caffeine speaking. She felt almost hungover with exhaustion.

What people could be this enthusiastic about—this early in the morning—she couldn't fathom. A group of women gathered in a circle, swarming whoever was at their center. The sun was barely up, and yet there were at least twenty people there, all practically vibrating with excitement and enthusiasm.

"We love you, Storm Stalkers!" an excited young woman shouted from the back of the crowd, jumping up and down with a sign perched over her head.

Storm Stalkers? Oh no....

"It's so nice to see fans all the way out here!" a voice boomed from the center of the crowd. Addie had to restrain an imminent eye roll.

Billy.

Yeah, Addie didn't have the kind of energy required for dealing with him right now, so she ushered Evie along. "Come on," Addie urged. "Let's go around."

"Is that him?" Evie asked as she followed quickly after her. "That Billy guy?"

Addie nodded. "Unfortunately."

They were only a few feet away when Billy's voice lashed in their direction. "Well, if it isn't Miss Walters! Fancy meeting you here."

Shit. She'd hoped that they'd sneak past without drawing his attention. Uneasy tension built as he parted the crowd and walked over. She was not in the mood to deal with whatever trouble he wanted to cause. The gleam in his eyes screamed of it.

"Good morning, Mr. Whitman," she replied flatly, shielding her eyes against the stream of light pouring through the tree line. The same light caught the golden hues of Billy's hair, let loose from the bun that he'd had it in the last time she had seen him. With his flowing blond waves, it felt like he spent more time in the ocean on a surfboard than someone who chased tornadoes.

"Alright, ladies," one of the other men standing in the crowd—who Addie assumed were part of Billy's team—said loudly. "We've got a busy day ahead of us, and while we would *love* to hang out and spend more time with our beautiful subscribers, we have some business to tend to. Maybe you could catch our next livestream later today?"

As chaotic as the crowd appeared to be, Addie was surprised when they actually *listened* and dispersed. The entire crowd was gone in mere seconds as they returned to their rooms, or whatever vehicles they'd arrived in. Addie had expected *some* protest, especially with how animated the people had been.

And as Billy and two other men came to stand in front of them, she almost wished they had.

"And who is this lovely creature?" Billy asked as he turned his attention to Evie.

Evie extended a hand in an air of professionalism that Addie hadn't expected, especially with how exhausted her friend had been moments before. "Evelyn Sanders. Camerawoman for Channel 5."

Billy took her hand, but instead of shaking it, he pulled it to his lips and pressed a kiss to it. "Charmed."

Gross.

"What are you two doing here this early? Come to the unofficial fan meet up?" Billy asked, smugness oozing from him like the strong aftershave that wafted from him. She suppressed a gag, but out of the corner of her eye, Evie rubbed her hand on her jeans with a frown. She barely managed to catch a laugh before it flew from her.

"Just heading to the lobby to check out with our team," she offered.

Billy raised an eyebrow. "Your team, huh? Tell me, how are you guys liking *the team*?"

"They've been nothing but great to us," Evie interjected. "We've gotten some great footage and have had a good time. It's nice to be around people who value intelligence as opposed to a team that might treat us like a bunch of blow-up dolls. Don't you agree, Addie?"

Billy's expression soured, but the comment didn't phase him long as he turned his gaze back on Addie. "Having fun with boring scenery shots?"

She rolled her eyes. "You know those are required for documentaries like this, right?"

He shrugged. "You only need a few, though with Ben's usual strategy, he likes playing it a little *too* safe. Am I right?"

Her temples began to throb rhythmically once again. A fog over her mind had settled in a way that made her already feel irritable, even more so for having to deal with someone like Billy on top of it. She wasn't in the mood for whatever mind games he wanted to play.

"Yeah, and how would you know what Ben's strategy is?" she asked and folded her arms across her chest.

Billy's eyes widened before he laughed. "Oh, he hasn't told you?"

Addie raised an eyebrow. "Told me what?"

He shook his head, the grin spread across his face widening further. "Shame on Ben. I thought he'd give me credit for helping him get his team started."

What?

Ben definitely hadn't mentioned that. Then again, Ben hadn't said much about Billy at all since their last encounter. He'd actually been pretty tight-lipped about the whole thing.

A fact she would remedy after they got back out on the road.

"It's also how I know that their equipment is old and out of date," Billy added as if noticing the skepticism plastered to her face. "They've been needing to replace that old Doppler for years."

The Doppler? Why would he mention that?

The clean-cut wire she'd seen the other day flashed in her mind. She opened her mouth out of instinct to mention it but snapped her jaw shut.

"Shame to waste such pretty little things on that lot anyway," the man to Billy's right said, low enough that she suspected he didn't mean for her to hear. His eyes flicked between her and Evie and licked his lips, as if he were looking at a prime piece of meat. It sent a shiver down her spine, feeling his gaze in all the wrong ways. Rude comments about her appearance weren't the only things she'd read on the internet about herself. But it elicited the same feelings—embarrassing, invasive, and just flat-out *gross*.

Billy's other buddy sidled up next to Evie and pulled her to him. "Come on. Don't be so stingy. We're not all that bad, I promise."

Normally, Evie would've sucker-punched a guy like this without breaking a sweat. But she didn't even move, almost completely frozen in place. Something flashed in her eyes that immediately had Addie seeing red—fear. *Frank.* It wasn't exactly hard to guess what Evie was thinking, and it infuriated her that these idiots would bring something like that back to the surface.

Without a second thought, she stomped over to the two and all but shoved herself between him and Evie. "If you guys are done leering, we're leaving." She sneered.

Before she could protest, Billy suddenly snatched Addie by the wrist, yanking her back. "Yeah, hold on. Let's chat a bit more."

"Hey—" Evie started.

"Jesus Christ, Billy," someone shouted from behind. "Can't you do your little fucking meet ups somewhere less inconvenient to *literally* everyone else?"

Addie looked over as Brody, Tony, and Ryan stormed in their direction. She was already fond of the team, but she'd never been happier to see them. Boys like this didn't respond when women said no, and as much as she hated that she couldn't handle this herself peacefully, she was glad for their arrival.

Billy smirked, fingers still wrapped around Addie's wrist. "You know how these things can get."

Glad for the distraction, Addie shoved herself away, satisfied by the grunt he made. "Next time you pull that shit, I'll deck you."

"So, she does have some bite to her after all. I like to see it." Billy chuckled, leaning forward until he was at eye level with her. "I'd love to see you try, sweetheart. I bet you pack a punch."

"If she won't, I will," Brody said as he stood next to her, adding a few hand motions that let her know he was adding something in sign language, though she had no idea what that was. But by the twitch in the corner of Billy's right eye, it seemed like he understood.

Addie looked between the two carefully. There was something there—something in Brody's eyes that didn't quite match his usual carefree tone. It was more like that glimpse she'd seen that first morning after their first deployment. A rattlesnake ready to strike.

"You're about as menacing as a golden retriever, Brody. Smart as one, too," Billy remarked.

"I wouldn't be throwing stones about *intelligence*, Billy," Ryan tossed in, rocking on his heels. "Glass house and all."

Billy whirled. "Why don't you come up here and say that to my face? I'll grab you a box to stand on, so you can reach it."

"Oh, we wouldn't dream of hitting your face, pretty boy," Ryan laughed and took a step closer. "We know how long you spend *primping* in front of the mirror before getting on camera."

"What the hell is going on now?"

Addie spun, instantly making eye contact with Ben as he and Grace walked in their direction. His hair was combed back, like he was fresh out of the shower, and the memory of the night before burned across her skin.

Time and place, Addie. Time and place.

His gaze softened on her before immediately hardening again when he turned to Billy. "Do you not have other things you could be doing?"

Billy shoved his hands into his pockets. "Oh come on, Ben. It's just some light banter. Nothing to get your panties in a twist about."

"Yeah, come on, Ben," the man standing on Billy's left said. "We were just chatting."

Tony scoffed, hovering just in front of Evie. "That's not how it looked from where I was standing."

Billy shrugged. "Maybe that's what they were asking for."

Evie's complexion paled at that comment, igniting a temper Addie thought she'd shed long ago. "I don't recall asking for you to put your fucking hands on me, asshole. Five year olds have better self-restraint."

A dark expression crossed Ben's features as his eyes shot to Addie. She didn't have long to think before he took the remaining few steps between them and pushed her behind him. It shocked any protest she could've come up with at the moment, taking note of their size difference as she stared up at his broad shoulders. The muscles there were tense, like he was ready to pounce at a moment's notice.

"Do what you want to annoy me," Ben snarled, "but leave them *out* of this."

Billy held his hands up. "Touchy, are we? What's the matter, Ben? Don't like it when others want to play with your toys?"

"Let's go, guys," Grace interrupted before Ben could reply. "As *fascinating* as y'all's dick measuring contest could get, we've all got a long day today, right?"

"I can arrange a private viewing if that's what you're after, Grace," the man on Billy's left said.

Good to know everyone in Billy's team was just like him. Perfect.

Ryan stepped beside his sister. "I'd like to see you fucking try."

Billy scoffed but smirked, as if this entire situation amused him more than annoying Addie and Evie. "See you guys around, then."

Ben remained where he stood, but Addie noted that his fists clenched on either side of him.

CHAPTER 15

Ben had been quiet since they'd taken off for their next destination. A storm to the north had cropped up with little time to talk about what happened. Addie expected jokes and teasing as always. Maybe for him to give her a hard time about having to step in—but there was nothing. He stayed completely silent. It was unnerving.

His eyes remained fixated on the road. Old-school country songs played over the radio, the only sound that filled the silence that stretched between them. It gave her way too much time to try and puzzle out this whole situation with Billy.

The tension between Ben, Brody, and the Storm Stalkers leader was palpable. And it seemed to be about something a hell of a lot more than some pissing contest about a documentary. It felt ... personal. Billy mentioned that they were all on the same team once upon a time, so what could've happened to sour things so much?

"Oh, I almost forgot," Ben said suddenly, surprising her from her train of thought. He reached into the backseat, digging about with a concentrated scowl before shoving a banana into her hands.

"A banana?"

Ben didn't look at her as he nodded. "Figured you hadn't eaten anything yet, so I grabbed it while we were checking out. Was gonna give it to you earlier, but, you know ... I was a bit preoccupied."

She stared down at the ripe yellow fruit in her hands—shame flooding her veins. "You didn't need to do all this. I can take care of myself, you know."

"If by *all this*, you mean the bare minimum, then sure. And I know you can."

"Then why?"

"Do I need a reason to care? You don't have to eat it if you don't want to. Just wanted you to have the option."

Heat pulsed up her neck and into her cheeks. *It was thoughtful.* "Thank you."

"Sure."

She needed something else to talk about to avoid the way her heart fluttered in her chest. The phone call she'd overheard between Ben and the mystery caller just before he'd joined her by the pool popped into her mind. What kind of business could he be doing in the wee hours of the morning?

"So..." Addie started, turning the banana in her hand. "Who were you on the phone with last night?"

"When? At the motel?"

"Yeah, before you came to sit with me. You were on the phone with someone."

He shrugged. "Just a business call."

When he didn't follow up with anything else, Addie huffed. She mentally put a pin in that topic. They had a while longer on the road, and Addie was too restless to fall back into silence again. So, she decided to move on to the next, more contentious question.

"Alright, if you won't answer that, how about this—what's the deal with you and Billy?"

Ben didn't turn. Instead, she noticed the whitening of his knuckles on the steering wheel. "He's an asshole. Not much to note there."

"Uh-huh. You forget that I've seen how you look when you're simply annoyed with someone—you look at me like that all the time."

That finally earned her a small smile that tiptoed into the dimples of his cheeks. "That's different."

"Then explain it to me," she said as she crossed her arms. "It's not like you have anything better to do."

Ben snorted, his grip on the steering wheel releasing enough that the color returned to his knuckles. The edges of his jawline softened a touch.

"It's nothing, firecracker. Don't worry about it," Ben finally said.

"First, stop calling me that," she scolded, but the noted lack of any force behind it made Ben's smile grow. "And second—you have to. You have no choice. I told you about my dad, so you have to tell me about you and Billy."

Ben winced. "Low blow."

"Yeah, well, if it gets you to talk, I'll go below the belt if I have to."

"Promise?" Ben asked, the corner of his mouth quirking as his gaze lingered on her. She wanted to smack the smug look off his face, but she was too busy fighting the burning in her chest.

"Don't distract me. It won't work," she insisted, adjusting the AC vent so that it would blow cool air onto her now heated skin. "Besides, I thought we were supposed to be on good terms now?"

"We are. I just didn't think that some minor flirting would distract you so much. I'll have to add that to my bag of tricks."

Minor flirting... That stumped her for a beat. Why would he flirt with her at all if he'd avoided kissing her?

"Is that how you flirt?" she challenged.

"And if it is?" he replied, his smile easy and natural.

Oh boy.

Seeing him smile like that softened the barbed-wires she'd placed around herself. And that scared her. She opened her mouth, closed it, and opened it again a few times before finally folding her arms across her chest. "You're still trying to distract me."

"Addie..."

"Come on. Just tell me. It can't be that bad."

Ben gnawed on his lower lip for a moment before sighing. "Billy used to work on our team. Not really that much *to* tell. He got a few corporate sponsors and a following with his streaming, and the rest is kind of history."

"I gathered that, but there's more to it than just that, right? What happened?"

"That's the thing. Nothing *did* happen that I know of. I met Billy around the same time that I met Brody. The three of us were decent enough friends, so we started this team together when we got out on our own. Everything was going smoothly up until Billy's mom got sick. He went home to be with her, in and out of surgery kind of thing, but she ended up passing away. After his mom died … he just didn't come back the same."

"What do you mean?"

"I don't know, it just wasn't like him. Started lashing out, particularly at me. Back then, I'd already taken more of the team lead role, so I don't know if that was it or if it was just easier to take his shit out on me." Ben shifted in his seat as he continued. "He'd dabbled with recording some of our chases when we first started out, and he'd gotten some traction online from that. But he started getting reckless, wanting to get more and more extreme shots, and didn't really seem to care who he put in harm's way to do it. Around that time, Grace and Ryan had started, and we didn't want Billy's antics to put them in danger too…. We had to make a decision that was best for the team, but he didn't exactly take kindly to us kicking him out."

"I imagine not."

"Then he got a few corporate sponsors who were willing to help him start a team of his own, so it wasn't like he was destitute. But he's sort of had it out for us ever since."

"What do you mean?"

"Started with just petty rumors that he would spread around to anyone willing to listen. How terrible we were to him, how we would *fabricate* data to match up with whatever we wanted it to say—stupid stuff like that. Then it started to escalate," he said, letting his words drift off for a moment before continuing once again. "This documentary with you and Evie is a lot more than just the fact that we needed the money. It's our chance to show the community that we aren't anything like what Billy has portrayed us to be."

Pieces of a puzzle she hadn't known she'd been putting together suddenly started to make sense.

"Well, if it's any consolation, I think that with the extra footage Evie has been filming of all of us together, it'll help disprove anything he's said."

"I can take a lot when it comes to Billy, I'm used to it at this point, but to see him talk to you like that," Ben continued as if he hadn't heard her, "and look at you like you're nothing more than a piece of meat—it really rubbed me the wrong way."

A stormy look that made even *her* shudder came over his features. She wasn't sure whether to be worried about what he was thinking or touched that he was *this* upset on her behalf.

"I'm a big girl, Ben. I've dealt with men a lot worse than Billy. I've read the bottom-of-the-barrel comments. There's not much Billy can say that I haven't already read a dozen times."

Ben's frown tightened. "That doesn't exactly comfort me—though that does explain a lot."

"Explain what?"

He nodded to the banana, still gripped in her hand. "The eating. The contacts. Is it because of what other people have said about what you look like?"

Addie's gut tightened.

"It's complicated," she offered, unsure what else to say, and went to divert attention from that. "Why does what Billy says to me bother you so much? You always say weird shit to me."

Ben notably wouldn't look at her as he replied, "It just does."

"What does that mean?"

"It just *does*, Addie," he ground out. "Drop it."

Oh, touched a nerve there. She wasn't exactly sure what nerve it was, but she couldn't resist the temptation to poke the bear.

"Are you angry, Ben?" she teased. *That's it.* Distract him so that he wouldn't see the conflict warring in her mind. That wouldn't backfire on her at all. Except it did when the deep void of his pupils turned on her. Dilating back like an all-consuming wave eroding the speckles of golden light in his irises.

"Boss," a loud voice boomed from the radio, causing both of them to jump in their seats. "Can you guys read us?"

Ben snatched the radio. "Yeah, yeah, we read you. What's up?"

"Grace needs to calibrate," Brody said, "and Evie was asking if Addie wanted to use the time to get some more talking segments?"

When Addie gave a thumbs-up, Ben flicked the turn signal for the approaching campground. "Yeah, pull in there, and we'll stop off for a bit."

CHAPTER 16

*A*ddie primped her hair as she faced the camera, holding up the microphone and waiting for the countdown. It was taking longer than usual, and she started to ask if everything was alright when Evie stopped and yanked the camera off the tripod.

"Sorry, give me a minute," her friend groaned as she fussed with the lens. "I think a bit of dirt got in here."

"Take your time! Need help?"

Evie shook her head, refusing to look up. "I'm good. It might take a minute, so you can go chill out for a bit."

Addie had hoped to have a quick check-in with Evie when they'd first pulled off, but Evie had stonewalled her, shutting the conversation down before it could begin by throwing herself into the camerawork. It hurt a bit, sure, but she understood. She knew Evie—she'd talk when she was ready. So, she gave her some space to work and took advantage of the free moment to herself.

She crossed the campsite parking lot, the thumping of her tennis shoes against the hard concrete grounding her nerves. Thankfully, the lot was empty aside from their own vehicles, which were all lined up neatly in a row at the end of the lot.

Addie made a beeline for a set of benches just outside of the log-styled guest area. A few minutes was exactly what she needed to collect herself. Her butt barely made contact with the surface when her phone dinged.

A muted groan hissed between her lips as she yanked it from her pocket.

John.

It wasn't anything egregious—only him checking on their status and requesting any preliminary footage for him to review—but Addie still didn't want to talk to him any more than was absolutely necessary. What had just happened with Evie and Billy only brought that anger she had toward him back to the surface.

She'd never been a particularly big fan of John to begin with—from all the snide comments he'd made about her appearance over the years, but now she outright despised him. The boys' club environment they'd cultivated had been suffocating, and she knew she would choke on the effort it was going to take whenever she *did* have to return.

It was a job. It paid the bills. A bit more and she'd be able to pay everything off. But she was starting to wonder if this job was worth all that it cost. Between her ever-depleting self-image and knowing what they'd done to her friend, she couldn't imagine having to be back there again.

Her fingers flew over the keys as she typed out a vague response.

The sound of Ben's laughter floated through the air from the ongoing conversation between him and Brody across the parking lot, though the actual conversation was sequestered into hand gestures and movements she couldn't understand. It was a pleasant melody that chased away the storm clouds in her head. She loved the deep timber of his voice, though she'd never tell him that. The way each word felt like a balm to her nerves, deep and soothing in a way that made the tension coiled in her neck ease.

Ben's gaze flitted in her direction, but she pretended not to notice.

It wasn't fair that she hesitated to fully trust him; she recognized that. Addie believed that people proved themselves through action, and his actions recently showed that he meant what he said. But she'd been fooled once before. What guarantee did she have that it wouldn't happen again? If working at the studio had taught her anything, it was to question everything. Every interaction. Every comment. Every motive. What was said to her face and what was said behind her back were often two different things.

Trusting him meant that it would be her fault if the other shoe eventually dropped.

Tony trotted out of the camper, entering her periphery as he headed to the building behind her. As he started to walk by, he stopped in his tracks, doing a double take at Addie. Registering him standing there, she looked up as he bent over, as if he were trying to get a better look at her.

"W-what is it?" she asked.

"Did you do something different? Something about you looks different today, and I can't put my finger on it...."

Ben answered before she could question what he meant, calling out from where he stood next to Brody. "She's not wearing those colored contacts."

"Oh! That's what it is! Something looked different recently, but I couldn't put my thumb on it until now. Why the hell would you cover those babies?"

"Says the guy with those baby blues? Please, mine are down right *spooky* compared to yours."

Tony made a face at her, one that pulled a giggle straight from her lungs. "Who the hell would call yours spooky?"

"Some viewers said I looked possessed."

Tony grimaced. "Harsh."

"Comes with the territory of being on live television, I guess."

"Want me to beat 'em up for you?" Tony joked, nudging her with his elbow. Addie couldn't help but laugh as she shook her head.

"No, but the sentiment is appreciated," she replied, and, despite herself, she smiled. Ben had said something similar. She hadn't believed him then, but a seedling of doubt had been planted. After all, she had never been self-conscious about them until she'd had to start getting in front of a camera.

Tony started to say something else as Evie stomped over. "I can't *believe* this!"

"What's wrong?"

"The footage! Some of it is gone!" Evie shouted as she threw her hands into the air.

Tony cocked his head. "What do you mean?"

Evie lifted the camera at her side up. "I *mean* that some of the segments Addie and I have filmed are *gone*! I had the talking segments on the memory card in this camera, and I looked at it after I cleared the dirt out of the lens, just to make sure everything was working, when I noticed some of the footage is gone. Poof!"

Addie pulled herself off the bench. "How much of it is gone?"

"Most of the ones of you talking. The one where you almost got your head taken off is still there, but a lot of the other ones we've taken on our own when things aren't as crazy? Most of those are gone."

"Is anything else gone? Like the footage of the tornadoes?" Tony asked.

Evie shook her head. "Thankfully, no. It seems like just some of the footage on this card was corrupted or something? I can't think of any other reason why segments have vanished like this...."

Grace's voice suddenly rang out from behind them. "We've got one! Confirmed a few miles north of here!"

"Never a dull moment around here," Brody laughed.

CHAPTER 17

"Stay on it, Tony!" Ben shouted into the radio as they flew down the road. "I don't want any surprises. Grace, you guys hang back and keep watch."

Hail the size of golf balls pelted the front window, making the already difficult visibility worse. Rain and hail destroyed their line of sight until it was only Ben's navigation system keeping them on their current path, as well as the spotty feedback Grace shouted out over the radio.

They were on the back side of the tornado if the damage they were avoiding was any indication, a beast curtained in dust and debris that managed to grow darker and darker.

Addie gazed out at the murky black wall of clouds ahead of them as she white-knuckled the passenger handle. Anxiety bubbled in her gut as she tried to focus. The first deployment they'd done had almost been a disaster *because of her*. She could've put Ben, Tony, and Ryan in danger if things had played out any differently.

Who was to say something like that wouldn't happen again? Only worse this time?

Before, she'd been itching to get back out into the field. Now she was unsure. What if she made the same mistake? What if all of those leering, awful comments about her at the station had been right? What if she was just some pretty face who didn't provide any real value?

She knew that those things people said didn't roll off her back as much as she hoped, but now she was sure they had instead clung to her like a second skin—sucking the life and self-esteem from her like a leech.

"What do you want to do, Ben?" Brody asked.

"Let's get a bit closer, then I'll make the call."

"Tell them I'm getting some *amazing* shots back here!" Evie's voice pierced through in the background. She sounded a bit more like herself.

No, Addie needed to focus. She studied the storm in the distance, watching the patterns and movements it made as she completely honed in on it.

Everything about this tornado was wrong—*felt* wrong.

When they'd arrived, it had more definition to it. A small little rope that exploded into something that was now shapeless, textureless. Now it was a near-solid wall of clouds and mist that curtained the contents held within. A dark and dangerous creature was hidden somewhere in the depths, just waiting to strike out.

The little "SW" at the bottom of the navigation system continued to needle straight ahead. They should be going northbound, following the trajectory most tornadoes did, but this one headed in the opposite direction. It would be one thing if she could *see* what the funnel was doing, but hidden by the curtain of rain, there was no way to predict where it would go next.

Trying to deploy with something this unpredictable would prove dangerous. Deadly, even.

But Addie hesitated to say anything—what if she was wrong? What if she made a bad call again, and they missed valuable data? Or worse, someone was hurt in the process?

Her breathing quickened as the car jostled her about, clutching onto the passenger handle tightly enough that her hand started to ache. The involuntary sound she made along with it seemed to catch Ben's attention as he turned to look at her. "What are you thinking?"

Addie chewed on her lip. "I-I don't know."

"You don't *know*?"

"Yes, Ben, I don't know!"

"Has Hell frozen over? Adelyn Walters doesn't have anything to say?"

She whirled on him. "Is this really the time to be making *jokes* like that?"

"If it means snapping you out of whatever the hell is going on in that head of yours? Then, yeah, I guess so," Ben ground out. "I don't exactly have time to play twenty questions, so tell me what you're thinking!"

Punctuating his point, hail began to pelt the hood of the SUV—each ping against it reverberating straight through into Addie's bones. This was the *worst* tornado to try to deploy with—but Ben would already know that. She saw his fingers squeezing and fidgeting with the steering wheel. She saw the hesitation as he looked from the radio receiver to the storm, like he was itching to call things off.

What he was looking for from her, then, she wasn't sure.

"I don't—I don't want to be wrong again," she said quickly. "Do what you think is best."

Ben shot her a sympathetic yet tight expression. "We don't have time to unpack *all* of that right now. Can you focus for me, please?"

Addie sat up straighter as the ball of nerves began to release her from its control.

She leaned forward in her seat, eyes to the sky once more. "I don't like this trajectory, and over there," she said as she pointed off to the west, "there are strong inflow jets pulling in. Whatever's in there is *big*."

"If it stays on the current heading, though, we might have an opening."

Addie shook her head. "We can't know that for sure. There's too much cloud coverage wrapped around it to tell what it's gonna do. Besides, I don't like how it looks on navigation. I'm more worried it's gonna pull an El Reno."

Ben glanced down at the navigation on the dashboard. "Good point. I think we should abandon deployment. Do you agree?"

Of course she did, but why was Ben asking her? Wasn't he the one who made a big show about who was boss and all that? Why did he suddenly want her input so badly?

"Ben—"

"Yes or no, Addie?" he interrupted, piercing her with a sideways glance.

She swallowed. "Yes. I think that would be the safest call. I don't like how—"

"Wind just backed—it's headed southwest now," Brody called out over the radio.

Addie grabbed the radio. "Are you sure?"

"Positive. Debris ball just lit up on echo."

Ben took the radio from her. "Bail to the north, we don't want to end up in the bear's cage. Abandon deployment. We can try for the next one. Tell Evie that we can focus on footage. Do we need to set up for any talking segments?"

Addie shook her head. "I don't think that would be safe. We don't know exactly where the core is or if there are multiple vortexes hidden in that wall. I can do a voice-over for whatever footage Evie is getting back there."

"You get that, Evie?" Ben asked into the radio.

"Loud and clear, captain! I agree with Addie," Evie called out in the background. "I'll keep the camera rolling, so we can get as much as we can."

"Alright. Tony, Ryan? You guys hang back and lead the RV," Ben instructed, his gaze hesitating on Addie for a brief moment before flicking back to the road. "Addie and I will see if we can head around to get a better view on the other side of it, but Brody, keep us updated if you see anything on radar."

Addie heard Evie in the background once more. "Will they be okay on their own?"

"You kidding me? With those two, it'll be like leaving two kids alone at Disneyland," Ryan shot back.

"Ding dong, they can hear you!" Grace said, sounding closer to Brody.

"That was the point!"

"We got you," Brody responded before anyone else could speak. "There's a creek a few miles in that direction, so you'll want to be careful. We'll be on standby."

The radio clicked as the live feed turned off.

Addie dug her phone out of her pocket, chucking it into the cup holder for the time being. "I'll record on my phone if we see anything and the rest can't get there in time."

"Stay on this heading, Ben. I think there's an opening for us up ahead!" Addie called out, hand bracing her against the dashboard as they flew onto another bumpy dirt road.

The tornado had grown further than what it had been just moments before, swallowing the skyline for an endless distance across the horizon. No rays of light poked through the front pushing forward. Despite it being early afternoon, when the sun would be at its highest and brightest in the sky, nothing from above the wall of clouds could be seen.

They'd managed to find a road almost directly following the wake of the storm. Ben's gaze was transfixed on the pavement ahead. Every bit of his concentration was devoted to avoiding debris littering the road in front of them. Fortunately, there was little of it aside from the scattered farming equipment.

Thank God it's nothing but cornfields and crops this far out.

"I see it," Ben replied and glanced in her direction. "Look, there's something I've been meaning to talk to you about...."

Addie shot him an exasperated look, waving at the storm just ahead. "And you choose *now* to talk about it?"

"Glad to see you've snapped out of whatever spiral you were in a few minutes ago," Ben muttered. "No, look, about the other—"

"What are you guys seeing up there?" Brody interrupted over the radio.

Ben scrambled to pick the radio up, his fingers nearly dropping it before he caught hold of it again. "Th-there's an opening we found in the back. We're in its wake right now, but stay back for now. This road isn't big enough to fit the RV. Follow Tony and Ryan in the other car."

She held back a giggle as he fumbled to put the radio back on the receiver. What the hell had gotten into him? "You okay, Ben?"

"I'm fine," he ground out. "Look, I just ... I don't … I just don't want to give you the wrong idea—"

Wrong idea? What did he—?

Oh.

Addie felt the pit of her stomach as it dropped out.

Last night. He didn't want to give her the wrong idea about *last night*. When she'd almost kissed him, when she'd almost wanted to tell him how her feelings for him were starting to change. How she had started to think of him differently and that it both terrified her and exhilarated her all at once because he was the *one* person she'd always admired and respected. Even when she'd told him otherwise. Even when she was angry at him, felt betrayed by him.

How she wanted to stay with him.

Everything bubbling up inside of her that had been primed and ready at the surface all squashed.

He didn't want to give her the wrong idea.

Because he didn't feel the same way.

She forced the smile onto her face and waved him off before he could finish, turning to hide the emotion already welling in her eyes. "Don't worry about it. No wrong ideas given. You were just comforting me last night."

Ben looked pained as he shook his head. "No, Addie, let me finish. That's not what I—"

Addie silently unclicked her seatbelt and rolled down her window. She would do something for the documentary at the very least. She needed to be careful and quick, but it would be an impressive shot for the documentary if her phone cooperated.

It wasn't the smartest idea, what she was about to do, but she needed this. She couldn't stand the embarrassment leaking from every single one of her pores. She needed to put herself back in the one element she knew she could count on. The storm.

No more feeling insecure about herself. No more wondering if she was good enough. The storm would decide that for itself. Everything else in her life felt out of control—and all she wanted was to feel the storm enveloping her in its chaos.

Ben's mouth was open with his unfinished statement, but he shot her a curious look when she pulled herself up and snatched her phone.

Addie shoved her body through the window opening.

She balanced herself on her elbows to point the phone's camera in front of them. Her knees folded in place beneath her in the seat.

"Addie! What the *hell* are you doing?!" Ben shouted as she steadied herself and clicked the red button to begin recording. Ben managed to grab her by the back of her jeans. She could feel the tug of it as he tried to get her to return inside—his fingers clenched into the fabric through one of the belt loops as he continued yelling at her from the driver's seat, though she couldn't hear him over the cacophony of sounds in the open air.

Rain pelted her relentlessly like tiny little bee stings that peppered across her exposed flesh. She had to squint to keep the stinging away from her eyes, her eyelashes and nearly closed eyelids serving as a makeshift umbrella.

Her skin tingled and buzzed with energy despite the bee-like stings from the rain, despite the pain churning in her gut. It was better to face it out here in the open—to let the tears streaking down her cheeks from the wind and rain intermingle with the tears she let flow more freely.

Her phone's camera managed to hold up beautifully, despite the conditions. She wasn't sure how the rain would affect the footage, but she also wasn't sure she cared. It felt more like an excuse now to let her feel the power charging around her.

A laugh bubbled out of her as she held her phone steady, letting her eyelids fully flutter shut as she *felt* the storm. The wind as it whipped her soaked hair across her skin. The orchestra of sounds roaring across the open field. The charge of electricity as a crack of thunder reverberated through the sky.

She felt alive.

She felt truly *part* of this majestic wonder of nature.

A sharp tug pulled her back into the cab. She landed with a thump into her seat, her phone clutched to her chest in surprise.

"Are you fucking *insane*?!" Ben shouted, one hand still clenched around the fistful of her jeans.

Addie's now soaking-wet hair clung to her face. The ponytail she'd tied her hair into nothing more than a fistful of dripping wet tangles.

"I-I got some amazing footage," she stammered, the adrenaline still pounding in her veins as she held her phone up. "It'll be a good segment."

"*Fuck* the documentary! You could've gotten yourself killed!" he yelled. If she weren't so embarrassed about everything else, she'd comment on the downright *distraught* look on Ben's face. Worry lines crinkled around his eyes, softening the hard expression he was giving her.

"We're far enough back that getting sucked out wouldn't be a concern, especially with how it looks like it's already starting to destabilize. I was fine, Ben."

"That's not worth getting thrown from the car you fucking *infuriating* woman. I don't—Fuck, *now* what?" Ben ground out, his attention diverted to something behind her. It was then that the sound of another vehicle fast approaching on their right blazed to life.

A pair of familiar-looking black SUV's quickly pulled up on their right, engines revving as the driver and its passenger of the lead vehicle came into view. "Looks like Billy and his team decided to join us."

Ben scrunched his nose to move his glasses further up the bridge of it, making the sneer he shot in Billy's direction all the more apparent.

"Great," Ben spat out. "*Perfect* timing."

CHAPTER 18

Billy waved from the passenger seat, wearing an unmistakable shit-eating grin. One of Billy's teammates hovered over the center console as they held a camera up, which made it clear that he was live-streaming to his audience.

"Ignore him," Addie instructed. "I don't want this whole documentary to get pulled just because the station caught us acting nasty. Regardless of how much he might deserve it."

The protest was practically on the tip of Ben's tongue; she could see it as he opened his mouth. Instead, he let out a frustrated sigh. "You're right."

They had bigger problems to worry about anyway.

The little dirt road they were on had gotten steeper as it cut alongside a nearby creek. A thick line of shrubs bordered the road on the right, marking the end of one property line, whereas there was nothing separating them from the incline to their left. Worse, the uptick in rain slickened the road itself and transformed the creek into a full-on raging river.

It didn't help that debris crashed down around them like hail, blown straight into them from the outer bands of the storm. Dirt and rocks pitter-pattered against the windshield as everything in the path they followed, which had been sucked into the air, collided back to the earth.

"Addie, Ben, how are you guys holding up?" Brody called out from the radio.

Ben lifted the receiver up. "We're following in its wake and have some debris. Where are you?"

"A few miles west of the system, on the main highway. Evie's been getting some great shots from here."

"Good. Keep on your heading, and let her get as much footage as she can—"

One of Billy's teammates chose that exact moment to lean out their window to whoop and cheer in excitement for their stream. Loud enough that it could apparently be overheard on the radio because Addie heard Grace groan. "Oh, don't tell me those idiots are out there?"

"Want me and Ryan to circle back and follow you?" Tony chimed in. "So they don't try to bully you guys off the road?"

"No, road's too narrow for many cars as it is. We'll be fine."

Addie continued watching the tornado, ignoring the nearby vehicles and chatter. The clouds that had been wrapped around the funnel like a menacing wall of devastation began to disperse. Like a veil lifting, it was just enough that Addie could locate the main funnel more clearly. Its movements became sporadic as it twisted and twirled in the open field a few miles ahead.

"The inflow band is going limp. I think it's starting to starve," Addie commented.

The shape of it narrowed down into a thin little rope that extended into the sky. It whipped about like a cowboy trying to lasso its last cow before calling it a day—careful and precise in its motion as it took final aim.

It was beautiful in its own chaotic and destructive right.

"Agreed," Ben said and raised the radio back up. "We'll circle back to you guys when its completely fizzled—Fuck!"

Ben clutched the steering wheel to avoid a tractor tire that had landed in the middle of the road. The black SUV swerved to avoid it as well, drastically and unexpectedly enough that Ben had to turn the wheel harder.

A scream lodged itself in Addie's throat as the car flew over the edge of the embankment, and, in a flash, Addie had a horrifying realization.

She'd forgotten to put her seatbelt back on.

There was no time to search for it as the vehicle slid, threatening to overturn and roll them down the rest of the way at a moment's notice. A pair of arms snaked around her middle as Ben yanked her to him sharply, holding on as she clenched her eyes shut.

🦌 🦌

*I*ncredible stillness.

It's what Addie opened her eyes to when she finally gathered the courage to.

She flexed her fingers once, twice, just to make sure that she wasn't dreaming.

The car hadn't flipped.

Her line of sight followed the trail of tire tracks from where they'd slid from the road down to where they rested, mere inches from rushing water. The SUV tilted in the direction of the embankment, further pressing her body back against a hard wall of muscles. The pair of surprisingly strong arms continued to brace themselves around her, holding her close. Unrelenting, as if afraid she'd be ripped from their confines.

Ben.

"Ben?" she asked, surprised at the shakiness in her own voice, as if it didn't belong to her. "Are you okay?"

An uncomfortable-sounding grunt reverberated through her back as he tried to adjust himself, still holding onto her with one arm firmly wrapped around her midsection.

"Yeah, I'm fine," he answered. "How about you?"

Addie released a shaky breath, shock giving way to an all-consuming relief that stole the breath from her lungs. And not for herself. Emotion crept up her throat and clamped her vocal cords shut, as if her body feared that uttering a sound would betray her. The last thing she wanted was for him to see the tears she was fighting.

He'd protected her... again.

"I need to hear the words, sweetheart," Ben prompted when she didn't answer. "Tell me you're not hurt so that I can start figuring out how to get us out of here."

Sweetheart? The laugh she choked out sounded wetter than she intended, but it helped clear her throat enough to speak. "Yeah, I'm okay. A bit shaken but not completely stirred."

Dull static whispered in the background from the radio, seemingly having switched frequencies. There was an odd sense of calm listening to it, the sound fighting off all the noise pinging around in her head. A welcome relief, given the circumstances.

Ben's other hand came up to grab her hip, a surprised squeak coming out as he wordlessly turned her to face him. The stern crease in his brow was the only indicator that he hadn't believed her.

Wild tangles of hair swirled around his head, even messier than it had been earlier when she'd rolled the window down to get that shot of the tornado. It reminded her of that boyish look he'd sported when they were in grad school, the one that she'd once wondered what it would feel like to comb her fingers through.

It made her all the more aware of how the lean of the SUV affected their positions, with her entire body pressing him firmly into the door.

Her gaze flicked to his lips. The way they were set in a firm frown, the kind that Ben always seemed to have whenever he fussed over her. Ben's hand cupped her face, his eyes roving over her as he inspected for injury, despite her words.

"Don't see anything, but that doesn't mean I'm not gonna fucking throttle Billy the next time I see him," he snarled.

Ben rubbed his thumb across her cheek in a tender move that ripped a sigh from her. The memory of that almost-kiss tingled across her lips as she diverted her eyes up to his. The familiar warm amber pooling there behind his glasses did little to hide the expressive quality to them—lighting up for a flash before becoming swallowed into the depth of black. His gaze flicked from her eyes to her lips then back. It was so quick, almost subconscious, that she would've missed it if he didn't do it again. This time lingering a bit longer on them before his gaze returned to hers.

The temperature outside was mild, but she shivered as she instinctively sank against him. There was something in the way he looked at her that melted her. Chasing the heat that radiated from him in droves.

There was a breath of hesitation as he leaned in, the tickle of his breath against her lips. Was he about to kiss her? God, she hoped so. It was the only thing she wanted, no, *needed*. Hooded eyes held her against him, as if the sheer will to not close them and drown in the kiss just millimeters away was enough to kill him.

If he was looking for her to be the rational one, the one to stop whatever was happening, he was mistaken. All she knew was that she *needed* him.

Before she could say anything, Ben captured her lips with his.

A need was born deep in her core—desperate for the taste of him, the feel of him, the *heat* that exploded and throbbed. The tension between them finally pulled taut and snapped into place, a desire that lurked in the shadows, waiting for the perfect moment to strike.

Ben's lips moved hungrily against hers like a man starved—like she was both his ruin and his salvation. He drew her further into him, and she happily succumbed. Kissing Ben was a wholly divine experience, and all other thoughts, all other worries, melted away until only he was there to catch her.

Ben drew Addie into his lap, yanking her legs around him to encircle his hips, like the air between them was his last. Her hands finally fulfilled her longstanding wish and tangled into his thick black locks—loving the way it felt between her fingers. Ben kneaded into the curve of her ass, his fingers digging into the flesh there like his life depended on it.

It was beautiful. It was perfect.

And then their moment ended as quickly as it had started when the sound of voices exploded in the distance.

"Ben! Addie!"

"Ben!"

"Can you guys hear us?"

The two ripped apart from one another like they'd scalded themselves. But the heat between them remained, both of them panting from both shock and arousal as they stared at one another. Ben's lips were a pinkish color from her efforts that did nothing to help quell the throbbing in her core—instead having to clench her legs together to avoid throwing herself on top of him.

Through the rearview mirror, Addie could see the others as they started running down the embankment.

"I need a fucking drink." Ben groaned out a laugh.

CHAPTER 19

"They can't get away with it!" Ryan shouted, a beer in one hand and pounding the curb of the bar with the other. "They did it on purpose!"

"You know we can't prove that," Brody said tightly. "Both of them were swerving out of the way of debris. Ben and Addie were just closer to the embankment than they were."

"There's no damage," Grace confirmed, "so it's not like we could argue that they did any actual harm."

"Evie wouldn't have caught anything on camera either," Tony, who hovered just behind Evie, added after swallowing a swig of his beer. "We were too far away and focused on catching the tornado as it fizzled out, so we didn't notice until we couldn't get a hold of them on the radio."

"Well, it's still bullshit," Ryan hissed uselessly.

Ben was oddly quiet at the other end of the group, looking off into the distance as if lost in thought.

He'd been like that since their kiss. Her lips still tingled from the memory of his lips on hers, but now her stomach twisted. She felt more confused than she did before because, for a moment there in that car, she'd thought maybe she hadn't been wrong. Maybe he actually *did* want to kiss her before.

But he hadn't said a word to her since.

Maybe he did mean what he said and was just overcome in the moment? That was what she thought at first on the long, silent car ride to the motel. Neither had said a word about it after the group had found them. The longer the silence had stretched, the more anxiety bubbled in her stomach.

Cold beer in hand, she tried to think of *anything* else to escape her head.

Addie was curious what footage Evie had taped during the chase. It had been such a whirlwind after they'd pulled the SUV away from the creek that she hadn't thought to ask. It was a bit surreal that, not for one second, did she think about the entire reason she was here in the first place.

It only added another layer of emotion as it all churned in her gut.

"Let's not obsess over what was," Ben finally said as he glanced at Ryan. "We had a successful chase. Yes, it could've been made much worse if the embankment hadn't been as slick as it was and the SUV had flipped, but it didn't. You guys are all safe, and we got some great shots for the documentary, so let's focus on that. Huh?"

He glanced in her direction, but she couldn't meet his eyes. Not yet. She'd process later when she was alone in her motel room. Until then, she'd do what she did best at work.

Fake it.

A TV-ready smile appeared on her face, the motion robotic. "Agreed. Let's have some fun! There's line dancing happening right behind us. Why don't we give it a try?"

Ryan chuckled and popped off his stool. "Fine, but don't blame me if I wipe the dance floor with you guys."

"You couldn't dance your way out of a paper bag," Grace scoffed as she sashayed into the crowd, her movements accentuating the soft curls of her platinum-blonde hair—let loose and free from its usual ponytail.

Ryan followed, the two already bickering before they disappeared.

With a shrug, Evie snagged Addie's hand and pulled her along. A night of a few drinks and dancing sounded like the perfect way to release the tension.

Evie easily parted the crowd, several heads turning to watch her as they passed. It was hard not to envy her as she dragged Addie. Evie's dark, tanned skin radiated an almost ethereal glow underneath the harsh bar lighting. Even her long black hair effortlessly cascaded down her back like soft waves beneath a starry midnight sky—peppered with flecks of starlight from the incandescent bulbs above the dance floor. Addie couldn't help the flare of envy she felt at how effortlessly beautiful both her and Grace appeared, with minimum effort no less.

All the time—the primping and prepping, the curling and swipes of makeup—it took for her to capture just a fraction of their natural beauty was an undertaking of mythic proportions. While Grace and Evie looked like mythical vixens freed from the constraints of everyday life, Addie glanced at the reflection of herself in a nearby window—wishing she'd had more time to freshen up.

Her hair was a bit less messy than it had been, though her stint outside the window in the wind certainly hadn't done her any favors.

Evie nudged her with her hip as they stopped among the other dancers starting to line up for the next dance, ripping her from her thoughts. "I never thought you'd be one to want to try line dancing."

"Figured it might be nice to blow off some steam."

"You thought right. I'm just glad *someone* suggested it," Evie said as the music picked up, and they began following along and mirroring the other dancers around them. "I've never line danced before, so I was just dying for an excuse to try it."

It was the first time since their run-in at the motel with Billy that Evie seemed to be more herself, much to Addie's relief.

"Well, then consider me the ring leader for our night of chilling the fuck out," she replied, laughing when she nearly tripped over herself trying to mirror a turn.

Evie threw her head back, the sound of her laughter ringing in Addie's ears. "Well, look at you, being all brave—got you cursing and everything."

"I'm not as much of a stick in the mud as you thought, huh?"

Evie's expression softened. "Addie, I don't actually think you're a stick in the mud...."

"You literally joked with Ben about it when you first met him. It's okay, though. You might be right. I'm not as much fun as I used to be."

"I shouldn't have said that," Evie said seriously. "I was feeling nervous and insecure being with a new team like this, especially after what happened with Frank, so I went for the low-hanging fruit at your expense. I'm sorry."

Despite the music and dancing around them, Addie stopped to look at her friend. "I-it's okay. I know I can be. I used to be a lot more fun."

Evie frowned. "But I like the person you are. I just wish *you* did."

Addie nearly tripped again, this time as the smile dropped from her face. "I don't know what you mean."

"It's okay if you're not okay, Addie," Evie replied, not missing a beat as she continued dancing alongside her. "I've tried not to pry too much, but I've noticed things that have worried me."

"How can you possibly worry about me? You haven't really talked with me about what happened at the motel, I didn't know what was going on with you and Frank, I've been a *terrible* friend to you, and—"

Evie held up her hand. "Addie, I didn't *want* you to know about what happened. Remember? And you might not think you're a good friend, but you are. I told you what happened and that I didn't want to talk about it any more, and you respected my boundaries. You knew why I froze when Billy's slimy friend grabbed me, and you didn't hesitate to intervene. I'm sorry I haven't really talked about it with you since. I've just been in my own feelings about it, but even then, you still didn't push me. You gave me space to figure things out. That sounds like a good friend to me. But I hope you know that I worry about you, too, don't you?"

Addie shrugged sheepishly, feeling like every eye in the room was on them as they stood awkwardly in the middle of the dance floor. "I-I know that...."

"Sometimes, I don't think you do," Evie continued. "I've been kind of in my own little world, trying to figure out my feelings, but I've seen that you haven't been eating much again."

Embarrassment once again flooded Addie's senses, and she wondered, if not outright hoped, that the dance floor would open up and swallow her whole. Just how many people had noticed?

"Did you tell Ben?"

Evie shook her head. "I didn't. He asked if I knew anything about it, so I told him that I'd noticed it, too. Look, I'm going to respect your boundaries, as you have with mine, if you don't want to get into it. I get it. It's a sensitive topic, and you seem like you have a lot on your mind right now—and not just about what happened earlier. Am I right?"

Was it so obvious? Addie couldn't help but wonder if all of her emotions were so apparent to everyone else. If everything she was thinking, worrying about, fussing over, was stamped onto her forehead in bright-red letters.

"You don't have to say anything," Evie continued, throwing her a wink. "Just know I'm here if you want to talk, okay? In the meantime, don't fake it. Just have fun. Stop overthinking everything."

Addie scoffed as they followed the group into another turn. Evie had always been free as a bird—so relaxed and carefree that it seemed like nothing could get under her skin. Though ... that wasn't entirely true, was it?

Tonight, Addie wouldn't be the uptight goodie-two-shoes that she pretended to be at the station, on camera. She'd just ... be.

Another turn and she caught the eye of Ben, nearly across the room.

Ben's gaze rested on her, as if he'd been watching her the entire time. He leaned back against the bar next to Brody and Tony, and Addie couldn't help the tingle across her skin. And when he smiled at her, the kind that creased his dimples into each cheek, she couldn't help but smile in return.

*A*s the music flowed, Addie *did* start to forget about all the things running rampant in her head. The easy melody and beat freed her body and coaxed her into moving to the beat. The stomping of feet and the reverberation of every clap before a turn. The steady vibrations coursing straight through her, relaxing the tension that had settled between her shoulders.

She laughed. She twirled. Everything else fell away for a little while.

Ryan and Grace, who had finally stopped squabbling, appeared in the crowd and made their way over. Of their little group, the siblings seemed to fit with the rest of the crowd the most.

Grace looked like the country-singer version of a Barbie doll, with her bright-blonde hair, pale skin, rosy cheeks, and soft-green eyes. It was hard to imagine her as anything but the tough-as-nails mechanic she knew instead of this blonde bombshell.

Even Ryan looked different. His normally untamed brown hair tucked beneath a cowboy hat, something that Brody had teased him about mercilessly on their way over there but actually suited him. It reminded her of that rough-and-tumble look from the day they'd met, this time paired with the casual jeans and simple white T-shirt.

Tony finally came over to join them, standing as close to Evie as possible, and Ryan grabbed Addie's hand as the song changed tempos and led her to the music. Evie and Grace just about doubled over laughing, but Tony soon swept Evie up toward the dance floor, leaving Grace behind. Not for long, Addie noted, as Brody walked in her direction from the bar.

She desperately tried not to trip over her own two feet. Ryan swept them both across the dance floor like a pro. Laughter bubbled out of her as he twirled her out, adding a dramatic gesture with his other arm as if he were on a ballroom showcase.

"I didn't know you competed!" Addie teased when Ryan pulled her back.

"Only when everyone else around here can't keep up with me," he replied, a mischievous grin overtaking his features. "Though, I fear our dance might be cut short."

She wasn't sure what he meant and was about to turn, but instead he quickly twirled her out in another spin. This time, she didn't have his hands to guide her along, leaving her spinning in place until another pair of hands grabbed her hips. Larger, warmer, more firm.

When her world stopped spinning, she let out a gasp.

"My turn," Ben said as he nodded at Ryan, who seemed less than perturbed by the change in dance partner, immediately shimmying in Grace and Brody's direction as they laughed.

Addie's expression remained frozen as Ben pulled her in close, his hands holding her against him.

She cleared her throat. "I didn't think you were going to dance."

He shrugged, beginning to move them to the beat of the music. "I needed the right partner."

"Am I the right partner, then?" she hummed, fighting the hurt and betrayal threatening to choke her.

"I think we make a pretty good team."

Addie scoffed. "Are you sure? Because I've gotten some mixed messaging on that."

Ben scrunched his eyebrows together. "What does that mean?"

She tried to look away, afraid that she'd already said too much. But Ben wouldn't let her escape his gaze, lifting one of his hands from her hips and tilting her chin back to look into those pools of amber. There was an unreadable expression in them despite the overhead lighting flaring in his glasses.

"Addie," Ben scolded, the deep rumble of his voice surprisingly gentle, "don't hide from me. I thought, by this point, you could be honest with me."

The sad part was that she wanted to. She wanted that more than anything. To be honest and be rid of this rock that had formed in the pit of her stomach. But the bigger part of her was afraid. Would it be awkward if she was completely honest? What if he flat-out rejected her? Would they be able to remain professional so that they could continue to film the documentary? There was so much riding on this succeeding, more than for her own career. The team needed this, to clear up the bullshit that Billy had placed around their name.

"It's just that ... I don't know if this is something we should discuss at all. Things have happened and ... and you don't need to explain why you did what you did or why you act like you care when I'm not sure if you actually do or not or—"

"Hold on, you think I'm ... what? *Pretending* to care or something? What kind of asshole does that?"

Shoot. Did he think she was calling him an asshole right now? She was already messing this up.

"I don't—Ben, I don't think you're a—"

"Well, only a dick bag would *pretend* to care about someone like that. Is that what you think I've been doing? Because, Addie, that isn't true, I—"

Before he could continue, she held her hand up and pressed it against his lips, stopping him. His eyes flared wide before softening. There was a sad expression in them that just about broke her heart entirely, but she knew that he *would* break her heart if she let him finish.

"It's okay. I'm sorry. You know how I get when I don't know what to say," she started, slowly pulling her hand away from his mouth. "I know you care, just not *like that*, and things just got a little chaotic in the car, and I don't want you to make excuses about why you kissed me, so just ... don't?"

He stared at her, the gentleness still lingering there in his eyes.

"I think I'm actually gonna turn in a bit early tonight, so I'll see you bright and early tomorrow," she said, taking advantage of his pause to pull herself away.

She turned and quickly trotted to the exit, bursting the doors open and out into the night air, ignoring the sound of her own name as Ben called after her.

CHAPTER 20

"Addie, wait, please," Ben's voice called out as she walked away, barely restraining herself from breaking out into a sprint. The sound of the pavement scuffling beneath her feet became her focus, pretending she couldn't hear him.

Rejection chased her, calling her name, and she wasn't ready to face it right now.

If he tried to explain why he'd kissed her, or God forbid, if he tried to *apologize* or something ... No, she couldn't take it.

A second time might break her.

Everything was too raw, and their earlier brush with danger had cut her nerves wide open. Exposed and electric.

A rumble of thunder shook the ground as she hurried. It would start raining soon, which honestly would be great. With enough distance, and rain coming down, Ben might not chase after her.

But that came to an abrupt halt as Ben easily out-paced her and placed himself directly in her path. "Would you hold on a second?!"

She barely avoided bumping into him. "Ben, please..."

"You can't just run away in the middle of a conversation, Addie," he said, the sternness of his voice not quite reaching his eyes.

The light of the streetlamp nearby provided a gentle glow for them to see by, but she wished they were shrouded in total darkness. She could disappear into the void and pretend like nothing was wrong.

"Ben, I can't do this right now," she started. "I don't want to hear whatever excuse you're about to make. Please, just let me go."

"Excuses? Why would I ..." Ben started before huffing out an aggravated breath. "Would you stop putting fucking words in my mouth and just hold on a minute?"

This was it. The end of the road, she could feel it.

Of course, he would want to make it clear that it didn't mean anything. He was the team lead. It was his job to make sure everyone was safe and professional—just because they'd known each other from a long time ago didn't mean she'd be exempt from that.

"Look, we have a serious problem—"

Here it comes.

"—because I have feelings for you, Addie. And you're making it *really* hard for me to tell you that when you keep trying to *run away* from me."

Addie blinked a few times as her mouth fell open. The clouds finally opened up as rain trickled down from above, a slow and steady stream that normally would've sent them running for the hills. But both remained rooted in place. Droplets of water weighed down her eyelashes, forcing her gaze to Ben's as if by some cosmic design.

"W-what?" she sputtered out.

When another crack of thunder shook the sky, Ben took a tentative step closer to her.

"I have feelings for you, Addie," he repeated, the rain spreading across his shirt and soaking it through—becoming a second skin of sorts within a few seconds. It molded to him, outlining every inch of his chest as it rose and fell.

It made her suddenly aware of the tightening of her own clothing against her skin. She felt it cling to her the more it rained, turning from a slow trickle into a downpour.

And yet ... neither of them moved.

"But... you said you didn't want to give me the wrong idea," she finally let out, unsure still if she'd misheard him. *Convinced* that she had.

"Oh, Jesus Christ, Addie," Ben sighed, rubbing the bridge of his nose just below his glasses. "You didn't let me finish. You'd just told me about your dad and the nightmare, and you were feeling vulnerable. I pushed you away because I didn't want to take advantage of you. I didn't want to give you the wrong idea that it was the only reason I wanted to kiss you."

Oh.

"And then ... earlier?"

Ben ran a hand through his hair, the water slicking it back. "I lost control of everything telling me I *shouldn't* kiss you. But kissing you was a curse to my existence—knowing what it feels like, what you *taste* like, the sounds you make? I'll never know a waking moment of peace if I don't get to experience it again. Look, I've been trying really fucking hard not to want you, but I do, Addie. I've wanted you so long that it *hurts*...."

"You can't—You can't mean that, Ben," she stammered.

"Oh, but I do," he hummed. His hands began to move, the motion hypnotic as he pointed to himself, crossed his arms across his chest, palms flat against it, then pointed at her. Continuing the pattern several times until he finally lowered his arms to his sides. It felt important, whatever he said, but with no context other than the given "you" and "me", she had no idea what he was trying to say.

"What does that mean?" she asked, her voice barely above a whisper.

"Maybe someday I'll tell you," he teased, a hint of amusement twinkling in his eyes. "Addie, you've had me from the day we met."

"You can't mean that, Ben. It's been *years* since we—"

He offered a small smile. "Believe me, I'm painfully fucking aware of that."

All this time?

"You never ... You never said anything...."

"When could I have? By the time I realized how I felt, the whole plagiarism thing was going on, and—I was confused. And then it was too late," he said, the downpour intensifying with each passing moment. "I knew I'd messed things up, so I didn't say anything. I let you go. I went on with my life, and it worked for a while. Life and work got busy, and grad school seemed like such a distant memory. And then I saw you again, after all these years, and everything came crashing back in—like it was yesterday."

"We haven't spoken in years.... And you told John you'd work with anyone but me...."

Ben shrugged, offering a small smile. "I wasn't expecting to see you, much less work together on this. And if I recall, you weren't exactly keen on working with me either."

Addie threw her hands up in the air. "Only because we drove each other *crazy*! And I thought you'd thrown me under the bus back then! I was *also* thrown into this situation at the last minute. And we've spent a good majority of the time arguing!"

"Arguing is just our form of foreplay," he replied casually, but she didn't miss the way his pupils flared at her. An involuntary shiver shot up her spine at the way his voice seemed to thicken on the word *foreplay*.

It was everything she'd secretly wanted to hear, amid all the fears and worries she'd been having ever since she'd walked into that conference room. The things she didn't even *know* she'd wanted to hear.

Hadn't she done the same thing?

She'd moved on with her life—tried to let the memories about him slip away.

And it had worked. She *had* forgotten about him. She'd forgotten how easy it was to be around him, how she could say whatever she was thinking without worrying that he would think less of her. Knowing that he would say something just as snarky back. That he would never question her intelligence, only challenge her.

Life had gotten messy—between having to leave her last team to take care of her dad, all the bills and medical costs that she'd been slowly drowning in, and everything at the station...

But all of those feelings came back tenfold. All those things she'd pushed down and tried to ignore.

All right here now, screaming at her to do something. *Say something.*

"I know this is a lot to throw on you, but I can't let another chance pass me by. I can't make the same mistake twice," Ben continued as he took a step closer to her, so close that she could feel the heat of his skin as it radiated off of him. "But I need to know how you feel. I need you to tell me what *you* want."

There were a thousand different things she wanted to say. A thousand things she *should* say, but nothing came.

Instead, she closed the gap between them. Ben's breathing hitched, and his eyes widened as she slowly took his face in her hands. Rain continued to pitter-patter around them in waves as the sky opened further, but neither moved to cover themselves. The rain washed away all the worries, doubts, and things they'd hidden.

"You mean that," she whispered, "true or false?"

His lips slowly curled into a smile—the kind that lit up his entire face despite the darkness threatening to swallow them. The kind that made her feel a bit weak in the knees.

"True."

She wanted to respond, to tell him all of the things she'd been feeling and holding back, but words felt too simple for what they needed.

With a gentle tug, she pulled his face down and kissed him.

His lips were supple against hers, relinquishing the obvious surprise at her boldness instantly. It became a gentle exploration as Ben easily took over with his height advantage. Softer, gentler than it had been when they'd kissed earlier. His arms circled her waist as he kissed her back, slowly winding them around her as if he were afraid she would turn and run for the hills. He tilted her face to better angle her lips—in a way that practically *begged* for permission—a slow dance that she willingly and eagerly submitted to.

She wanted more—*needed* more.

Ben hauled her up against him, and she had to choke back a laugh as she lifted a foot into the air. She shivered, from the top of her head down to her toes. Whether it was from the rain peppering against her skin, the cool night's air pricking it up into little goosebumps, or the rampant heat coursing through her body—she wasn't entirely sure. But nothing ever felt this incredible, this *intense*.

When they finally parted to catch their breath, Ben didn't lower her back to the ground, continuing to hold her there against him with her feet dangling above the hard pavement. The nearby lamppost cast shadows of her dangling feet next to them.

"Do you think Brody will mind staying with Ryan and Tony tonight?" she asked a bit breathlessly.

Ben pulled his head back, cocking it to the side a bit as he scrunched his eyebrows together. "Why would he…"

His sentence trailed off, and she felt a hint of satisfaction seeing the flustered expression on his face when he cleared his throat.

And the lust as it overtook him and completely blew out his pupils.

"Addie, we don't—"

She shook her head and covered his mouth with a hand again. "You told me to be honest about what I want. And what I want is you."

CHAPTER 21

The two had barely parted lips long enough for Ben to kick the door shut behind him. Mutually greedy hands grabbed and pulled at one another as they tried to shed each other's their soaking wet clothing.

"Are you sure?" Ben asked against her lips once more, nearly tripping over himself as he tried to kick off his wet shoes.

She clenched his shirt in her hands. "I've never been more sure of anything."

"Hit me if you change your mind," he replied with a husky laugh.

She giggled. "Doubt I'll want to, but I appreciate the offer. You're sure Brody got your message?"

"He acknowledged," Ben said as he peeled his socks off. "He's steering clear."

She wasn't sure she wanted to know exactly what he'd told Brody. It would only be a matter of time before *everyone* was aware, including her two roommates who would be wondering where she'd disappeared to.

Tonight was for them.

Tonight was for all of the time lost between them.

Ben ripped his shirt over his head, tossing it with a wet thud into the corner of the room. He rushed back to her, as if the space apart was sheer torture, but she held him at bay with a hand. Confusion wrinkled his brow for half a second before he stopped. His gaze heated when she didn't move her hand away, keeping it in place with fire burning in her fingertips.

She wanted to see him.

She'd wondered about all these muscles he'd gained. What they looked like, what they would *feel* like, and she was certainly not disappointed. Her fingers fanned across his chest, the hair there tickling the palm of her hand.

His chest rose and fell beneath her, practically panting as she touched him. Even giving her a small nod when she glanced up at him, silently asking permission to continue. The wanton look in his eyes gave her a thrill, knowing how much—from that look alone—he wanted to touch her too. Instead, he gave her the time to explore first.

She traced along the hard edges she found there, following each to completion.

The hard line from his neck to his shoulders, making his frame larger than it had been once before.

The rounded muscle of his arm, strong and corded with tension as he held himself still. Like *not* touching her was torture.

That kind of power can certainly go to a girl's head.

Ben's stomach quivered when her hands went lower, tracing along the muscles of his abdomen. Greedy for the goosebumps that rose with a flick of her wrist. Her fingers were on the button of his jeans when he finally moved, snatching her wrist and pulling it up.

"Not until I see you. I will absolutely not be rushing this part. I want to see you, *all* of you," he breathed, pulling back from her touch and grabbing the hem of her shirt.

It took a few rough tugs for the wet material to finally relent, clinging to her like a second skin, before it finally joined his on the floor.

Ben's nostrils flared at his sudden intake of air.

Confused, Addie looked down at herself, realizing that the white bra she'd put on that morning had also been soaked through. Her nipples, sharp with desire, showed through the already thin material.

Ben cupped her breasts, giving them an appreciative squeeze without a word. Her back involuntarily arched beneath his touch, but he was there, ready for her—capturing her in his arms to prevent her knees from buckling in on themselves.

When he unhooked the clasp and her breasts spilled out into his eager hands, seeing the color of his eyes almost completely lost to the blackness of his pupils, she forgot what she was thinking about. She could get drunk on that look alone, let alone the feeling of Ben's hands on her. It was addictive, like a drug she could never get enough of.

Her nerve endings sang when he brought his mouth down to suck on one pebbling nipple, a groan vibrating through her skin. She arched further to give him more of herself. To push herself more fully into his embrace as he swirled his tongue and massaged the other with his large, calloused fingers. It wasn't the first time in her life that a man had touched her in this way, but it was the first time that it was done with such a skilled hand. As if he had a map to her body and knew exactly where her treasures lay.

"I've wanted to do this for so long," he whispered fervently against her, his hot breath tickling her sensitive skin. "Every perfect fucking *inch* of you."

Her toes curled at his words. "You know exactly what to say to take my breath away."

"And I'm just getting started."

He guided her backward until she felt the back of her knees hit the edge of the bed, seconds before he gently pushed her onto it. She landed with a soft thud on the bed, a giggle erupting from her when Ben fell upon her, tearing and tugging at her soaking-wet jeans. They were more difficult to remove wet, but Ben was a man on a mission. Silent and singularly focused on his task.

She assisted the best she could as he peeled the layers away, another shiver wracking her spine when the cool air finally greeted her skin and she was completely bare. It was then that the flush of embarrassment at being so open and vulnerable in front of him hit her. She felt exposed, like every single one of the insecurities that had built up in her head over the past few years were on full display.

Ben surprised her with a kiss, a hungry animalistic one that drove out any thoughts other than him. When he pulled back, he smiled, but the heat was still there in his eyes.

"You are so fucking beautiful," he said appreciatively, his voice thick and husky. The sound of it rang perfectly in her ears as the heat in her belly increased tenfold.

He grabbed her hips and yanked her to the edge of the bed before she could form a response, lowering himself before her. She was about to ask him what it was he was doing, but her jaw hung open—the words dying somewhere in her throat—as his tongue delved straight to the core of her. His chuckle was dark and dangerous but unrelenting as he found her sensitive bud. Lapping at it until she was a writhing mess beneath his skillful tongue.

"What ... What are you doing to me?" she managed to choke out.

He paused and looked up at her. "You sound like you've never had someone go down on you before."

She shook her head a little shyly. "Most of the guys I've been with weren't really interested in that. They just wanted to get in and out if you know what I mean."

Ben's face soured, forcing a giggle out of her. "You know what, don't tell me that. I'd rather not hear about what you've done with other men with your arousal soaking my chin."

A lightning bolt of desire shot through her at his words, and she tried not to sound breathy when she spoke. "You started it...."

"I know. Now, hold onto the sheets. I'm going to get you ready for me," he commanded.

His tongue returned to her, quickly finding her clit once more and drawing delicious circles around it.

He chuckled low in his throat as he added a finger. Her eyes rolled back in her head at the feeling, and she opened her mouth to voice the soundless word that tried to escape. The digit easily glided inside of her and hooked upward to rub a spot that had her seeing stars.

Her fingers unabashedly ran through his hair as she held his head against her, her thighs trembling at the sensation.

A coiling tension began building inside of her, a delicious magical sensation that grew more and more taut with each passing moment. Nothing had ever felt so good in her life, and she didn't want it to end.

When he groaned against her cunt unexpectedly, as if bringing her to her peak was the sweetest pleasure that he, himself, would experience, the tension snapped and her orgasm exploded. She clutched at the bedsheets as she cried out, chanting his name like a prayer as she was completely swept away by the sensation.

When her vision cleared from the haze and her body thrummed with its recent orgasm, she looked down at him. A breathless laugh and smile escaped her as she did. She'd never felt anything like that before, and she embarrassed herself on how much she wanted to experience it again.

Ben repositioned himself, crossing his arms, settling over her thighs so he could look up at her, and giving one of her thighs a gentle kiss as he did.

"That was..." she started before closing her eyes and letting out another laugh. "I don't know if incredible would be the right word...."

His fingers danced across her stomach, tracing indiscernible lines on her skin.

He grinned, giving her a little wink that already had her core clenching in anticipation. "Catch your breath. We're not done yet."

"But I want ... I want to see you too. It's not fair you're only getting to see me."

His laugh was rough, laced with desire. "You test my patience like no other, Addie."

He didn't deny her, however.

Ben pulled away and moved to the end of the bed. A momentary worry hit her as she thought he would leave her like this, and she sat up to protest. But she stopped when he turned and quirked an eyebrow at her, his hands working on the button of his jeans.

Thunder crackled outside, accompanied by the drumming of rain against the nearby window as it turned into a torrential downpour. A flash of lightning cast light around Ben's frame, further illuminating his body.

Seeing the look he gave her, she sank back on her knees and watched him strip. His movements were rough, impatient. That knowledge sent a new thrill through her, and she bit her lip.

When he did finally manage to lower his jeans down his hips, kicking them away, her mouth felt dry at the sight of his cock springing free. It curved upward, almost hitting his stomach with his own desire—twitching once under her intense gaze.

His desire for *her*.

The few other guys she'd been with before paled in comparison.

"You're gonna give me a complex if you don't stop looking at it like that, Addie," Ben said heatedly but feral pride twinkled in his eyes.

She smiled. "Is that—is that going to fit?"

He growled as he fell upon her once more, pushing her back onto the mattress below so his body covered hers. "You can take me."

Being skin to skin with Ben was as magical as she'd thought it would be, loving the feeling of his body against hers. It felt so good, so *right*, that it surprised her when Ben suddenly froze.

"Wait, hold on," Ben said with an air of frustration as he tried to pull back. "I don't have a condom."

Addie shook her head and slammed her lips against his. "I have an IUD," she assured him when she released his lips for air. "We don't need one."

The pressure of his fingers digging into her hips increased tenfold as he kissed her again. "*Fuck*, Addie," Ben groaned as his eyes rolled back into his head. "Are you really about to let me fuck you bare? Are you sure?"

Addie had never been more sure of anything in her life. The only other thing that she was that sure of right now was kicking herself for not doing this with him *sooner*.

"I'm sure," she answered, her voice barely above a whisper.

No further persuasion was needed as Ben grabbed onto his cock, running it up and down her pussy. The motion was slow and teasing at first, deliberately torturous in the best way.

Addie started to pant when he circled her clit with the tip of his cock, already sensitive—continuing up and down, up and down, until she was nearly delirious with desire. Her nails dug into the flesh of his shoulders as she clawed at him, wanting him closer, *needing* him closer.

Ben started slowly pushing inside of her, like he was trying to acclimate her to his length. But it was such a beautifully delicious burn as her body adjusted to his that all she could do was to hold onto him. She dug her fingers into the flesh of his arms as he hovered above her, leaving crescent moon marks there. The feeling of fullness was the most exquisite thing she'd ever felt.

When he seated himself fully inside of her—stretching her to the limit—she let out a gasp, unable to contain it. Ben furrowed his brow in concentration, his arms trembling as she realized that he was waiting for her to give him permission to move so as not to hurt her. The thought touched her in ways she couldn't express and stirred the hunger lingering low in her belly.

"I'm okay," she whispered.

Lightning flashed outside, accompanied by the sound of thunder cracking once more—the rumble of it shaking the ground. Then, just as suddenly, the lights in the room flickered out completely and cast the two of them into complete darkness.

They were still connected, with Ben's cock seated inside of her, both of them now a bit thrown at the sudden loss of light. Ben's face was just about the only thing she could see in the darkness, hovering above hers as he, too, adjusted to the lighting.

"Sh-should we stop?" she asked quietly. "Until the lights come back on?"

He leaned over and gave her a quick kiss. It was tender, loving. Something she hadn't expected from this borderline frustrating man. Though, there was a lot about him that had surprised her.

"We don't need the light for what we're about to do," Ben said before he began to move. He started to withdraw from her, the slow drag causing her body to cling to him, begging him not to pull out. But he didn't, not completely. They both groaned at the movement until he was almost out, and then he thrust his hips forward, grinding against her as he did.

"How?" Ben panted.

She blinked. "How what?"

"How can I make you come again?" The smile was slow and feral. It instantly had Addie tingling in all the right places. "I need to feel your cunt clenching my cock as you come."

Oh boy. If he kept talking like that to her, he wouldn't have to touch her. She was already about to combust once more with his gravelly voice. Never in her life would she have thought Ben capable of uttering such dirty things, but she liked it. She liked it *a lot*.

She held onto him for dear life as he adjusted his angle and thrust again, the harsh motion hitting somewhere deep inside that left her panting.

"*That*," she whimpered helplessly. "Whatever you just did ... Do it again...."

He gave her a wicked smile and repeated the motion, slamming against that magical spot again. She cried out as stars entered her vision, her toes curling and clenching.

"Good girl," he whispered into her neck, kissing where her pulse thrummed.

Lightning lit the room once more, silhouetting their figures in the night. A darkly erotic image of their bodies moving together in the shadows, frantic in their need. It only added to her pleasure as she saw the raptured look etched into Ben's features. His mouth was slightly agape as he watched her—a long, drawn-out groan hissing out as they moved together. She closed her eyes once, twice, as pleasure blinded her—unable to keep them open as it wracked her body.

Her fingernails dug into his back. She heard his accompanied hiss of pain, but he didn't protest. Instead, his pace began to increase. A frenzy of flesh pounding into flesh. His cock angled in such a way as to bump up against that spot over and over.

"Ben..." she moaned, feeling that delicious tightening deep in her belly once more. But she didn't have long to process before it slammed into her, rolling through like a tsunami. Wave after wave of pure bliss cascaded over her, enough that she was sure she screamed his name.

Ben buried his head against the crook of her neck as she rode out her orgasm, continuing to pant and moan as he, too, began to chase his release.

"Come for me, Ben.... Please, I need to feel you come inside me...." she whispered, unabashed in her desire. It worked, too, as his thrusts became desperate, pounding her down into the mattress like a madman on the verge of insanity.

Despite her sensitive body, she encouraged him. His cock continued to hit that spot inside of her and only added to her spasming around him. It felt endless, like she would drown in the sensations his body was giving hers.

And she wanted him to drown with her.

She watched him through hooded eyes as she clung to consciousness. She was sure she'd pass out from the pleasure she felt, but she held on. She wanted to see him pushed over the edge as well. To see him experience rapture as she had, and she wouldn't miss that for the world.

His eyes caught hers when she felt his cock start to pulse inside of her. Their eyes remained locked, as if he, too, wanted her to see him fall over the edge and groan out her name in completion. His hips bucked against her wildly, sporadically, as he climaxed.

She'd never heard a sweeter sound in her life. The unabashed pleasure in his voice, the vulgar sounds her pussy made as he thrust erratically inside of her, the sounds of their combined panting pulsing in the air around them. She didn't think she'd ever hear anything as incredible.

CHAPTER 22

*A*ddie opened her groggy eyes, albeit reluctantly, as she roused from the deep slumber she'd fallen into. The morning fog took a few seconds to clear from her vision, but as she blinked, she could see the scant hints of early morning light as it peeked through the blinds. Another few blinks and she registered that her head was resting against something warm and pliant. There was a gentle motion of her head as it followed the movement beneath her. Up and down. Up and down.

The sound of breathing brushed close to her ear, and a shy smile pulled at the corners of her mouth.

So, it wasn't a dream after all.

The warmth of Ben's chest as she rested against it was comforting, and she let out a little sigh as she settled against him. She wasn't sure when she had passed out the night before, remembering only that she'd started to feel the tugs of sleep after their third round.

Well, whenever it had happened, Ben had tucked her into his side —her head against his chest, just over the thumping of his heart. It was slow and steady, like the beat of a drum. A soothing balm to any nerves that might've otherwise peaked.

This had been the first night in longer than she could remember that she'd had such a peaceful night's sleep. Truly *peaceful*.

No nightmares.

No waking up at two in the morning, drowning in sweat and panic.

Nothing but sweet dreams and a warm embrace. And from the sure and steady sound of his breathing, he was likely still asleep.

It was a welcome change, although the tug into the real world caused her some anxiety. They'd admitted that they had feelings for each other, they'd slept together, but what exactly did that mean for the two of them? Their history made things a bit ... complicated.

It had been a while since she'd last been someone's girlfriend, or anything close to that, so she wasn't sure what the terminology was for what they were to each other now. Or what he wanted them to be. Not to mention the complication that they worked together. He was her boss in this setting. That would complicate things, right?

And as much as she wanted not to—she couldn't help but remember the stack of bills sitting on her kitchen counter. If things between them went south again, for whatever reason, that could put all of that in jeopardy.

Addie shook her head. She was thinking too much—jumping ten steps ahead. Cuddled up against Ben with his arms wrapped around her, she didn't *want* to think about anything else.

He'd shown her through his actions that he meant what he said. That he cared for her.

They could talk more about their situation later.

First, she needed to splash some water on her face and get something to drink. Then maybe she could get some more sleep. She gently untangled herself from his embrace, careful not to disturb him. She began sliding to the edge of the bed when he suddenly moved behind her, and she let out a surprised gasp.

Ben yanked her back in place, shoving his face into the back of her neck and grumbling into her hair. "Where do you think you're going?"

She giggled. "I was just gonna get something to drink."

He shook his head, pulling her into him more firmly. He was surprisingly strong for this early in the morning, but he was unrelenting. When she moved into position, a dull throb of pain coursed up her spine from her core, causing her to wince.

Ben's head shot up immediately. "What's wrong?"

"Just a ... um ... You know, a little sore," she said apologetically. Then again, she wasn't sure she *was* entirely sorry about it, given how it happened. She'd happily take this pain if it meant Ben shoved himself into her again, his cock already stiff from the early morning as it pressed insistently against her thigh.

"Stay there. Don't move a muscle," Ben ordered as he pulled away, the warmth of his body leaving with him. "Let me get something for that."

She whined a protest, but it quickly morphed into a sound of approval as Ben walked to the bathroom, still completely naked. She'd seen all of him before, but in this early-morning light, she wanted to appreciate every inch.

The dark black hairs trailing down from beneath his navel, down the vee of his hips, all the way to his thighs and beyond. The tawny complexion of his skin, almost golden in the early morning light. The corded muscles of his back—strength and power emanating from each one in a way that sent an interesting shiver down her body.

And that ass.

It was so supple and perfect—like a shiny red apple just waiting for her to bite.

Who knew she would think lewdly like that? She wasn't a prude by any means, but sex had never really been something she thought of or discussed very often. Now that she'd fully experienced sex with Ben, however, that was likely to change.

It was...

Well, it had been absolutely incredible.

When Ben turned and walked back to the bed, Addie felt a flush of heat rushing straight to her core.

Oh, the front view was *much* better.

How the hell did that thing fit last night?

Ben chuckled as he grabbed the edge of the blanket, abruptly ripping it off of her and snaking a hand around her ankle. "Behave."

She giggled again when he pulled her closer to the edge of the bed, prying her legs apart and bringing the warm, wet washcloth up. She winced when he began wiping between her legs, both in surprise and embarrassment.

"Ben, you don't have to," she tried to argue, attempting to pull herself up on her elbows but failing when he yanked her closer. "I can—"

"Just shut up and let me do this," he interrupted. "Hold still."

It was sweet. Sweeter than she ever thought such a gesture would be. The hint of embarrassment was still there, being so open and exposed, but the overwhelming warm flutter in her chest overruled it.

"How are you feeling otherwise?" he asked, his concentration still focused between her legs.

She tried not to squirm with such a heated gaze aimed directly at her pussy, but she cleared her throat. "I'm okay. You?"

"Never been better," he hummed. When he finished cleaning her, he tossed the used rag onto the bathroom counter and rejoined her back in bed—pulling until she was once more in the same position she'd been in moments before, with her head resting against his chest.

"Okay?" Ben prompted when she sighed.

She smiled lazily. "Yeah, I'm okay."

"Good. Get some more sleep for now," he said softly. "We can talk more after you get more rest."

Talk? Uh-oh.

Addie shook her head. "I don't think I can go back to sleep now. What did you want to talk about?"

"About what I said last night."

Oh no. Was he going to change his mind? Tell her he didn't really mean it?

"What about it?"

"I told you that I have feelings for you, but you didn't say how you felt. We sorta ... you know ..." Ben said, his voice sounding surprisingly shy given the fact that they were currently twined together, naked. "I just need to hear it from you."

Addie opened her mouth and closed it. She hadn't expected that. She was pleasantly surprised—but surprised nonetheless.

Hadn't she said anything?

She thought about it for a moment, trying to scour her memory, but she quickly realized she *hadn't* said anything. She'd just expressed herself the best way she could in the moment, which apparently had been to just grab his face and kiss him.

She felt that was a pretty direct way to tell him without *having* to tell him how she felt, but he was also right. They had a pretty bad track record.

"I have feelings for you, too, Ben," she replied quietly. "I'm sorry I wasn't more direct last night."

Ben chuckled. "I have absolutely no qualms with *how* you did it; I guess I just needed to hear the words."

"Did it help?"

"It did."

She nodded with a smile. "Where do we go from here, then?"

"How do you mean?" he asked, tucking his free arm behind his head.

"I'd like to point out that regardless of our relationship, we have this documentary to finish. We work together for the time being. We need to *finish* this documentary because I need to pay the bills I have waiting for me at home…."

Ben hummed low in his throat. "I see your point. What would make you feel more comfortable, sweetheart?"

Addie worked her lip between her teeth, momentarily ignoring the shiver racing up her spine that him calling her *sweetheart* elicited. What *would* make her feel comfortable with this whole situation? It would be hard to pretend like nothing was going on between them. The rest of the crew already knew she was in here with him, so that ship had long sailed. But it would be harder to focus on the task at hand if she was distracted at all times.

At the same time … she didn't want to let this go. She didn't want to let *him* go.

"How about this, then—let's just see what happens? I know I don't want anyone else but you, but if we need to keep things casual for a bit until we figure this out, you know, *this*," she said as she pointed between the two of them, "just until we finish this documentary up, and then we fully dive in?"

"If it means I get you, I'll do whatever you want, Addie," Ben said, pulling her closer and pressing a kiss to her forehead.

A loud bang shook the front door just feet away. Addie squeaked as she hopped up, instinctively clutching at the bedsheets and holding them up against her exposed chest.

"Don't you move," Ben scolded gently as he got out of bed and grabbed a fresh pair of jeans, quickly tugging them up his hips. "I'm not done with you yet."

Addie took the chance to lean over and glance at Ben's phone on the night stand to see what time it was. It was just after six in the morning, which likely meant it was either one of the crew coming to heckle or something was up.

The front door swung open as Ben leaned against the frame.

"This better be good," he grumbled to whoever was on the other side. Addie held a hand over her mouth to stifle the laugh that rose at his borderline grumpy tone.

"Sorry," the voice—the one that sounded like Ryan—said, "some of us are trying to *work* and not—"

"I dare you to finish that sentence," Ben snapped.

Addie could hear Ryan's laugh as another voice joined, definitely Grace. "We've got some readings you might want to see."

CHAPTER 23

Ben tossed her a wink over his shoulder as he left, but Addie wanted to find out what was going on. If it was readings on the storm, she wasn't going to miss that conversation. So, she decided to get dressed and follow after them.

She fumbled around the room, trying to find something to throw on. Her clothes from the night before were still soaking wet in piles where she'd last thrown them. And it wasn't like she could exactly walk out naked, so Addie raided the bag of Ben's clothes nearby.

The early morning light was enough to provide some guidance, but Addie blindly grabbed the first pair of shorts and shirt she could find. Ben was much taller than she was, so finding something to fit over her frame wouldn't be too hard. She quickly yanked the items on and stumbled out the door, trying to figure out which direction to go.

"We have to stop running into one another this way," an unpleasant voice called out.

Addie inwardly groaned as she turned to see Billy closing in on her from across the parking lot.

"That would be preferable," she returned with a forced smile. "But we can't seem to escape bumping into you just about every other stop, can we?"

"Same storm, same location, coincidence honestly." Billy smirked. "Nice legs, by the way."

Addie felt the heat rush up her neck and to her cheeks. What she thought was a pair of shorts was decidedly *not* shorts but instead a pair of Ben's boxers. She hadn't seen the telltale slit down the front until now, and without a pair of underwear underneath them, she suddenly felt exposed. Fortunately, Ben's shirt on her was baggy enough that she simply tugged the fabric lower to cover anything exposed there. It had been one thing for Ben to see all the parts of her that she felt self-conscious about; it was another for someone like Billy to see them too.

But Addie refused to let her self-esteem overtake the situation, and she *absolutely* would not give him the satisfaction. She folded her arms across her chest defiantly—the old Addie wouldn't care. Why should she now?

"Thanks. And thanks for stopping to make sure we were okay after your team sent us spinning. It was really sweet of you," she said, her voice dripping with venom.

The shrug he gave only pissed her off more, coupled with his casual grin, and she was clenching her fists behind her back. "You know how it is in the field. Accidents happen."

"Uh-huh," she hummed. "What are you doing up this early anyway?"

Billy rocked on his heels as he dug his hands into his pockets. "Business call. I would ask you the same, but I think I have an idea what *you've* been up to."

Addie rolled her eyes. If he wanted to bait her, he would have to try harder. "Is that just where your mind lives? In the gutter?"

"If it's where I'll find you," he purred, taking a step toward her. "I'll be happy to go there."

Gross. "Charming."

He shrugged. "If you need a bed to warm, mine is available. I have no doubt I'll leave you far more satisfied. Ben and I have shared a lot in our life. What's one more thing?"

As gross as the statement made her instantly feel, it caused her to raise an eyebrow at him. "What exactly have you *shared*?"

The face he made at that was the first time she'd seen him look anything other than smug or cocky. A flicker of something she couldn't quite pin but she'd absolutely seen. Uncertainty? Panic? But it was gone as quickly as it had appeared, leaving questions in its wake.

"Look, sweetheart, I don't want you to get caught in the crossfire," he shot off, his smug demeanor sliding back into place. "You seem like a nice girl. I don't want any bad blood between us, so keep your head down, huh?"

Addie narrowed her eyes. "The *crossfire*? What exactly would I be in the crossfire of? If you think I'm going to take kindly to threats of *any* kind, whether to myself or my team, you're sorely mistaken."

His grin widened, which only pissed her off further. "I see why Ben's so fond of you now. I remember him telling everyone all about the dark-eyed pain in the ass he used to know. Glad to see he didn't exaggerate."

"I'm full of surprises. I guess I just don't understand why you seem to hate Ben so much, then."

Billy opened his mouth to respond but was interrupted when Brody appeared from around the corner. "Jesus, why is it that every time I turn around, your dumb ass is here?"

Billy clenched his jaw for a fraction of a second before taking a large step back from her. Brody came to a stop next to Addie, a hard expression in his eyes despite his smirk. She knew a little about the dynamic between Ben and Billy, based off of what little Ben had told her, but she knew even *less* about Brody and Billy. They had all three been on the same team, and while it sounded like Ben caught most of the flack from Billy, Brody couldn't have been totally immune from Billy's antics.

The two stared each other down, eyes narrowed before Billy broke first and scoffed. "Don't flatter yourself, Brody. We're following the storm, same as you."

Brody grinned and crossed his arms, the warmth of his tanned skin contrasting with the lighter, more pale color poking out from beneath his shirt sleeve. "Having a nice early-morning chat, then?"

"Exchanging pleasantries, that's all," Billy tutted. "I have things I need to get done, though, so I'll leave you ladies to it."

Addie turned to Brody as Billy walked away, not caring to watch him leave. "Thanks."

Brody shrugged, turning his red baseball cap to the front as a trickle of early-morning light spilled through the nearby trees. "I heard the tail end of it. You didn't need my help."

"No, but it's still appreciated," she replied with a smile. "Where are you going?"

"Ryan came banging on my door, saying that they wanted to show Ben and me something, so I was headed that way. You?"

"I heard about it, too, and wanted to join if that's okay?"

"I don't see why not."

The two strolled in silence across the lot. A few rays of sunshine peeked across the horizon, illuminating the pavement in front of them—a stark contrast to the harsh streetlamps overhead. The occasional chirp of grasshoppers nearby filled the silence between them, but Addie had too many questions to let that silence stretch too far.

"Brody, can I ask you something?"

"Hm?"

"Ben told me a little about the history between you two and Billy, but that was so long ago. Is there a reason there's still so much tension between you guys?"

"Other than the fact that Billy is just a reckless idiot? I wish I could say I knew, but I really don't," Brody replied with a shrug. "It felt a bit like night and day. He was always a pain in the ass but in that kind of goofy way that made it fun to be around him. Then one day he's just … I don't know, he's just different."

"Ben told me that after Billy's mom died, he just wasn't the same. That he was angry all the time?"

Brody folded his arms across his chest and stared into the air for a moment, his eyebrows scrunched in concentration until he finally shrugged. "Yeah, but … I don't know, it was more than that."

"How do you mean?"

"It's hard to explain.… Billy wasn't always that bad. He had a hard life before he met us—raised alone by his mom, who was in and out of rehab most of his life. But when we met, we were all thick as thieves. A real team. Then his mom got sick, and he went back to take care of her for a while before she passed. Ben insisted he take some time after the funeral to grieve and get back on his feet, but Billy refused and came back almost immediately after." Brody rubbed the back of his neck as he continued. "Then it just went downhill from there. It felt like Billy was specifically angry at *Ben*. I mean, he got snippy with all of us, but he *really* went in on Ben for some reason. He'd pick fights, accuse him of poor leadership, that kind of thing."

"Huh. Yeah, that is weird."

"Why are you asking?"

Addie shrugged. "I don't know. I just get this weird vibe from him."

"That would be the asshole part of him, most likely."

Addie laughed and nudged him with her shoulder. "You know what I mean. He said something about sharing Ben's things, and it really rubbed me the wrong way—and not in the way you'd think. He always just seems to be…"

"Right there when things go wrong?"

Addie stopped. "Exactly! But how did you…?"

Brody shrugged. "I've had my suspicions. A while back, while we were prepping for you and Evie to join, we bumped into Billy and his team. He and Ben got into an argument, and while it didn't *quite* go to blows, it got close."

"Over what?"

"He was angry that we got the contract and made some loosely veiled threats."

Addie cocked her head to the side. "What kind of threats?"

"Billy found out that Channel 9 had also reached out to Ben for an exclusive about the storm front, right after we accepted the contract with Channel 5, so I think he was just extra butthurt because Channel 9 has sponsored some of his stuff before."

Ah. Channel 9 was her station's biggest competitor by far in terms of local weather. She remembered a few conversations she'd overheard with John and a few of the higher-ups about Channel 9 copying some of their work. She didn't think it was copying so much as there was only so much they could cover in one state at a time, but from the sounds of their conversation, they were *convinced* that they were trying to steal content.

"Ben turned them down, as we'd already locked into our contract," Brody continued, "but they've been pestering him about changing his mind—especially after they found out about the documentary."

That phone call she'd overheard that night by the pool ... Was that who Ben had been talking to?

"Does Ben know? About your suspicions?"

"He's aware. I think he just doesn't want to worry anyone if it's not true. There's enough bad blood between our teams, so we don't want to make things worse."

She frowned. "I guess that makes sense."

It did, but it didn't ease the flicker of frustration that Ben hadn't mentioned any of this before.

As if reading her expression, Brody laughed more heartily and nudged her shoulder with his arm playfully. "Don't give him a hard time about it. Ben can be protective to a fault over people he cares about, and I think he cares about you a *lot*."

This time, Addie didn't fight the blush as it rose to her cheeks. "Y-you think so?"

"Oh, I *know* so. Did you forget who he had to kick out last night?"

Oh... Yeah, she'd forgotten about that.

"Don't tell anyone.... I know they probably already assume, but Ben and I want to take things slowly while we're working together...."

Brody nodded thoughtfully. "Understood. I'll keep quiet about that as long as you don't tell him I told you about all this? He'll have my neck for it."

Addie laughed. "Deal."

"That is one beautiful storm cell," Ben said as Addie followed Brody into the RV. "I'm willing to bet that it'll spin off four or five today alone."

Beautiful storm cell was an understatement—it was everything Addie had seen back at the station. A supercell primed and ready for action, and if one of the bigger bands south of the main cell was any indication, it wouldn't be more than a few hours before the action would begin.

Addie pointed to the cluster. "This one is pretty promising."

Ben shook his head, a hint of pink dusting the tips of his ears as he avoided eye contact with her—though his smile had notably widened a bit. "I don't know. The one a bit further east of that looks like it's gonna gear up sooner."

"Not likely. It doesn't look stable enough, and it's smaller. If we're wanting to deploy, we have a safer bet with the one north."

"Right," Ben said, "but there's the river over there to give it the moisture it needs to grow."

"Not unless the one further north chokes it out with its size, and with the way the winds are shifting, the moisture's gonna go in that direction anyway."

The tension between them felt natural, though it had the opposite effect it would have in recent times. Normally, she would be annoyed at arguing with him like this, but all it made her want to do was to drag him back to the motel room.

Maybe Ben was right.

Maybe arguing *was* their weird form of foreplay.

Brody, hands on his hips, huffed out a laugh. "I think Addie's right. The one further north might have a better chance of churning out something worth deploying for."

Ben rubbed the back of his neck as he looked at her, but the soft heat in his eyes felt incendiary—so much so that Addie couldn't help but glance away in an attempt to be less obvious to the others gathered around them.

"Well, if you force my hand, I guess we'll go with Addie's suggestion. Everybody, start packing up, and let's be ready to roll out of here in half an hour," Ben said. He turned and walked past Addie, slyly running his hand along her backside as he did and throwing her a knowing cat-like smile when she flushed harder at his touch.

Tony cleared his throat as she followed after Ben, catching his words as they drifted into the distance behind her. "Are we … Are we just not gonna say anything?"

Grace turned with a mischievous gleam in her eyes. "I don't know, Tony. You wanna say where Evie is?"

"Some things are better left unsaid for the time being, dude." Ryan's chuckle rose up behind Addie as she fought the urge to hide, already following behind Ben.

The door clicked closed behind her, wheezing out an anxious sigh. She had to retrieve her wet clothing, but she wasn't in any particular rush when, as soon as that lock clicked, Ben was on her again.

She let out a delighted squeak when he practically yanked her back into his arms and pulled her in for another kiss. His lips were so warm and inviting that she barely felt her feet leave the floor when picked her up. Heat flamed to life between her legs once again, instantly ready to explore Ben's body further in the light of day. She knew Ben felt the same, feeling the hardness of him against her thigh as he continued to kiss her.

But they had to get ready to leave, so as much as she wanted Ben inside of her—and hitting that spot that she'd only read about in romances—they'd need to part.

She was the first to pull back, unable to hold back the giggle when he let out a small groan in protest.

"Good morning, by the way," she whispered, a breathless quality to it.

He smiled. "Good morning."

CHAPTER 24

A few miles ahead, the clouds above them swirled ominously. All the conditions were right for something to spin up, large and strong enough for them to deploy.

It only took a few hours for Addie's prediction to come to fruition as the crew flew down the highway. And now Addie wanted a clean slate. She needed another chance to prove to herself that she did still belong in this world. A world she'd been devastated to leave in the first place.

"Do we have all the equipment ready?" Ben asked into the radio.

Radio static crackled and popped in tune with Addie's ears popping at the drop in pressure.

"Brody?" Ben prompted when the radio clicked and whirred, but no sound came through. "Damned thing is jammed."

Ben hunched over the steering wheel, his gaze flitting from the road to the churning clouds above them. The muscles of his neck corded in concentration, his arms flexed as he gripped the wheel tightly.

He was distracting—unwillingly dragging her attention from the storm.

His hair was unruly compared to how he'd been wearing it the past few days, likely in the rush to throw everything into their vehicles and hit the road once again. She liked it, though—this recently-pulled-from-sleep look. It reminded her more of the grad school boy she'd had a crush on.

It was embarrassing how much she wanted him again. She'd never thought of herself as a particularly sexual individual, but it was like he'd awoken some sleeping giant. Always there, lying in wait, but completely dormant.

His hands on her skin were addictive, and she wanted to taste...

Addie cleared her throat. What the hell was wrong with her? They agreed to be professional through all of this because there was still a job to do. Though, the occasional bump in the road didn't exactly help the dull ache that had formed where he'd been the night prior. She needed to distract herself.

Addie attempted to clear the lump in her throat. "You asked me this once before, but I'm curious. What made you want to get into chasing?"

Ben chuckled and glanced in her direction. "Is this our version of pillow talk now?"

"You won't get any better."

Ben's grin widened. "I wouldn't dream of it."

She elbowed him. "Come on. I told you about my dad. Your turn to share. What got you into this?"

"My mom."

Addie quirked her head to the side. "Your mom?"

If she wasn't mistaken, there was an almost misty quality to his gaze as he fixed it ahead. "You'd have loved her. She was just as ... spunky ... as you are."

"Loved ... as in past tense?"

He sighed. "As in past tense."

"Oh, Ben..." she said, a heaviness suddenly clanging in her chest. "When did she ...?"

"Well before you and I met. When I was about ten, I think."

Why did she not know that about him? What *else* did she not know about him?

"Do you mind if I ask what happened?" she asked carefully. She could see the emotion swirling in his amber depths, so she wasn't sure she wanted to push too hard.

She knew all too well how difficult it had been to talk about her dad.

"It was a long time ago. You don't have to treat me with kid gloves," Ben said, turning his gaze to her and giving her a small smile before returning back to the road. "She was killed during a tornado. It was why I got into chasing."

Guilt clawed to the surface. How could she not have known something like that? How could she never have known that about him?

Frustrated tears threatened to surface, but she quickly flicked them away. "That's ... That's terrible."

Ben ruffled her hair with his free hand. Any other time, she would've shoved his hand away, made some snide comment about touching her, but she didn't. A new sense of comfort in his touch curled her into it instead.

"It's alright, sweetheart. Don't cry," he said softly, the worry line between his eyebrows furrowing as he looked at her.

She sniffled despite herself. "I'm not crying."

"Yes, you are, and that's okay. I appreciate that more than you think," he assured as he pulled his hand back to rub a loose tear from her cheek. She didn't push him away then either, instead enjoying the sensation as his hand cupped her cheek. It was heart-achingly tender, and should have embarrassed her for how good it felt, especially considering the topic of conversation.

"C-could she not get to shelter in time?" she asked, forcing as much of the emotion out of her voice as she could. "I know you guys mentioned wanting to help with some research on building better warning systems?"

Ben shook his head and pulled his hand back in place. "It wasn't that she couldn't get to shelter; it's that she didn't know she needed to get to shelter in the first place."

Addie's forehead wrinkled in consideration. "How would—"

"She was deaf," Ben said, causing the ache in Addie's chest to clench harder. "My parents divorced not long after I was born. My dad moved around a lot because he was in the military, so I was with him when it happened. It came in the middle of the night. Most places only have the siren to warn people—they aren't equipped for those with hearing disabilities. She wouldn't have known it was coming."

Oh.

That was worse than what she'd imagined. Ben's poor mother. Addie couldn't imagine how awful that would be.

Morbid as it was, she only hoped that it was quick.

"I'm so sorry, Ben."

Another realization dawned on her. *That was why he knew sign language.*

He shrugged, the gesture too practiced for him to really not have any feelings on the subject. But if that was what he needed, she'd give that to him. "These things happen, but it's also why I'm such a stickler for safety—don't want anyone to get caught off guard."

"So, you lived with your dad after?"

"As much as one can with someone with his job," Ben replied with a laugh. "You should've seen how his colleagues reacted the first time they saw me hanging around to wait for him on base after school."

"Why's that?"

Another shrug. "I look more like my mom. She was a first-gen Filipino woman, and my dad was the curly-haired, blond American guy who swept her off her feet. So, you can imagine how much of a sore thumb I was standing next to him."

He acted so casual about it, but she could hear the lingering pain in his voice. "I'm sorry, Ben."

"It's alright. He and I didn't get along well, especially after he eventually told me why they got divorced—years after she'd died—but we're on better terms these days."

"What happened?" she asked, curiosity making her bold.

A soft chuckle rumbled in his chest. "Tale as old as time, I guess. Military man leaves his wife in one place, deploys, and gets himself a girlfriend there. My mom apparently found out when the girlfriend called the house. I was young when it happened, so I don't remember it. I'd basically only ever known them as divorced, but my mom never said anything bad about him."

"That's … That's so awful. I'm sorry, Ben," she said, feeling the hurt that something like that would do to a person. Knowing exactly how he would feel. "My mom left when I was little, and my dad was the same way about her. After she left him alone to raise me, he never had a cross word to say about her."

Ben finally looked in her direction, taking a hand off the wheel to quickly flick another tear that rolled down her cheek. "I hate that we have that in common, but I appreciate the sentiment."

"Hello? You guys there?" A sudden voice crackled through the radio.

Addie snatched the radio up off the receiver, clearing the emotion from her throat before switching it on. "Yeah, we read you now."

"Good. *Someone* forgot to charge the battery for this one last night," Brody ground out on the other end—an accompanying grumble of protest echoing somewhere in the background.

"How's everything looking on radar?" Addie asked.

"Looking good. Only a matter of time now."

The clouds began to shift, the dark-gray tufts rolling across the sky angrily. Addie held her breath as the makings of a funnel began to appear, out in the field off to the left of their little convoy. Her heart pounded in her chest, drowning out the sounds of the storm around them.

It was beautiful. Simply incredible to watch. The funnel slowly began to lower from the sky. Bit by bit, second by second, the vortex made itself known. It twirled about in the air like that of a circus acrobat. Twisting and twirling with such graceful movement that, if it weren't a wild force of nature, it would have looked practiced. Honed. Sharpened by a millennium of practice.

With the way it remained suspended above the ground, teasing the earth below like a lover, Addie began to wonder if it would fizzle out before it touched down. When a plume of dirt and dust finally kicked up on the ground, she slapped the dashboard excitedly.

"Hell yeah! We got one!" Ryan called out over the other radio with excitement as he and Tony followed in the car behind Ben's.

It didn't take long for it to strengthen, the spinning and twirling vortex starting out as barely more than a whisper before it exploded into a cacophony of roaring winds and black clouds. It was a masterpiece in its own right—a perfectly clean-cut vortex that felt almost picturesque.

Addie turned and grinned at Ben. "You think you want to deploy for this one?"

He raised an eyebrow at her. "Think you can take orders this time? Or are you gonna leave me standing in a field?"

She laughed. "Not unless you give me a reason to."

"Then I think we should deploy," he said as he took the radio from her. "Ryan, Tony, you guys good to go?"

A whoop cleared through the radio as Tony laughed. "Yeah, I think we're ready."

Ben grinned. "Alright then. You two, follow me. Grace—you, Brody, and Evie, hang back to start getting our readings and some shots for the documentary."

The engine roared as Ben stepped on the accelerator, leaving the RV in the dust as Tony followed closely behind.

The familiar sensation of butterflies fluttered inside of Addie's gut—the mixture of excitement and nerves pinging through her body. The rush. The adrenaline. God, it was the most addictive drug on earth.

"Let's do this!" she called out, slapping the dashboard with excitement.

"That's my girl," Ben said quietly, just barely above a whisper, then he grabbed the radio and spoke more clearly. "Alright. You know the drill. Tony, you follow until I give the word. We drop the equipment, and we clear out before it takes us with it. Got it?"

"You got it!" Ryan shouted in the background.

"Yeah, we got it, boss," Tony echoed, sounding both annoyed and amused.

CHAPTER 25

"Do you think we have enough space to deploy in that area over there?" Addie asked as she pointed. The open clearing, fit snugly between two farm plots, had the kind of low-cut green grass that made traversing easy when time was a valuable resource. A perfect spot for what they needed to do without anything knocking their equipment over.

Ben sized it up. "If we can time it just right, I think we can. You ready?"

Addie didn't exactly have long to think about it, with an unseen timer counting down the seconds she had to reply. Was she ready? What if she made another bad call?

As if sensing her internal battle, however, Ben reached over and gave her hand a firm squeeze. "You've got this, firecracker. Don't worry."

It was exactly what she needed to hear, so she let her insecurity whistle past her lips on a deep breath out. "Yeah. I'm ready. Let's do this."

With another firm squeeze, Ben grinned. He threw the steering wheel in the direction of the field with one hand and snatched the radio with the other. "Follow me, Tony. We're gonna deploy in this field over here."

"Roger that, boss!"

"Evie, make sure you're rolling too."

"Already on it!" Evie called out in the background.

The SUV leapt across the bumpy dirt road, jostling the two of them as Addie's stomach shot up and lodged itself in her throat.

She looked up at the swirling vortex in the distance, trying to gauge exactly how long they would have until they absolutely needed to be out of the way. With the current trajectory, there was no doubt it would head in their direction. It was building in power, slow moving, based on the increasing amount of debris being sucked up into the sky.

"We likely have less than three minutes," Addie said as the SUV bounced off the dirt road and out into the open field.

"All the more reason to do this as quickly as we can so it doesn't pick us up with it," Ben said, though Addie could hear the slight tremor in his voice. Whether it was from anxiety or adrenaline, she couldn't quite be certain, but she leaned toward adrenaline when his wide smile nearly cracked his face. A gleam sparked to life in his eyes as he watched the storm ahead with childlike wonder and awe.

Addie knew how much she missed doing this, but it was easy to tell how much *he* loved doing this as well.

Ben applied the brakes, coming to an abrupt stop. "Let's go!"

The moment she exited the vehicle, the wind and taste of dug-up earth assaulted her senses. Her hair—which she'd barely managed to pull into a loose bun on top of her head—immediately wisped and tangled out of the rubber band. There wasn't any time to deal with it, just hoping more than anything that it didn't impact her vision too badly.

The ruddy taste of clay and soil assaulted her senses, the granules pebbling against her teeth before she could close her mouth quick enough. The gritty texture was like that of a body scrub but felt all wrong as she ran her tongue across her teeth to wipe it away and spit.

She grabbed onto the side of the SUV to steady herself and made her way back to the trunk, using the solid structure to guide her under the force of the winds battering her body.

Her ears had long popped from the drop in pressure, but the sound of the storm—as it howled like a wolf serenading a full moon—encased Addie like a cocoon. Warm and devilishly tempting to give in to the will of nature. The way the wind pushed and shoved against her felt like a dancer pushing and pulling their lover across an open ballroom. All give and take, all power and strength.

It was exactly how she remembered.

She felt *alive*.

Ben greeted her as he came around to the back of the vehicle on his side, the two quickly grabbing the trunk latch and throwing it open.

The roar of the funnel made it difficult to hear, but Addie could see Ben's lips moving as he grabbed one side of the equipment. He began pointing to her side, making a flipping motion, and she immediately understood.

She flipped the switch to arm the equipment just as Tony and Ryan ran up to join them. Even with the four of them lifting it up and out of the trunk, Addie's arms strained under the weight. She knew these things were heavy, but it had been long enough since she'd last had to pick one up that she'd almost forgotten just how *hefty* they were.

Debris sprayed against her back as she faced away from the wind, shuffling in unison with the others until Ben seemed satisfied with their position. When they'd lowered it to the ground, Addie quickly went about checking to make sure everything was ready.

Orange lights whirred to life as Addie continued on one side of the equipment, while Ben worked on the other side—both trying to make quick work as Ryan and Tony spotted for them.

At this distance from the funnel, Addie could feel the intensity of the storm buzzing around her. It inched closer and closer toward them like the killer in a scary movie—tall and menacing in the darkness, waiting for the perfect moment to strike. Stalking their prey as they zeroed in on their victim.

Both terrifying and exhilarating all at the same time.

This one was *definitely* stronger than others they'd seen so far. It was almost hard to breathe as the funnel attempted to suck the oxygen straight out of her lungs. It took focus to force breaths in and out, shoving the air into her lungs despite the will of the storm.

Only the bigger and badder twisters had power like that, so it lit a greater fire under her butt.

When she flicked on the last indicator, she looked up at Ben. She gave him a thumbs up, making her way around the equipment. Ben called out for Ryan and Tony, and the four of them rushed back to their vehicles.

Ben didn't wait for her to buckle up, immediately throwing the car into drive the moment she shut the car door behind her—and effectively peeling out of the field behind Ryan and Tony.

"Are you okay?" Ben asked in panting breaths.

"Never better!"

Ben nodded but said nothing, instead focusing on the road ahead. Addie didn't mind as she rolled down her window and stuck her head out. She wanted to keep an eye on the equipment—the orange whirring lights fading farther and farther into the distance as they tried to put space between them and the twister.

The now black funnel cloud had grown in size. It blended a bit more into the blackened clouds around it, but Addie was able to make out enough of it to know it was *big*. Not only big, but its shape had morphed. It had shifted into a full-grown wedge, causing a new wave of nerves to bubble in her gut.

She wasn't as familiar with the area, but it was much more populated than some of the previous ones they'd chased. She only hoped that it stayed out in the fields like this instead of heading into town.

The vortex churned the ground as it bared down on the equipment, and Addie could vaguely make out those little flashing orange lights as they lifted up into the air.

"It took it!" she whooped out, turning to Ben with a grin and clutches his arm before she can stop herself.

Ben let out a cheer and snatched the radio. "Can you confirm, Grace?"

"I can! It's already reading as high as ten thousand feet!" Grace called back, the sound of applause and cheers ringing out in the background. "Great job, guys!"

God, she missed this so much that it ached deep in Addie's chest.

Something hot and wet began to soak her cheeks, a smile bubbling to the surface as she laughed. She *could* still do this. It sounded so silly for her to think, but the sensation was overwhelming. She'd outright convinced herself that she would mess it up somehow. That if she couldn't even do something as simple as a deployment like this, then how could she ever dream of being back in the field again?

But she'd been wrong. She had been able to do it—with ease. It had been so natural, so second nature, that she started to doubt the little voice in the back of her mind. If she could be wrong about something like this, something so logistical and concrete, maybe there was more about herself that was wrong too?

Ben turned to look at her, a soft chuckle escaping him as he rubbed one of her cheeks with his thumb. "Adrenaline does funny things to you, it seems."

"Thanks for letting me come this time," Addie teased.

"Couldn't leave my girl behind, could I?" Ben replied with a grin. A delightful shiver raced down Addie's spine, leaving her a bit more breathless.

CHAPTER 26

Addie flew out of the SUV as soon as Ben parked it alongside the RV, far enough away from the storm to allow a moment to celebrate their victory. Then she practically leapt into Evie's waiting arms.

"Did you see that? Did you *see* it?" Addie cried out as she collided with Evie.

"That was *amazing*, Addie," Evie exclaimed as she picked Addie off the ground and spun her around. "And holy *shit*, I got it all on camera! The buildup, the deployment, it was all incredible!"

Out of the corner of Addie's eye, she could see the monitor inside of the RV—data already pouring in. Numbers and variables streamed down the page like a waterfall of invaluable information.

Ryan rushed over next, jumping up and down with excitement. "Holy shit! Did you *see* that thing?!"

A barrage of gargled noise suddenly pierced through the air, causing Grace to break away from the group. "Don't uncork the champagne without me!" she called over her shoulder and trotted over to the RV.

Addie joined Ryan by jumping up and down, the two holding hands and cheering as they did. They looked more like teenagers than fully grown scientists, but no one seemed to care. Deploying at all is a celebration in and of itself—especially one that went as smoothly and safely as that one just had. It's a lot easier in theory to deploy equipment like that in the field, but no amount of practice could help with fighting against the elements, time, and strength. Each and every successful deployment was a triumph—but deploying on what was likely a pretty hefty tornado on top of it? It was any scientist's dream come true.

When Evie jumped in to join, Ryan's excited cheers turned into high-pitched squeals that could've easily damaged any nearby dog's eardrums. The sound only caused Evie and Addie to wheeze with laughter, desperately trying to stand up straighter as Ryan's movements became more and more exaggerated.

It didn't take the rest of the crew long to join in, the three stragglers racing over to hop inside. Tony snuck up and surprised Evie by sweeping her feet from beneath her and lifting her up, spinning her about in the center of the group. Even Ben, who had been relatively tame in his reactions in comparison, bumped shoulders with Brody.

It warmed something deep in Addie's chest as she took a step back to catch her breath and watched with amusement. She often found herself missing her old team after she'd joined the news station—missing that sense of camaraderie that is often found in teams like this. It's hard not to when each person has to depend on the other to help keep one another safe.

But this felt different from that. It tingled a long-dormant part of her that she hadn't felt since the day she'd watched as her father was lowered into the ground.

Ben jumped out of the tangle of limbs and bodies as he, too, went to catch his breath, his chest rising and falling rapidly as their eyes met. His smile felt as bright as the sun as he looked at her, something so loving and soft that it almost made her blush, but she didn't dare look away. She wanted to remember this moment for the rest of her life.

Of her here with this little family she'd found with them.

"I can't fucking believe this!" Grace's voice boomed from the RV, the celebrations immediately ceasing as Ben and Brody rushed over—quickly followed by the rest of the crew.

"What is it?" Ben asked.

Grace pounded the keyboard in front of one of the monitors. "This is fucking perfect! We get the biggest fucking tornado that we've ever deployed for, and our fucking recording equipment stops working."

"*What*?!" Brody exclaimed.

Ryan ran a frustrated hand through his hair. "You've *got* to be fucking kidding."

"I wish I was," Grace said, leaning to point at the last line of data on screen, "but look. It collected as it went up, held stable for a few minutes, and then the data just abruptly stops here."

"How the fuck does machinery *that* sturdy 'just stop'?" Ryan demanded.

Grace shrugged. "It shouldn't have. Either something *in* the funnel damaged it, or something happened to it *before* it was picked up."

Before? How could that be? She'd been the one to arm the system, and it had worked perfectly fine then. It was certainly possible that something could've collided with it and damaged it in the air, though it would be extremely bad luck if that were the case.

No, something about the whole thing felt off. It was entirely too coincidental, especially coupled with the other strange things that had been happening with their stuff. Her skin prickled uncomfortably, but one look over at Brody—whose face had darkened considerably—told her she wasn't the only one suspicious.

Ben, now standing next to her, rubbed his face. He pinched the bridge of his nose for a moment before the steady, sure look in his eyes returned. "It's not what we would've hoped for, but we *did* get some data—"

"Do you think they'll take it since it'll be only partial data?" Tony asked.

Another breath and Ben put his hands on his hips. "I don't know for sure, but any data is better than none at all. They'll still want to see what we have even if it's not a completely full cycle. Besides, Evie, you were able to catch the whole deployment, right?"

Evie gave a thumbs up. "I did. Footage is clear as a bell too."

"Good. Then even if we have *no* data, we got what we needed," Ben replied.

Wanting desperately to ease the disappointment, Addie smiled. "Besides, we're nowhere even close to the end of the season, so it's not like this will be our last deployment. Right?"

Ben looked visibly relieved. "Exactly. I'll make a few calls to see about getting more equipment for our next deployment. In the meantime, let's celebrate the win for what it is and keep our eyes out for any other cells today."

"Do you think they're gonna give us more equipment after this?" Ryan asked, the muscle of his arms tense as he folded them across his chest.

"Of course they will," Brody stated with confidence. "Once we close shop for the day, I'll work on getting the data sent over."

"I'll start making some calls here in—" Ben started before a sharp intake reverberated inside the crowded space of the RV.

"Guys, we have another problem," Grace interrupted.

"What could it possibly be now?" Ryan asked.

"I think one of the towns nearby was hit," she said solemnly.

A pin could have dropped in that moment, and it would've boomed through the silence that sliced through the group, a tonal shift so abrupt that whiplash instantly set in.

"How bad?" Tony asked.

"I don't know. I haven't heard any reports coming out yet—but based off the trajectory, they were likely side-swiped, so I don't know for sure."

Brody and Ben exchanged a few signs at one another, a silent discussion between them that lasted all of two seconds. "Pack up, then. We're gonna head over to see if anyone needs help. Grace, you hang back with the RV until we can see how much debris is on the road. Tony, Ryan, and Brody—follow behind me."

"Can I come? I want to help," Evie asked.

Ben nodded. "Yeah, hop in the back of the SUV with me and Addie."

Electrical wire popped and crackled nearby on the ground when Addie and Evie stepped out of the SUV. The sound caused Evie to startle and edge closer to Addie, just as Ben rounded the vehicle to join them.

They had only managed to get to the edge of town before the roadway had been completely impassable—a large oak tree having fallen in the middle of it and taking a few power lines down. Ben had radioed back to Tony, Ryan, and Brody, who followed closely behind them, and the three soon joined them just in front of the massive trunk blocking their way.

"That doesn't look good," Tony commented as he came to stand next to Evie.

"No. No, it doesn't—especially with the power lines down like that," Ben agreed as he turned to face Addie and Evie. "Alright, you girls stay here. We'll go check it out, so stay here with the cars, and we'll be back in a—"

"No fucking way," Evie interrupted firmly.

"Yeah, we're coming with you guys whether you like it or not," Addie added.

Ben shot her a pained expression. "Addie—"

"No, we'll need all the hands we can get, so don't even give me that look."

"Yeah, I'm not staying here either," Evie said.

Concern lit up Tony's already bright eyes. "Evie, it's going to be dangerous...."

An unspoken tension passed between them, one that Addie was absolutely going to ask her friend about later.

Evie shot him an unexpectedly soft smile. "I'll be fine. There might be spaces you boys can't get into that Addie and I can, so y'all are stuck with us."

"At the very least, we can send them back to Grace to call for more backup if needed," Brody said, shrugging casually when Ben shot him a tight expression.

Before anyone else could protest, Addie started to make her way through the land mine of cabling, hopping over one cable into another safe patch of pavement. The cars wouldn't be able to pass through the cables, but with careful footing she could easily walk around it and head further into town.

She wasn't going to wait for Ben to make up his mind. There could be people that needed help. Nothing else mattered except for that.

"Goddammit," she heard Ben mutter loudly somewhere behind her, along with the echoing sound of his boots scraping against the pavement. A game of hopscotch seemed a small price to pay if the town on the other side of the tree looked even a fraction as chaotic as the roadway did.

It took a few moments of bated breath and careful planning, but when Addie finally made it to the other side and looked up, she was glad that she was there to help.

It was a relatively small town from what she had seen on the map, which wasn't surprising given the area, but knowing the *exact* size of it would've been impossible in its given state. The main road, already blocked by the large oak tree behind them, led straight to the heart of downtown. At least, that was what Addie assumed, as she could faintly make out the "Town Hall" sign dangling off to the side of a building less than a few hundred feet directly in front of them.

Wood splinters littered the ground like party confetti—a mixture of tree bark, branches, and structural wood beams that were practically indiscernible. Leaves were completely absent, making any standing trees appear skeletal as they loomed over the sides of the road like a bad omen.

Most of the power lines going into town seemed to have held up for the most part, though a few posts leaned precariously to the side, as if another minor gust of wind would be enough to topple it over.

"Oh my God...." Evie whispered next to her.

Ben came up and let out an exasperated breath, a first-aid bag that Addie hadn't even seen him grab clutched in his hands. "Alright, everyone, spread out. Bring anybody here to the town hall area for safety until more people show up to help. Brody and I will start on clearing out some space here for a makeshift triage area for first aid."

Addie nodded—not waiting for instructions before instinctively choosing a direction and making her way toward one of the residential side streets.

She didn't wait for the boys, but she heard Evie coming up behind her. "I'm coming with you."

It appeared like the tornado had blindly chosen which houses to leave—and which it would level to the ground. It was an unfair game of chance that no one wanted to play. The raw smell of earth meant that it hadn't been too long since the tornado had come through, so it was likely that most people were still bunkered down in storm shelters.

Addie made her way to the first house, the most intact one she could see on this street, and began calling out.

"This is … This is awful.…" Evie said, her voice so quiet that Addie almost didn't hear her.

It absolutely was. What had likely once been a beautiful and thriving town was now nothing more than dust riding on the wind. They'd have to rebuild from the ground up. *If* they could build back up again.

"As beautiful as these storms we chase are, we often forget the toll they take," Addie replied, wiping away the sweat building on her forehead with the back of her hand.

Out of the corner of her eye, Addie saw the slightest of movements and whipped in that direction. A metallic storm shelter door slowly swung open, catching the light of the sun peeking through the storm clouds as it clanged against the hard dirt. Addie and Evie immediately started rushing over in that direction as an elderly couple slowly emerged.

No words were exchanged as Addie and Evie offered their hands to help the couple over some debris littering what was likely the couple's backyard. The older gentlemen tottered in Evie's grip as he kept turning his head to check on his wife, his white hair caked with mud and dirt.

Addie climbed over one of the larger branches to help the wife, who seemed to be less able to traverse the landscape like her husband had, and offered her arm. The woman, with her short, curly white bob, gave her a warm smile and accepted—shaking a bit whether from age or from the scare of the storm, Addie couldn't be sure.

"We barely got downstairs...." she offered as both Evie and the woman's husband helped to pull her over the branch.

Addie didn't doubt that, and she hoped everyone else had enough time to get to safety like this couple had.

"You got them?" Addie asked Evie as she hopped back over the branch.

"Yeah, I've got them," Evie replied. "I'll help them get back to Ben if you want to go ahead and keep looking."

"Sounds good. I'll just be down this street if you want to come back down this way," she replied, wiping a bit of dirt from her hands onto her jeans.

Evie looked paler than she had previously, though not in a sickly kind of way—more in the overwhelmed kind that felt all too familiar. It had been a really long time since Addie had last had to do anything like this, her first time having been the first year of chasing right out of college, but it was hard to forget the feeling.

She wasn't sure what her friend was thinking or how she was feeling, but neither of them had the luxury to discuss any of that. The two exchanged glances, a small smile passing between them, before Addie started to head to the next house.

CHAPTER 27

The next few houses were mercifully empty, as were their shelters. The further down the road she traveled, the worse the damage seemed to get. The scientific part of her brain attempted to kick into overdrive as she tried to focus on her search—wondering if this was the part of the town where they'd been sideswiped.

The humidity from the storm lingered in the air, clinging to her skin in the ever-warming afternoon heat. She swiped the sweat from her forehead once more, stopping to take a moment to assess where to go next.

To her right, the road appeared to head back to the main road they'd been on earlier. Looking to her left, a few more houses could be made out among the downed trees and other debris.

Left it is.

The duality of the job wasn't lost on her as she stepped over another large branch in the middle of the street. That less than an hour ago, they were standing in a field, celebrating the same tornado that had just ruined the lives of dozens of people.

It was a cruel sort of irony that twisted the knife of guilt into Addie's stomach.

It was easy to see the beauty of nature, the majesty of a storm as it swept across the open plains of Oklahoma, and hell of a lot less painful than this.

An eerie silence had swallowed the whole town—occasionally pierced by the sounds of people calling out for loved ones, a baby crying for its mother, and the soft weeps from those whose entire lives had been destroyed. Even the cracking and crumbling of someone's house as it finally gave in on itself and collapsed to the ground like a house of cards. Sounds that would haunt Addie in her sleep until the end of time.

Exhaustion and heat pebbled sweat across her forehead, but she pushed on. By the fading sun, it had to have been hours since she'd last seen the rest of the team. The triage area they'd set up had been packed with people the last time she'd gone back.

The last she'd been there had been to help a younger woman, no older than she herself was. She'd been so optimistic when Addie helped her out of her shelter, blocked partially by a nearby fallen tree. Blood oozed from a cut on her forehead from some debris, but had been otherwise unharmed. But she was alone. Her husband had been in town when the tornado hit. Something about groceries for a dinner he had been planning. Addie couldn't be sure. The woman was talking so fast that she'd been practically babbling. Likely a result of the adrenaline swimming through her veins.

She'd been so optimistic that he would in town waiting for her, or that he was out looking for her, so *sure* that he was there that even Addie started to believe it.

Addie had gone back out to search for more people, wishing the woman luck as she left. But when she came back later, that same woman was sitting on the hot concrete sidewalk, sobbing into her hands next to the grocery store. Or … what was left of it.

The bitter sting of tears had burned in Addie's eyes as she'd forced herself to turn back around and look for more people. She waited until she was around the corner before she let out a sob. She didn't want the others to see her cry.

The beauty and majestic side of nature was worthy of awe, of respect.

The human side of nature was cruel and unforgiving.

There had only been a few stragglers heading to town hall since then. By her count, she'd only seen a few dozen people at the makeshift triage area. There were a far greater number of houses than that.

Addie's T-shirt was completely soaked through with sweat, but she continued on. If there was even a remote chance that anyone else needed help, she would take it.

"It's why teams like ours are so crucial for advancing the art of storm chasing—" someone said solemnly around the corner, exhaustion causing Addie to doubt whether she was actually hearing someone or just hallucinating. She wiped the sweat off her brow and continued, stepping into view of the scene unfolding.

Billy stood in front of one of the demolished houses, his cameraman posed and crouched in the street as he pointed the camera directly at Billy.

Addie *knew* she had to be hallucinating now. She was positive that her team were the only ones on site for the time. Brody had told her, upon her last drop off, that emergency services were still en route.

So she walked on, putting one foot in front of another as if in a trance.

"That's why, with your help, you can make a difference. Majority of proceeds from today's sale of the merch on our website will go to— Well, look who is here!" Billy called out upon spotting her approaching.

She wasn't dreaming. They really were here. And they were ... filming?

"Billy?"

Billy waved at his camera guy, who lowered the device from his shoulder. "We'll pick up in five."

"What the hell are you doing here?" she demanded, her words beginning to sound slurred.

The rest of his crew busied themselves with their equipment, which they had strewn about like they were on a movie set instead of a disaster area.

Billy grinned at her, that slimy kind that made her feel like gagging. "What does it look like we're doing, sweetheart? Filming? You know, same thing you do?"

There were so many questions running through Addie's mind, but she didn't have the patience to restrain the unbridled anger pulsing beneath her temples. "That's—that's not what I meant. How ... How long have you guys been here?"

Billy gave her a look, his eyes scrunched. "A few hours, maybe?"

A few *hours*? They'd been here this whole time filming when there have been people still in need of help?

"People are still missing and in need of rescue!"

Billy shrugged, nary a dent in his impish grin. "It seemed like y'all were doing just fine with the cleanup, so we thought we'd take the opportunity to help out *our* way."

Cleanup? How the hell could he say that? There were still people missing! There was no *cleanup* happening. And how the hell could he possibly be *helping*, standing out here filming some poor family's destroyed house?

"Help *out*? How the hell are you helping out?" she demanded. She was far too exhausted, far too tired, for whatever bullshit Billy was up to.

Billy placed a hand over his heart, looking suddenly devastated. "We're just trying to raise money to help people here rebuild. How could you be so upset over that?"

"There are people that are still missing!"

"Gotta help some way, right? Besides, I wanted to get some practice for when you and your friend join us."

Addie blinked. Then blinked again. "What the hell does that mean?"

Another impish grin, this time more foul. "I guess you'll find out soon enough. In the meantime, if you'll excuse us, we have work to do."

She stomped away before he could say anything else—putting as much distance between herself and Billy before the urge to punch him became too overpowering. She didn't trust herself to not say, or do, something she would regret. She knew that berating him, or knocking the fucker out, would only hurt her team. But that didn't stop the ache in her fist from how tight she coiled it just to release the tension in her chest.

Hot tears pricked her cheeks as she angrily sobbed, continuing to storm around another house until she was out of sight. Then, and only then, did she let her rage bubble out. She kicked at a pile of rubble and clamped her teeth around a scream of frustration, the sound of the wooden discards clanking against one another as it toppled to the ground.

Addie wobbled on her feet when she attempted to take another step. She braced herself against the crumbled remains of the house she stood next to. Goosebumps skittered across her skin as a cool wave passed over her.

When had she last had water? The thought occurred to her that the fuzzy quality to her vision likely wasn't from irritation but dehydration.

Shit. She needed to get back to take a quick break. She'd be of no help to anyone if she passed out.

Being in the station, under the hot studio lighting and a secure roof over her head, she often forgot how important her job could actually be. Especially when dealing with pigs like John, or Frank, or, hell, any of the random men commenting "nice ass" on her reports online.

It was teams like *Billy's* that had given their entire line of work a bad name. Thinking of him taking advantage of this to sell a few extra shirts made her skin crawl. Meanwhile, teams like Ben's did incredibly important work helping to keep people safe, to keep them informed.

Did these people get that warning? Had they been given that chance?

Something shifted in the distance, and Addie glanced up to see Ryan. He noticed her as well and started walking over the debris cluttering the road.

He cocked his head as he neared. "Addie? Addie, are there people over there? I thought I heard you. What did you—"

She didn't hear the rest of the sentence before blackness finally overtook her.

"Ben, I'm fine," Addie protested as he wrapped a cool cloth around her neck. "I want to get back out there to—"

"Oh, you've helped enough for one day," he admonished, shoving her protesting hands away.

When she'd woken up in the RV moments ago and tried to sit up, to see what was going on, Ben appeared next to her in a flash. From the frown plastered to his face, he wasn't particularly thrilled with her.

She rolled her eyes. "I'm fine, Ben."

Ben's expression was tight. "Yeah, well, I'm not taking the risk."

"Ben, I passed out because I was hot and exhausted. Plus, I'd just run into Billy, and he pissed me off."

That seemed to get Ben's attention as his expression grew darker. "Billy?"

"Yeah, he was out *filming*! Can you imagine that?! Dozens of people missing, injured, and he's busy trying to get viewers to buy his fucking *merch*. Oh, but don't worry! A *portion* of the proceeds will go to the families he's exploiting here!" Addie fumed, her head getting light once again, and she forced herself to take a breath. "I got so angry that I stormed away, so that's why I overheated. He's such an ass! Do you think you can teach me sign language, so I can say that to his face whenever I want?"

"Tempting as that may be," Ben chuckled, "we've got more important things to worry about right now than him, so I want you to stay here and get some rest, okay?"

"But—"

Ben crouched in front of her, and the sudden shift of his tall stature lowering so quickly startled her. "You're gonna sit your ass in this bed until I say otherwise, got it?"

Addie's eyebrows shot up, turning to look at him. *Really* look.

The statement itself was stern and unrelenting, angry even, but the tone was soft. As if trying to pillow the harshness of it. A very un-Ben-like move when he normally had *no* issue telling her exactly like it was. An unsure gleam in those pools of amber.

He was worried about her.

Addie tried to frown but failed miserably as a small smile cracked through. "And you say *I'm* the stubborn one?"

Ben pulled her in and kissed her. It surprised her for a second before she leaned into him—his lips lingering on hers just long enough to leave her breathless.

"You still are," he whispered, finally relenting and returning her smile. "When was the last time you ate?"

She pursed her lips as she thought back. "Not sure. I-I promise I wasn't trying to skip, though. We just left in a hurry and—"

He leaned to press his forehead against hers. "If I give you a granola bar, will you promise to eat it for me?"

She nodded sheepishly, feeling like a scolded child. "Yeah. You don't have to treat me like a baby."

"If being concerned for your well-being means *treating* you like one every now and then, well, you better start getting used to it." Ben's smile widened. "Is this what it's gonna be like being together? You gonna give me a heart attack every other day?"

She smiled. "Not every other day. Once a week, tops."

"Duly noted." He chuckled and shook his head, pulling a granola bar out of the nearby cabinet and pushing it into her hands. "Now, stay here, eat this, and rest for a bit, okay?"

She opened her mouth to protest, a response on the tip of her tongue, but stopped. Maybe she *did* need a few minutes. Her head still felt fuzzy, and the cold cloth on her neck had already grown hot to the touch. She wouldn't be of much use to anyone if she passed out again.

"Just for a little while…" she muttered, ripping the wrapper open. Ben stood there, waiting until she'd taken a generous bite from the bar before chuckling.

"That's my girl," he said, tossing her a wink and disappearing through the door.

As if she wasn't hot enough, hearing Ben call her "my girl" was enough to raise her temperature even higher.

Addie barely had another bite of granola in her mouth when Evie stormed inside dramatically. She'd tied her hair up into a ponytail since Addie had last seen her hours ago, and pebbles of sweat marked her forehead and upper lip. The bright-pink tank top she'd worn was now a muted blush color, almost a dusty orange, having gotten in a fight with dirt and muck and lost.

But Addie was glad to see her nonetheless.

"What the hell, Addie?!" Evie demanded, stomping her foot as she did. "Tony told me that you passed out?"

"I'm fine. Just got a little too tired and hot," Addie said.

A hiss slid between Evie's lips as she plopped down in the seat next to Addie. "Well, that may be the case, but—"

Addie laughed. "I'm not going to apologize, so you're wasting your breath at this point."

"I don't..." Evie started, her voice sounding a touch calmer when she started again. "I don't want you to apologize. You have nothing to apologize for. I'm sorry. It's just ... I mean, you're my best friend, and it scared me when I heard what happened and—"

Despite herself, Addie smiled. "I'm your best friend?"

Evie gave her an incredulous look. "Of course you are. What kind of stupid-ass question is that?"

Addie barked a laugh, the sound loud enough that she worried that anyone standing outside the camper would hear. "Wow, it's nice being Evelyn Sanders's best friend. Is this what it feels like to be famous?"

"Yeah, laugh now, but because you are now my literal captive audience, you and I are *definitely* gonna be talking about the situation with you and Ben."

Addie had another bite halfway to her mouth when she froze. How on earth was she supposed to respond to that? It was only a matter of time before the questions came; she'd just hoped she'd be better prepared.

"I don't kiss and tell," she relented.

Evie slapped her shoulder. "I *knew* it! Come on. Spill it. Tell me *everything*!"

"That's not what I meant. You know it's just a phrase."

"It's not *just a phrase* if you two have kissed. Or, you know ... maybe more?" Evie said, puckering her lips to the side and looking away.

The moment was broken anyway when Addie's phone began to ring. She groaned, frustrated by the interruption, and pulled it out of her pocket. Then she grew even more frustrated by the name on the caller ID.

"John always has the *worst* timing, doesn't he?" she commented.

Evie groaned, too, with an exaggerated roll of her eyes. "Always."

Addie giggled as she clicked to accept the call. "Hello."

John didn't miss a beat, an exasperated sigh curling through the receiver. "It's about time. Where the hell have you been? I've been trying to call you for over an hour!"

Addie pulled the phone away from her ear and tapped over to the call log which showed four missed calls in the past hour. "There was a tornado that went through a town we were near, so we came to help out. I've been a bit busy. What's up?"

"Are you alone?"

That got her attention—and not in a good way. "It's just me and Evie right now. Should I be alone?"

"So long as the rest of the team isn't near, it's fine."

"Why? What about the team?"

"Look, Addie, I'm sure things have been going swimmingly with the chases. Evie sent me a bit of the footage, and it's looking great."

"Then what's the concern?"

John sighed. "We got ... How do I put it? Well, we got some information recently that's been pretty concerning."

Addie blanched. "What kind of information?"

"Have there been any unexpected incidents during filming? With some of the equipment and such?"

Addie started, switching the phone to her other ear and standing up.

She felt like she needed to move—needed to not sit still for the time being.

"Nothing concerning that I've seen, but in-field issues are common with chasing," she offered, not wanting to confirm anything concretely. From the urgency—and a hint of frustration—in John's tone, it couldn't be good

"Well," John drew out. "We were given information that it was on purpose."

"On *purpose?*"

"Did you hear anyone talking about Channel 9 while you've been with them?"

Addie recalled her conversation with Brody, but she had no idea how John would know any of that. "No, not at all."

"Well, apparently, Channel 9 approached the team for a similar project but at a much higher bid than we offered," John started. "We now think that in order to get out of the contract with us, they've been sabotaging the documentary."

This time, Addie did gasp. "*What?*"

"There's pretty damning proof."

"Well, it's not true! These guys have been working so hard to make sure everything goes smoothly. They would *never* do anything like that."

John sighed on the other end. "I know you might have formed relationships with these people, so I understand your hesitation…"

Addie could hear the *but* coming a mile away. "But…?"

"*But,*" John continued, "there's enough evidence that some of the higher-ups are concerned. They want to fully investigate for legal purposes, but as a precaution, they want us to play safe.…"

Addie's stomach dropped. She really didn't like where this conversation was going. "Well, what are they suggesting we do?"

"They want to transfer you two to another team for the time being."

Addie stood so quickly that the blanket Ben had wrapped around her instantly pooled to the floor. "No way. They can't expect us to just hop ship to another team halfway through the season. You can't let them transfer us!"

"This isn't really up for discussion, Addie. I'm not particularly thrilled either, given how expensive this is going to be. But for "*safety*," they want to set up the transfer to Bill Whitman and his team by the end of the week."

No, no, no, no. This couldn't be happening. There was absolutely no way she would ever work with someone like Billy.

"Look, if there's any *sabotage* going on, it's Billy and his team behind it, I know it. He has history with this team," she said, starting to pace the length of the RV as Evie watched on curiously. "He used to work with our two team leads before he split off on his own. Every time we run into him, something always seems to happen to our stuff. He even ran us off the road during a chase out in the field. He could've seriously hurt me or Ben."

"Addie—"

"John, I have asked *very little* of you since I've started at this station," she continued, the words spilling from her, "and even less so when I was tossed on this assignment last minute. So, I'm asking for you to believe me now. I'll find a way to prove that it was him."

She held her breath as silence came from the other end of the phone. It was just about the only thing John *would* actually give a shit about in this whole situation.

"I think you should let me take care of all of this. This really isn't up to you."

Addie clicked her tongue indignantly. *This fucker...*

No, Addie wasn't about to meekly accept things anymore. She absolutely wasn't about to let Billy ruin everything for Ben and the rest of the team, not after they'd worked so hard to get to where they were. Old Addie was back with a vengeance.

"Fine, then I'll quit."

The other end went deadly silent for a moment before John spoke again. "What?"

"You want to play hardball, fine. So can I. Give me a chance to prove that the accusations are false, or I'll quit," she snapped.

"Addie..." Evie whispered, her brows furrowed together.

"Are you insane?" John spluttered. "You can't quit *now*, in the middle of production—"

"Exactly! You just told me how expensive it is just to transfer us to another team. Imagine having to find an entire-ass replacement for me. And like you said before, no one else has experience in the field like I do."

Addie could picture how red John's face was getting by the increased volume of his voice. "You can't throw things in my face like that, you—"

"All I asked for was a chance, and you wanted to be a dick about it. So, here's how it's gonna go," she spat. "Either you give me a few days to prove this team's innocence or I walk. Your choice."

"Addie, what are you doing?" Evie whispered, louder this time, as she reached out to touch Addie's arm.

If she were honest, she didn't know. It just sort of … fell out of her. All her cards to play were scattered on the table; everything she had was now on the line. But the thought of letting someone like Billy get away with this just didn't sit right with her. Not after everything this team had been through. Not after how she'd seen Billy's team today. No way in hell.

The clicking sound of John sucking on his teeth reverberated through the phone, and Addie instantly knew that she had him. "You know you and I will have to have a talk when you do finish this assignment."

She'd figure out something else with her debts if that time came.

This was something worth fighting for.

The only regret she had was that she hadn't fought for *herself* sooner than this. But it was too late to take it back now. She was in, all or nothing.

"I'm aware. Do we have a deal or not?"

A hefty sigh wheezed through the line. "You can't let your team know. It'll tamper any evidence you get."

Addie practically jumped into the air. "I won't say a word—only Evie and I will know."

Another pause, one that caused all the nerves in her body to coil into springs, ready to pop off at a moment's notice.

"You have two days, Addie," John finally said. "After that, start packing."

CHAPTER 28

"Well, that was … interesting?" Evie offered, rubbing her palms together.

Addie collapsed onto the chair with a heaviness that weighed down her soul. "How on earth am I going to convince them of what's been going on?"

"Well," Evie said, "let's start by telling me what the hell has been going on and what you just put your career on the line for?"

"They want to transfer us to Billy's team because they got a report that Ben and the team are trying to sabotage the documentary."

Evie's lips curled. "What the hell? Why would they even think that?"

Addie rubbed at the spot on her temple as it began throbbing. "Channel 9 wanted to do a documentary too."

"So?"

"They wanted to work with this team, but Ben turned it down. *Someone* claimed that they actually accepted the offer and have been sabotaging things so that they can get out of the contract."

Evie jumped out of her seat. "That's ridiculous! They would *never* do anything like that. Who the hell called them?"

Addie scoffed. "Who do you think?"

"Oh, that motherfucker! When I get—"

"I mentioned my suspicions to Brody after I bumped into Billy this morning, just before we left for today's chase," Addie interrupted.

"Oh shit," Evie whispered. "The deployment equipment?"

Addie nodded. "I think so. When the Doppler went out, I noticed that the wiring looked odd—like it had been cut, not frayed. Then with your camera losing footage after we bumped into them in the parking lot…"

"That motherfucker!" Evie boomed, slamming her fist against the cushion. "I *knew* that wasn't just an error!"

"Exactly, but I have no idea how I'm gonna *prove* anything. We can't even tell the team what's going on because John said that would discredit anything we find. This is all such a mess," she ground out as she rubbed a frustrated hand over her tired eyes. "If Billy has been able to sneak without getting caught, catching him now is gonna be nearly impossible."

"Then we'll have to come up with another plan. How long do we have?"

"Two days."

Evie winced, and she plopped back in the seat next to Addie. "Crap…. And if they told him that we're gonna be switched to his team by the end of the week, he might not even try anything else. He wouldn't need to—he got what he wanted."

"Right, so we have to think of another way to get him to mess up."

Evie straightened in her seat with a sudden smile, as if a light bulb had flashed above her head. "We have to get him to confess. On camera, too, so that way we have proof that can't be easily disputed."

Addie's eyebrows shot up her forehead. "You're joking…. You think he's going to admit to any of this?"

Evie shrugged. "It's the only foolproof way. He's not going to do anything else if he thinks he's won, so why not get him to admit to it? He's got a big ego—we know that already—so if we confront him with the evidence of what he's done…"

"We don't have any evidence, though. That's the problem."

Evie's smile widened. "He doesn't know that."

Addie drummed her fingers on the table. It was so crazy that it might just work. If Billy thought there was even the slightest chance he'd been caught, he'd lose more than just a contract. Word would get out—he'd lose his sponsors, his team, his *reputation*.

The problem would be the precise balance between confrontation and understanding. If he felt ganged up on, he'd clam up completely, and they'd lose their chance forever. Addie and Evie couldn't tag-team him, good-cop-bad-cop style. It had to be just one person to do it.

Someone he needed on his side.

And who better than someone he would have to share the limelight with?

"I'll have to be alone with him," Addie said with finality, her decision already made.

"I can come with—"

Addie shook her head. "He's not gonna feel comfortable enough to say anything if anyone else is around. It has to be just me. He told me recently that he didn't want any bad blood between us. I can use that to my advantage and make him think I'm on his side. That way, when I confront him, he might be more likely to try and convince me to keep quiet."

"What if he doesn't go that route?" Evie asked, eyebrows drawing together. "What if he gets aggressive?"

"It's a risk I'm gonna have to take. I don't like it, either, but we don't have many other options—especially in the time frame we have."

"I *hate* that you have a point."

Addie chuckled. "Trust me, I'm not thrilled about it."

"Ben is gonna have a *cow* when this does eventually come out."

Oh, he'd have more than a cow, but that would be a bridge they'd cross when that time came. Ben already saved her ass more times than she could count—it was time she returned the favor.

"Let me deal with Ben."

Hesitation swam in Evie's chocolate eyes as she chewed on her lip. Conflict warring across the features of her face. "What's the plan, then?"

"I need to get him alone, where Billy is focused solely on our conversation."

Evie hummed in her throat. "Maybe you should reach out and let him know you need to meet? He'll think you want to talk about the transfer."

"Not bad. I'll have to convince him to meet alone, without his team. They might keep him from talking if they know what he's been up to."

"Good point. What about our team? Won't they notice if you just disappear?"

They definitely would, especially Ben.

"That's where you're gonna have to come in. I'll see if I can meet him early enough that everyone else is asleep, but you'll have to distract them if anyone starts asking. Just long enough that I can sneak out, meet with Billy, and sneak back."

A mischievous grin lit up Evie's face. "That's if you can sneak away at all...."

This time, when Addie rolled her eyes, it felt like they went back into the socket. "Don't start with that again."

"Come on. Give me *something*. I'm your best friend. You have to share! I'll tell you whose bed *I've* been in while you've been *not* in yours."

That caught Addie's attention. "Excuse me, what?! When did you and Tony—"

"Started last week." Evie gave a casual shrug, like she was reporting the weather. "Didn't want to make a big deal about it, so we've kept it quiet."

Now Addie understood that weird tension between them from earlier. Damn. "And you've been giving *me* a hard time?!"

"You're just so fun to tease." Evie giggled.

After their plan was agreed on, Evie wandered out to continue helping with the rescue efforts, effectively leaving Addie alone with her thoughts. A dangerous place for her to be.

Only a few hours ago, she'd woken up in Ben's arms. Happy. Safe. Now everything was wrong. The sound of firetrucks and police sirens had long diluted the silence that had filled the town—making it nearly impossible for Addie to relax completely. She needed to do something, to feel like she was being useful even if she wasn't out helping.

The nearby computer screen bleeped as the next set of Doppler radar data processed. Well, she could keep an eye on the storm cell to make sure nothing else was coming their way.

She snatched the blanket Ben had left behind and wrapped it around her shoulders. When she inhaled the scent enveloping her, it brought a smile to her face. It still smelled like him. Earthy, spicy—like the open plains of Oklahoma just after a rainstorm.

Thinking of him, her chest ached. She rubbed it absently as she tried mentally drafting the apology she'd have to issue him. He'd be furious with her for keeping something like this from him. She knew he would be, and she honestly wouldn't blame him for it either. If the roles were reversed, she'd be mad, too.

But she couldn't risk it. She hated that anything John said made sense, but he'd been right about this. If any of the team tried to help expose Billy, it would look like they were shifting blame.

No. It had to be her.

Billy didn't know Addie very well, which would work in her favor. All he knew was that he needed her for this documentary.

This wonderful, beautiful thing that had developed between her and Ben could survive this. She had to believe that. It would break her heart if it didn't, but if that was the price she had to pay to make sure Ben and his team weren't screwed over by Billy? She'd have to learn to live with that.

Time and time again, Ben had put his neck on the line to help her—saved her on more than one occasion. So, the one time she could actually do something to help? She was going to take it.

Before she completely lost her nerve, she picked up the phone. It only took two rings before the dial tone stopped and a voice echoed through. "Hello?"

"Can I speak to Bill Whitman, please?"

"And you would be...?"

She sighed. "Adelyn Walters."

"Well, well, well," Billy greeted, smugness oozing through the line. "Look who's finally giving me a call. Already dying to get onto team Billy?"

It was a good thing she was alone, as she'd have to train her face not to grimace. "We have a lot of things to sort out before the end of the week, and I have something I need to discuss. It's important."

"Oh yeah?"

"Can we meet in person? Alone?"

A pause, long enough that Addie feared she'd already messed up, when Billy scoffed. "Well, that is a surprise."

"Can we meet or not?" she huffed. If she tried to schmooze up to him too much, he'd get suspicious anyway. That's what she tried to convince herself of as she shoved the annoyance out of her voice.

"I have some free time tomorrow. The boys have some errands they have to run in town."

Perfect.

"What time?"

"It'll be early, but I can swing by after I drop them off, around six?"

"That's fine."

Honestly, the sooner she could get this whole thing over with, the better. She'd feel a hell of lot less guilty if she could get in and out before anyone even noticed she was gone.

A chuckle on the other end. "Alright. See you tomorrow."

The line went dead, and Addie placed the phone on the table. There was no turning back now.

Her eyes flicked back to the monitors to watch for any movement of the storm, but she had a hard time focusing. Her eyelids drooped without her permission, and a yawn ripped from her chest. She wanted to fight it, to stay awake in case anyone needed her. She'd already passed out once from exhaustion, and she didn't want to do it again. And the war between her and her eyelids was a losing battle.

Well... A few minutes of shut-eye might not be such a bad idea.

Her loose curls were still damp with sweat, but not so wet that it was uncomfortable, when she leaned back to rest her head against the wall behind her. In fact, it provided a bit of cushioning against the hard surface—a makeshift pillow that caused her body to relax as she slowly relinquished her body to sleep.

CHAPTER 29

Addie sat up sleepily and rubbed the grit coating her eyes. An unfamiliar, darkened room greeted her.

How long had she passed out for?

She stretched her back, arching into it, as she wondered where the rest of the team had gone.

The door across from the bed rattled, drawing her attention when it popped open and a tall figure stepped inside. Silhouetted against the shadows surrounding her, it took her a moment to realize who it was as the door shut behind them.

"You're awake," Ben said, sounding both surprised and relieved all at once.

"How long was I out?"

"A few hours."

She ripped the blanket off herself and threw her legs over the side of the bed. "Where are we?"

Ben lowered the paper bag onto the desk, just to the right of the door. Another step and he flicked the lights on, flooding her senses momentarily as he spoke. "Our motel, since we'll be staying in the area with this cluster of storms coming in."

The entire day rushed back so quickly that she sucked in a breath.

Oh yeah. The phone call. John. Billy.
The meeting tomorrow morning.

"You look worried. What's on your mind?" Ben commented, tilting his head as concern traveled across his face in ripples. He narrowed his eyes, but she turned so he couldn't see. How could he tell that just by looking at her?

She forced an eye roll. "Ben, I'm fine. I don't know what you're talking about."

The frown deepened. "Then tell me what you're thinking."

She needed to change the topic, quickly.

"I'm *thinking*," she started as she spun to face him, crossing her legs as she did. "That if we're going to be here *alone* tonight, there are quite a few things we could be doing."

Her attempt at humor didn't work. His hands went to rest on his hips, the full force of his eyes glaring at her. "Don't do that."

"D-do what?"

"I let you make the terms for what's going on between us, and I'm still fine going about it that way if it's what makes you comfortable. *For now*. But don't use that as a *distraction* to avoid telling me something," Ben ground out. "This isn't just sex for me, Addie. You know that."

She *did* know that. Of the two of them, he'd been the most open about what he wanted. She was the gun-shy one. But thinking that she inadvertently made him believe otherwise, that her feelings for him were so surface level—just to avoid dragging him into the situation with John and Billy—caused the guilt already pulsing beneath her temples to double.

"I know," she said—not defiantly but gently enough to soften the intensity in his gaze a fraction. "I'm sorry."

She closed the space between them in a few steps, circling her arms around his neck—and having to stand on her tiptoes to do so. His skin was hot to the touch, enough so that she could practically feel the sizzle of it against her own.

His arms wrapped around her waist without a word. The day's frustration hardened into place as his features etched into a frown, but she saw the cracks beginning to form. The warmth in his eyes. The way his fingers dug into her skin, like he was afraid she'd pull away. The breakdown into something softer, something just for her.

"Then tell me what's going on," he said, that final hard line crinkling between his eyebrows.

She couldn't tell him about the situation with Billy. What she *could* do, however, was to admit the other thing on her mind. That, she could give him. She owed him that much.

"Ben, it's just been … it's just been a long day, and seeing how badly damaged that town was…" she admitted.

Ben's arms tightened around her gently, a knowing squeeze that reflected the emotion welling up in his eyes. She knew he felt it too. It would be impossible not to. No matter how many times it happened, nothing could prepare them for seeing damage like that up close.

"It's never easy, no matter how much I see it," Ben said, low and steady. It grounded her. That low rumble in his voice that eased the ache between her shoulders. She was safe there in his arms. He wouldn't let anything happen to her—and she believed that.

"Are *you* okay?"

"Me?" he asked incredulously. "Oh, I'm fantastic. We deployed on one of the largest tornadoes ever, lost most of the data, nearly got electrocuted playing Tetris, my girlfriend works herself to exhaustion—" Ben's mouth clamped shut as his eyes widened, causing her to giggle. Her insides immediately turned to mush. It shouldn't affect her this way. They'd agree to take things slowly, but he'd said it so easily, so *confidently*, that how could it not?

Her smile turned feline. "Is that what I am? Is that what you want, Ben?"

He looked pained as his grip on her somehow tightened even more. "More than *breathing*. I want you to be mine, sweetheart. I think I've made that pretty fucking clear."

"I know… I know I said I wanted to keep things casual because we're working together, and it'll complicate things, but…" she started, biting her lower lip as nerves trapped her voice. "I think I want that too."

It scared her to no end, but it was true. She couldn't promise anything different, knowing what tomorrow brought—but she could be honest about what she wanted.

When the worry lines on his face faded and those dimples crinkled into a smile so bright that it lit up the entire room, nothing else mattered.

A mischievous twinkle glimmered down at her. "True or false?"

Her smile felt a little watery as tears pebbled to the surface. "True."

He kissed her before she could say anything more. A rough, desperate kiss that curled her toes in the most delicious way. She could feel him already hardening against her thigh when he lifted her—wanting, needing him. Her hips ground against him, just as desperate.

"I need you," she whispered against his lips. "Right now."

He pressed his forehead against hers, both of them panting as those pools of amber seared straight to her core. "You have me. All of me. Whenever you want, however you want. I'm yours, Addie."

And have him she would. The only sure thing she knew right now was this electricity sizzling between them, and she wanted to let it course through her until it pulsed true in her veins.

Their hands instinctively found one another as she reached to grab the hem of his shirt, needing to remove every barrier keeping them apart. She needed to feel his body against hers—to send her to nirvana as she chanted his name.

Ben didn't protest when she practically ripped at the material, wanting, *needing,* to feel him. He moved just as hungrily, helping with her efforts until he was able to throw the shirt across the room.

He grabbed at her clothing to do the same, but she stopped him. She shoved him back onto the bed before he could manhandle her further. There was something she needed more, and she was determined to get it.

He landed with a soft thud on the edge of the bed, his eyes wide and curious. There were many things she wanted to do to this man in the time to come, but she would start with this. She hadn't gotten to see all of him the night before. It had been dark for most of it, with his body covering hers as he fucked her relentlessly into the mattress.

Not that she was gonna complain about that.

But she wanted to explore him more now. The shock on his face lasted all of ten seconds before she fell to her knees before him. Her fingers wrapped around his girth, reveling in the feeling of his cock in her hand as an undone moan flew from his lips. Her eyelashes fluttered against her cheeks, and she looked up to see his features contorted into pleasure.

"Addie, you don't—" he stammered, his words cut off on a breathy exhale as she pumped the sensitive flesh. "*Fuck...*"

His fingers dug into the sheets, head thrown back in unabashed desire and pleasure. She quickly found a rhythm that he seemed to like —with just enough pressure that he squirmed beneath her greedy hands.

Then curiosity got the better of her.

She needed to taste him, as he'd tasted her. Her tongue started at the base of him and slowly traced upward to the tip. His hips bucked, but he didn't stop her. The little helpless sounds when she swirled her tongue around the crown of him was enough that she could feel the slickness between her own thighs.

She repeated the motion several times until he was panting, the muscles of his legs bunched together like a cord ready to snap.

When he reached for her, she popped up to her feet. She was drunk on the power he'd given her, and she wanted more.

Ben leaned back on his elbows, his chest rising and falling rapidly as he fought to steady his breathing. A feral gleam flashed at her, a dark chuckle shaking his chest. His cock twitched upward, hitting his stomach with a dirty, dull slap—the sound echoing in the darkness. Propped up by one elbow, he raised his other hand and curled his index finger—beckoning her to him. Pure sex and fire dancing in his gaze.

The heat radiating off of him was like a match to her fire—burning hotter and brighter than before. Her clit throbbed tortuously, alive with a pulse of its own. She was nearly delirious with want, and she was more than ready to ease the ache between her legs. Without warning, she pushed him back and climbed on top—wanting nothing more than to watch as she sank down on his cock.

A dark look swam in his hooded eyes, mouth slightly agape as he watched her. He didn't try to take over, instead remaining still. Tension coiled in his muscles, tight and trembling like a cobra ready to strike. And yet he remained completely still—letting her take control and explore him at her leisure.

"Take what's yours," he said—a command, not a request. One she was more than ready to obey.

She slowly sank down on his eager cock, both of them hissing in pleasure with each inch that went inside.

It was slow, it was torturous, and it was *perfect*.

Exactly as she remembered—if not even better—because now she could clearly see him in the light of day. The way their bodies pressed together, chest to chest, hip to hip. The way it felt so incredibly right, yet erotic, all at the same time.

A bead of sweat trickled down from her forehead, following the line of her body with ease. Ben followed the motion of it eagerly, enraptured by it like he was jealous that he wasn't tracing her body in the same way. When it pooled between her breasts, her nipples tingled in response—pebbling harder until she was sure they were digging into his chest.

All so blissfully perfect that she was drunk on it.

Ben dug his fingers into the flesh of her hips, nearly bruising in its intensity—only adding to the pleasure already crackling within her. His jaw clenched, like the effort to let her have all the control in this position was killing him.

The problem was that she *loved* seeing the borderline feral look in his eyes. The barely bridled passion that he held back *for her*, so she could take what she wanted—what she needed.

She leaned back, using his thighs to help prop herself up as she bore down on him. Her hips moved with a rhythm all their own as a gasp slipped from her own lips. The tip of him was hitting *exactly* where she needed him to, and she could feel herself already hurdling toward her release.

Ben suddenly pressed just above her pubic bone, a little ways above where they were joined. A lightning strike crackled up Addie's nerve endings where he touched, where his cock was buried, and pressed exactly where she needed most.

A strangled cry wrangled its way through her—her body involuntarily spasming around him from the sensation.

"You like that?" Ben hummed, rubbing circles there.

His fingers pressed harder when she didn't respond, causing her vision to blur as a guttural groan ripped from her lungs. Unable to do anything other than blindly nod as he chuckled darkly.

That was all it took.

Lights flickered in her vision, and waves of pleasure took her under. And yet still, Ben continued rubbing, taking her peak higher and higher until she chanted his name desperately—another orgasm surprising her and blasting through. It overtook her so quickly that she was left reeling.

When the pleasure became too much—*too powerful*—Ben sat up and moved to grip her hips harder, aiding her as she continued to ride him.

"I like hearing my name on your lips when you come," he growled just before he, too, was overtaken with pleasure—biting down on her shoulder with a shuddering groan.

She was limp against him as she came back to her body. Panting breaths and her own mewls of contentment were the only sound between them as they both fought to catch their breath.

She could live a thousand lives and never get enough of this, enough of *him*. If she were to choose a way to go, death by orgasm from Ben sounded just fine.

They were still joined, and she could still feel the fluttering pulse deep inside her pussy. She *really* liked that feeling. That contentment and pleasure wrought on Ben's face as their eyes found one another again. About to move off of him, so they could take a moment, Ben suddenly clutched onto her.

"We're not even *close* to being done," he ground out as he flipped them so that he was on top, bearing her down into the mattress. Then, and only then, did he set upon her like a ravenous wolf.

CHAPTER 30

It felt wrong as Addie tip-toed out of the motel room at a few minutes before six.

They hadn't gotten much sleep the night before, and it had taken every ounce of her strength to pull away from Ben's warm embrace. Soft snores rumbled through his chest as he held onto her, an arm slung around her. He was so deliciously warm against her cool skin that all she wanted to do was wrap herself in him. If it were any other time, she would have.

She was on a mission now—and if things went her way, she'd be back before he even woke up.

A black SUV was already waiting for her when she rounded the corner to the lobby. The outline of it was silhouetted through the glass-doored entrance, dark and ominous for such an early time of the day, and she couldn't help the nervous uptick of air as she attempted to steel herself.

She yanked the phone out of her back pocket and quickly set about what she needed to do.

"Text me if anything happens," Evie had instructed her quietly when she'd stopped by her room moments prior. "Are you sure I can't come? I don't like you being alone."

"No," Addie stated adamantly. "I told him it was just me, so he might get suspicious if you show up."

Wind kicked up around them, and Evie wrapped her arms around herself. The skin of her exposed shoulders rising into noticeable goosebumps. "I'm getting second thoughts about this plan of ours.... What if—"

"Relax," Addie tried to assure her. "If things go my way, I'll be back before everyone else gets up, and they'll be none the wiser."

"Yeah, but—"

"Unless you *want* to get stuck working with Billy?"

Evie made a face and shivered. "I'd rather put myself directly in the path of a tornado."

"Alright, then."

"Be careful?"

Addie shrugged casually, like this was the easiest thing in the world. "Not a problem."

Of course, Addie wasn't sure if their plan would actually work or not, but they had to try. Without involving the rest of the crew, they were limited on both time and resources to come up with anything better.

Nerves were already starting to bubble to the surface as the dark black SUV pulled into view, despite her earlier bravado. She tapped over to the audio recording app on her phone and pressed play before tucking it back into her pocket.

That should cover everything for now.

She walked into the bright morning sun, shielding her eyes as the crisp air hit her skin. It had thankfully cooled down from the previous day, but the weather looked ominous as dark clouds loomed off in the distance. She'd need to keep an eye on that when she got back—looking promising for later in the day.

The driver's side window rolled down and Billy's grinning face greeted her. It was a harder struggle than she thought to *not* roll her eyes.

"Get in."

She hadn't been sure what to expect, but when she crawled into the passenger seat and closed the door, the sleek and neat interior of the SUV was not it. She expected it to be messier, more ransacked, like his personality would indicate. But everything inside was absolutely pristine—neat as a pin.

Before Addie could change her mind, the engine roared to life, and Billy stepped on the gas.

"Alright, what did you so ominously need to talk to me alone for?" Billy asked, his smile smug.

A single trickle of water rolled down his neck from the still-wet tangle of hair tied up into one of those man-buns Addie so detested. Droplets of water peppered his shoulders, the spots on his white wife beater darkened to an off-gray. Complete with cargo shorts, it reminded her of that initial picture she had of someone who seemed more likely to be coming off a nearby beach than a storm chaser.

It oddly helped Addie feel a bit calmer, mostly because she could actually see his face more clearly. It'd be much harder to try to read his expressions with his hair in the way.

Addie knew how to act the part. The friendly weather-woman in front of the camera—the one who offered a small smile and subtle wave of the hand, but spoke with confidence. The one with a bit of bite to her that Billy banked on getting. A no-bullshit approach would be easier than trying to placate his ego.

"There's a storm brewing a bit south of here, so let's make this relatively quick. Park over there, so we can talk," she said flatly.

Billy merely chuckled. "So demanding. Look, we can keep this brief, but I need to head back to follow the storm. You're gonna have to come hang out with me for a bit."

Though she trained her features for neutral—panic gripped her.

"This won't take that long, and I have things I have to take care of because of *someone*. So, just find a spot to park, and we can get this over with," she insisted casually.

"Well, since you're gonna be transferring to my team soon, it might be good for you to get familiar with our setup anyway. Don't worry. I'll bring you back after I make sure the readings are okay."

A response prickled within her, but she stopped herself short. Being in a familiar setting, Billy might feel like he could let his guard down further. She would be in *his* space. He'd feel like he won, and that could be quite promising for her purposes.

She forced a shrug. "Fine, but it better be quick."

Billy's camper was even more spacious than she expected. Sure, she knew that it would be big, but when they pulled up, she had to suppress a gasp. It made her crew's RV look tiny—this one large enough to easily house a family of five without issue.

The entire drive there had been silent, but she could practically feel the pride radiating from him when they pulled up.

New-car smell permeated the air as she stepped inside, like the entire vehicle had been freshly driven off the lot. Billy's car smelled similar, which let her know that both were either new or they were just that meticulous with keeping it sparkling clean. Though, she couldn't picture Billy to be one to scrub a camper from head to toe every day.

Monitors lined the wall, easily double the amount her team had—and twice the price. Her team's looked … well loved … while these appeared to be fresh from the package.

Each desk sported some of the latest and greatest gadgets money could buy. Expensive laptops and drones. A variety of filming equipment, cameras, and tripods that Addie could rotate out each day of the week and still have equipment left over. There were even a few gizmos she had only ever seen advertised.

All the fancy bells and whistles that practically screamed "corporate sponsor."

Billy leaned against the wall. "Pretty neat, huh?"

She nodded, albeit reluctantly. "I'd say.… I've never seen some of this tech in person before."

"One of the perks of taking sponsorships these days, I guess."

"You guess?" she prodded as she fiddled with one of the drones perched on the nearby table.

"Being in front of the camera isn't always the first thing I want to do when I wake up in the morning," he said, flashing a grin at her. "I'm sure you can relate."

"I've gotten used to it. Gotta pay the bills somehow."

Billy scoffed, a knowing sound that felt strange coming from him. "That we can agree on. Now, what is it that you so desperately needed to talk to me about that you wanted to be alone?"

Here it is.

This was the part where she needed to play her cards just right. Anything too *in-his-face* and the situation could turn on her. Anything not forceful enough and he could dodge her questions, and she would walk away with nothing.

She needed to be distant. Aloof even. If she appeared too emotionally invested in the situation, he could use that against her.

"How'd you disconnect the deployment equipment?" she asked, turning to look at him. It was the first time he appeared surprised, though he tried to hide it quickly behind a smile.

"The deployment equipment?" he repeated, though she didn't miss the slight twitch in his eyebrow as he raised it.

She hummed low in her throat. "Yeah, how'd you do it? I'm genuinely curious."

Billy folded his arms across his chest and scoffed. "Don't know what you're talking about, Walters."

"I think you do," she said, brushing her fingers along the edges of a drone next to her. "You did something similar with the Doppler before, so I'm just curious how?"

A muscle in Billy's arm ticked, but the rest of him was impassive. "That Doppler has been on the fritz for years. If Ben and his team can't maintain their own equipment well enough for them to run properly, that's on them. Not sure why it has to be *my* fault."

She turned and leaned back against the table. "I used to work on some of the equipment with my old team and noticed the wiring."

"So?"

"*So,*" she emphasized, "I can tell when a wire is frayed or damaged by age and when it's been completely severed. Happened *after* we bumped into you guys. Then again with our camera footage. Bump into you at the motel and come to find some of our footage is missing. Then, after we deployed our equipment in the field, it suddenly stopped working not long after it left the ground. Also after we spoke to you. Interesting coincidence, don't you think?"

Another shrug, this time a bit more confident. "Or just that, a coincidence."

"Look, we both know Evie and I have to transfer to you guys. I have bills to pay, so if we're going to work together, I don't want any surprises. Tell me you didn't hold onto any evidence that can come back and bite us in the ass?"

That seemed to intrigue him a bit as he cocked his head to the side. "Us? I seem to recall our last conversation having taken place with Ben's shirt on your back?"

She pinched the bridge of her nose to appear annoyed. "Don't want to get caught in the cross hairs, like you said, remember?"

He sniffed. "And I'm supposed to believe that?"

This was the part she was going to hate the most, the part that made her skin crawl, but it was the only way she could think. When she'd talked to Brody about the dynamic shift between Ben and Billy, it had planted this small seed in her mind. This was something personal between them. It had to be, otherwise it wouldn't make any sense for Billy to single out Ben as much as he apparently did. So, if he was trying to sabotage the team now, a part of that might still be in the works.

That was the angle she had to play into.

"Did Ben ever tell you about what he did to me back in school?"

Billy pursed his lips. "Vaguely."

"Then you understand why I might be simply playing nice?" she cooed, forcing a coy smile onto her face. The words tasted bitter leaving her lips, enough so that she wanted to gag and immediately take them back. It made her feel dirty using that against Ben, but it was her best chip to play. She only hoped he'd never have to listen to this recording.

Billy pressed his lips into a thin line, his expression tight. He studied her, his eyes narrowing as if trying to scan for the slightest hint of weakness or vulnerability. Despite how disgusted she felt with herself, she refused to let her mask slip even a fraction. All that time in front of the camera had prepared her for a moment exactly like this, and she would use that to her full advantage.

After what felt like an eternity of him studying her, she saw the moment when he decided to believe her. His body relaxed a fraction and sank back against the wall behind him, a light chuckle rumbling through his chest.

"I underestimated you, it seems."

"Happens more often than you'd think," she replied, not allowing the relief to show. "Now, how confident are you that you didn't leave any evidence behind? If *I* can figure out it was you, don't you think someone else might, as well?"

"I was careful."

Now she was starting to get somewhere—she needed to push a bit harder. "How careful?"

"Careful enough."

Addie rubbed her temples. "Well, I need to know if I'm getting in the middle of some schoolyard bullshit. There's clearly something more going on than just money. I don't know what the deal is between you and Ben, and frankly, I don't care, but I need to know what it is, so we can avoid getting that thrown in our faces."

Billy's grin had notably disappeared. "Let's just say that Ben and I go *way* back, further than either of us even know."

Unable to help herself, she rolled her eyes. "Way to be cryptic about it."

"I always seemed to get the short end of the stick in life, while Ben always manages to come out on top, so I wanted to even the playing field."

She feigned annoyance, trying not to look too invested. "Meaning?"

"Meaning that Ben has been in the way my entire life, even before I knew we were related."

The last word felt thick and heavy in the air.

"R-related?" she repeated, unable to mask the surprise. She worried instantly if that would be what got her caught, but seeing the amusement light up on Billy's face, he wasn't surprised at her reaction.

"I know. Surprised the fuck out of me, too, when I found out," Billy snorted. "My mother never would tell me who my old man was, so of course she waits until she's on her fucking deathbed to do it. Fucker knocked her up while on deployment then ran home to his wife and son. She tried to tell him about me, but he didn't want anything to do with either of us. Even when Ben's mom divorced him for cheating on her, he refused to acknowledge either of us. He chose Ben and *his* mother over me and mine...."

Billy is Ben's half-brother.

Addie had never met either of Ben's parents. She remembered the conversation they had about him in the SUV, about how different he looked compared to his dad. And now she could see it. The long, blond waves. His nose. The amber eyes so much like Ben's...

Why had she never seen it before?

"Then I find out," Billy continued incredulously, "that my own fucking sponsors would rather work with him than with me? They chose him over me ... *again*. No, absolutely fucking not. I just ... I couldn't let him take one more thing from me...."

Billy straightened, as if he, too, were surprised at all the words pouring out of him. But with a clearing of his throat and crack of his jaw, the smug demeanor slid back into place. Like it never left in the first place.

She knew that she needed to mirror him if she was going to get through this, despite the shock coursing in her veins. She'd have to save that for later. She couldn't act like she was emotionally invested in this conflict, or he would know. Cold indifference. Even if she was barely holding on by the skin of her teeth to the cool and collected persona she'd walked in with.

"So ... daddy issues?" she forced out.

Billy chuckled. "I guess you could say that."

"Regardless," she continued, fighting the burning ache in her chest. "How can you be so sure you were careful? Depending on how you messed with the deployment equipment, if you used any of your own computers here for that, you could leave a digital footprint behind."

Billy scoffed. "I'm not *that* sloppy."

"How'd you do it, then?"

"I cut a few wires and unscrewed some screws. Figured it would either fall apart immediately in the field or would stop functioning soon after liftoff."

Thunder cracked once more, loud enough that Addie could feel the vibration of it beneath her feet.

She tapped her chin in consideration. "What about Evie's camera?"

"Oh come on. That one's easy. I just snuck in when no one was watching and deleted footage. Left enough to make it look like it had glitched or something."

"Smart."

Addie wanted to smack the smug look that overtook his features at that. "Child's play, really. I left enough bread crumbs so that I could get my own *evidence* and send it over to Channel 5 to make my claim. It looks like anyone could've done it, but I have the pictures, not them."

A motive and confirmation of what he'd done? *Bingo*. Got him. "Good. One less thing to worry about."

"Trust me—unless you or I get loose-lipped about it, they'll never find out."

It was at that exact moment that the phone in her pocket decided to ping, startling both of them.

"Are they looking for you already?" Billy asked.

Panic surged to the surface as she fought to smile. "They might be. I mean, I obviously couldn't announce where I was going."

Billy narrowed his eyes at her, but didn't say anything as he turned to head to the door. It was long enough for her to quickly fish her phone out of her pocket, pretending like she was merely checking the notification she'd gotten when instead she was frantically trying to stop the recording.

Her fingers trembled as adrenaline surged through her veins, fighting the panic as she ended the recording and immediately sent it to Evie. She wanted that recording as safe as humanly possible.

The best decision she could've made when the phone suddenly flew from her hands as Billy whipped about and snatched it.

Billy thumbed through her phone, a deadly quiet looming over him like a storm cloud. His expression went from suspicion to shock, to confusion and panic, and then finally landed on anger so quickly that it had her head spinning.

"You were fucking *recording* me?!" he exclaimed, an incredulous expression crossing his face at the message as the read receipt flashed beneath it.

The implications that she was alone with this man, in the middle of nowhere, slammed into her.

"I ... I don't ... It must've ... I don't know—" she stuttered, trying to figure out what to say as she took a shaky step backward. Billy stood between her and the exit, and there would be no way out unless she got around him. Everything went south so quickly that she was still grappling as she stumbled back into the closest door.

Thunder rumbled in the distance, booming even closer than it had last. A crack that managed to snap her out of shock enough that pushed Billy out of the way to try and escape. Her nails clipped his face as she scrambled to get around him, but he moved just as swiftly. He used his body to block her, shoving her hard enough that she fell backward into the enclosed space behind her.

She gasped, grabbing at the closest surface. A counter-top on one side, and a shower curtain on the other, stopped her head from slamming against the wall. It wasn't enough purchase for her to recover quickly enough to escape, and before she could find her footing, the door slammed in her face.

"Hey!" she cried out, finally standing to her feet.

A heavy clunk shook the floor on the other side of the bathroom door. The door handle jiggled the way it should, but the door wouldn't relent when she pushed.

He'd locked her in the bathroom.

"Billy! Let me out of here!" she shouted, banging her fists against the solid metal surface.

"Just fucking sit tight until I can clear my head and figure out what the hell to do with you!" he yelled back, a waver in his words.

Curses echoed around the sounds of her fists banging against the door, her only indication he was even still there. How the hell had things gone south so fast? She thought she'd been so careful. Had he seen her phone when she pulled it out of her pocket? Had he snatched it to confirm she was telling him the truth?

She had no idea, but when she heard footsteps tapping farther and farther away, a new panic gripped her. "You're not … You're not gonna fucking *leave* me in here, are you?!"

"Don't fucking move. I'll be back. I just … *fuck* … I need to think," he stammered back, his voice growing farther away until a loud click and thud sealed her fate.

Billy was gone.

Addie slammed her fists against the door. "Billy! You let me out right fucking now! Billy?!"

Fuck, this complicated things a bit....

CHAPTER 31

𝒜ddie used her shoulder to slam her body weight against the door. But again, for the dozenth time, it didn't budge. She slumped back, allowing herself a moment to breathe before trying once more.

She really fucked this up.

Spectacularly so.

At least she'd been able to send the recording to Evie before Billy had taken her phone. She only hoped that the recording was clear enough. She'd had to tuck it in a way that Billy wouldn't see it sticking out of her pocket but enough for it to capture the sound. Even then, without hearing it for herself, she couldn't be sure.

Worse yet? Billy *still* had Addie's phone.

There was no way to even let anyone know she was here.

Evie would be worried that Addie had sent the message before getting back and without any other context. It would undoubtedly raise the alarm, but what could she really do? Even if they managed to figure out where the phone was—it wouldn't be anywhere near where Addie actually was.

It was in Billy's truck, heading God knows where.

A frustrated sob hiccuped out of her. Everything made sense now, given what Billy had told her. Storm chasers were a tight-knit community, and trust among any given team was practically law. Having any team put another in danger, on purpose, was a red flag. But downright hatred on a personal level? That was a different story.

Billy would eventually come back. Dread coiled up her spine, unsure what he would do *when* he got back. She'd betrayed him with that recording. All she knew was that she didn't want to be here when he did.

She sagged back against the wall and fought the sob caught in her throat. She had no idea what to do. The door was sealed shut. Even with all of her strength, it was unlikely to budge. And her only source of light was the one overhead—blinking and flickering precariously each time she slammed into the door. There wasn't exactly a window she could crawl out of.

She was in some RV park, that much she did manage to gather on the journey there. But where exactly that was, she had no idea. It was at the far end of the lot, away from other vehicles and cars, so no one would hear her shouting either. She kicked herself for not paying more attention to where he was taking her. She'd been so focused on trying to figure out what to say that she hadn't taken the time to study her whereabouts.

Stupid.

Naive too.

How could she *not* think something like this could happen? Honestly, who did she think she was? She was a weatherwoman for Channel 5—not some secret covert spy. The fact that she'd convinced herself so surely that Billy wouldn't suspect what she was doing was all the proof she needed to know that this wouldn't work.

All because she wanted to feel like she could help—like for once, *she* could be the one to protect the people she'd grown to care about. Some help she was, sitting on the floor of this dingy bathroom.

Ben's sleeping face from that morning flashed in her mind.

Ben.

Addie patted both of her cheeks roughly to snap herself out of the pity party spiral she was going down. Knowing Ben, he would be angry that she was talking to herself like this instead of figuring out a plan. She could almost hear him chastising her for it now.

Right now, she needed to focus. She and Ben were not going to finally come together after all these years just for her to wind up losing him this way.

No fucking way.

She got herself into this mess; she'd just have to get herself back out.

Exhausted from her previous attempts, Addie wobbled up onto her feet to try the door again. As she gained her footing, an alarm blared just outside—sudden enough that it caused her to jump back.

Shock and her situation muddled her thoughts, standing still to figure out what that sound was. Frozen in place, it wasn't until another sound swallowed the first. Louder and blaring, Addie's ears rang as it pierced straight through her, causing her blood to freeze in her veins.

A siren.

A tornado had spun up.

And it was close.

"You've *got* to be fucking kidding me right now!" she screamed in frustration.

This was bad.

Really, *really* bad.

She had to figure out how to get out of this damned bathroom before she got swept away. Before she had the chance to tell Ben that she loved him.

Shit.

She'd gone and fallen in love with that irritating, infuriating man.

The realization of it slammed into her like a lightning strike. She was in *love* with Ben....

She thought back to the young grad student with the secret crush on her biggest rival in class—had it been all the way back then? Maybe, in her own way, she always *had* been in love with him.

Addie's entire body suddenly lurched to the right, slamming her into the bathroom wall.

The camper had moved, which was a really, *really* bad sign. If debris was knocking the camper about, ... she was already too late. It was close by. She whispered a prayer into the space, standing shakily back to her feet. Let it be a low-level one. Please, let it be less than an EF2.

Anything more than that and the camper could easily be picked up and thrown about like a child's bath toy.

Addie threw herself frantically against the door, a frustrated whimper coming out when, once again, nothing happened. The bathroom was so small and narrow that even with all her body weight, she didn't have much in the way of a running start. She chewed on her lower lip as she tried to think of another plan, steeling her nerves when an idea struck.

She braced herself against the back wall, opposite the door. Her arms strained beneath her weight as she lifted herself up, bracing one hand against the shower wall and one against the bathroom mirror. She grunted and started propelling her legs into the door.

Were there any shelters nearby? If she made it out in time, she could try to run for cover. That might be pushing her luck, if the ever-increasing roar of wind was any indication. The camper had vibrated around her, racing up her arms and making her teeth chatter.

Another slam against the door and the vibrations finally got the better of her, causing her grip to slip as she fell back to the floor.

She couldn't give up. Wouldn't give up. She had to try.

As she went to stand again, a loud thud from outside caught her attention. More debris? About to try to position herself again, she stopped when she heard something else. It was faint, quiet enough that she shouldn't have been able to hear it.

"Addie?!"

Addie blinked once, twice.

No, there was no way.

It had to be a trick of the wind as it howled around the camper. No one knew she was here. Billy wouldn't come back to get her now. She had to get out on her own.

She focused and lifted herself up again to begin kicking, getting one firm kick before the vibrations rattled her out of position once more. She collapsed back against the wall, and she fought to catch her breath.

"Addie!"

She froze. That time she was sure of it, she *did* hear someone.

And she recognized the voice instantly.

"B-Ben?!"

CHAPTER 32

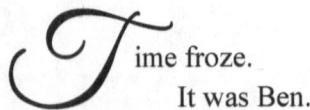

Time froze.
    It was Ben.
He was here.

A sob ripped out of Addie as she pounded her fists against the door.

"Ben!" she screamed. "I'm in here!"

Banging echoed from the camper door, no acknowledgment. Could he not hear her? She had to find a way to draw his attention, or he might move on to search elsewhere.

"Goddammit, the fucker locked the front door!" he shouted, as if to himself, followed by more banging.

If that statement held any weight, Addie was more screwed than she'd originally thought. She turned to start pounding a fist against the wall behind her, hoping that the metallic sound would be enough that he could hear. It was a shot in the dark considering he was on the opposite side of the camper, but it was her only option.

"Ben!" she shouted again, hoping to bring his attention back to where she was. "Ben! I'm in here!"

"Addie?!" His voice was closer to her than before, as if he'd abandoned the front door and found his way along the camper to the exact spot she was at. She could practically feel the heat of him from the other side of the wall. Enough so that tears streamed freely down her cheeks.

"Addie," he said, his voice so close that she was sure he'd pressed up against the camper. "Addie, are you okay?"

"I'm okay...."

"Where are you in there? Can you get the front door open for me?"

"He shoved me into the bathroom, and I think he pushed something in front of the door, I can't get it open."

A thick string of curses spewed out of him, muffled and distorted through the thick material separating them. "When I get my hands on that little *fucker*..."

She had no idea how close the funnel was, but judging by the panicked edges to Ben's tone, it had to be a lot closer than she wanted it to be. Would they have enough time to get out? Or did being here at all already seal Ben's fate with hers?

She wasn't going to let that happen.

"Ben, you need to go!" she shouted into the wall. "Get out of here, and get to a shelter! I'll be okay!"

His response was immediate, and she could swear she felt the slam of his fist against the siding. "Not fucking *happening*, Addie! Just ... hold on. Let me think!"

Addie clenched her eyes shut. "Ben, please, you need to get out of here!"

"I'm not leaving you here!" he shouted. "Just—just hold on sweetheart. I'm coming!"

She didn't see or hear it as much as she *felt* him move away. The loss of that was enough that her entire chest hurt, and she bit her lip to keep a sob from coming out.

Broken glass crashed in the distance, followed by a quick succession of thuds that tracked closer and closer with each passing second. Addie's ears rang as she threw herself to the bathroom door.

Ben angrily grunted from the other side of the door. Wood scraped against the floor like a nail dragging across a chalkboard. She moved aside just in time for the door to fly open, Ben's wild and worried eyes landing on her. He was nearly white as a sheet, panting from the exertion, but she didn't have time to look at him when he instantly yanked her to him.

"Thank Christ..." he huffed close to her ear, trembling as his arms secured her to him. "Do you *ever* fucking think before you act?"

She wanted to stay there in his arms, to feel that sweet and loving heat radiate straight through to her core, but time wasn't on their side.

Something warm and sticky dropped down her arm, and it was then she noticed the shattered glass littering the floor near a broken window. The realization hit her as she glanced down at Ben's knuckles.

He'd punched the window out.

"Oh my God, Ben! Your hand!" she cried out, trying to grab his hand, but he pulled it from her grasp.

"Come on," he instructed gruffly, "we don't have time. We need to go."

She grabbed the lock, the one preventing Ben's entry, and threw it open. As she did, the door almost flew out of her grip—the wind ripping it from her with such force that it dragged her closer to the exit.

Addie then finally saw the beast lurking nearby—a thin rope twirling about in the nearby field as it bore down on them. Ben snatched her arm as she flew forward, both pausing to look up at the angry funnel barreling in their direction.

"*Fuck!*" Ben shouted as he shoved her back and yanked the door closed. "It's already here. We're gonna have to bunker down!"

"Here?!" Addie screamed, the sound barely audible above the roar of the wind. He fumbled shakily with the door's lock and slammed it down, testing the handle once before turning to grab her hand.

"We don't have a choice, firecracker," Ben bit out as he pulled her to the nearby metallic table, the one holding up several weather monitors. "Get under!"

The table was wide and long enough that the two of them could fit, though it would be a bit of a squeeze, but Addie wasn't going to complain. She quickly crawled under, grabbing the singular metal pole anchoring the table into the floor like a lifeline.

Wind lashed out at the camper, more jarring this time, and she screamed. The window frames groaned under the pressure as they bent violently. It only took a few seconds for all of the windows to blow out, one by one popping and shattering under the pressure. The spray of broken glass and metal scattered across the floor nearby.

Ben crawled into the space to join her, clutching onto the metallic pole as he scooped her up in his embrace, anchoring both of his arms around her like a shield. It was only a few seconds, but it felt like an eternity as they braced for the worst.

"I've got you, sweetheart," Ben shouted. "I've got you!"

Every moment of their time together flashed before her eyes. Seeing him again for the first time, after all these years. Arguing until they were both red in the face. The smile on his face after a successful chase. Rain as it pounded against her skin when he told her how he felt. Making love with him in the darkness, with nothing but lightning to guide their way.

She needed to tell him.

Before she had no time left.

"I love you," she cried out when the camper rocked violently to the left. "I'm so in love with you! I'm sorry I didn't say it before when I had the chance!"

Ben blinked as he met her gaze, an unreadable expression crossing his features before he shook his head. "Don't tell me that now—say that again later, when we're out of this. Don't tell me that because you think we might die."

"But—"

He sealed her lips with his before she could finish—stealing a feverish, desperate kiss.

"Hold on!" Ben shouted as a final warning when the camper finally rolled onto its side.

CHAPTER 33

A washing machine.

That was the closest that Addie could think of that came even *close* to what it felt like when the camper rolled. Once, twice, then a few more times until she completely lost count. Unable to tell which way was up, disorienting to the point that all she could do was close her eyes and hold on.

The only constant was Ben's arms around her, holding her close—refusing to let go despite the wind trying to tear them apart. The sound of equipment exploding and crashing almost drowned out the wind whipping them about. *Almost*.

The wind closed around her, smacking both of them about like balls in a pinball machine.

Up and down, up and down, spin, spin, spin. Ping. Ping. Ping.

Her voice was hoarse from the screaming, though she couldn't remember when she started.

When the camper finally came to a stop, teetering back and forth before settling onto the ground, it took her a moment to realize it was over. She was flat against some surface, but she didn't dare open her eyes—terrified that opening them would throw her back into the cycle.

What had been deafening mere moments ago vanished to an eerie kind of silence that sent a shiver down Addie's back. Silence. Complete and utter silence. It was terrifying in its own right. Seconds ago, a tornado had battered them about like a kid playing with a bath toy, and now? Now it was quiet. Deadly silent.

But it was over.

The tornado had moved on.

She needed to open her eyes—needed to get away in case it circled back. Blinking them open slowly, the shadow of Ben hovering over her blotted out the light shining down. Mangled rays of it streamed through the broken tatters of a window directly above them.

Ben's glasses were still perched on his nose, but there was a notable crack down the left lens. Trembling arms held himself above her, his eyes clenched shut.

"B-Ben..."

Those beautiful eyes of his snapped open. Flecks of gold pierced her, scanning, searching, ensuring she was actually there. With a few quick movements, he yanked her into his lap. He didn't say anything as he inspected every inch. No morsel of exposed flesh went untouched, but she searched just as frantically. She needed to make sure he wasn't hurt—that they were both, indeed, alive and relatively unscathed. She winced when he touched a spot on her cheek, but she continued searching.

There was a cut just above his left eyebrow that had started bleeding. She reached for it, to swipe the already drying blood away with her thumb, when he stopped her.

He stole the fraction of space between them. His lips were hot and scouring as he devoured her repeatedly in fierce, rapid-fire kisses that did little to seek comfort but more to reaffirm presence.

I made it in time.

You're here.

You're real.

You're safe.

Emotion welled in her throat before it finally broke free. "I'm sorry...." she sobbed between kisses—truly meaning the words as she sank further into his arms. "I'm so sorry...."

"What were you thinking? You could've gotten yourself killed!" he barked, his lips still against hers. "Don't you *ever* fucking do that to me again. I could've lost you, you insufferable woman!"

"I know. I'm so sorry...." she sobbed against his lips, too far gone in emotion to care that she was crying.

He continued his assault of desperate kisses all over her face. Her lips, her cheeks, her eyelids, her forehead—anywhere he found purchase. He wasn't looking for her to answer, merely allowing the adrenaline and relief to swallow both of them whole. All she could do was nod as she continued to hiccup sobs between kisses.

They were okay.

They'd survived.

A throat being cleared finally broke the two apart. They looked up to see Ryan and Brody hovering over the front door, which was now above them.

"They're here!" Brody shouted over his shoulder. "We got 'em!"

"Oh, thank *God*," another voice replied—Tony, most likely, from the deep timbre of it. "Are they okay?"

Brody turned back to them. "You guys okay?"

His hands still glued to Addie—uncaring of who saw—Ben replied, "For the most part."

"They're okay!" Brody called out.

"Good!" Evie's voice rang out even closer than the other two. "Make sure to tell Addie that I'll kill her *myself* when I get my hands on her!"

Addie winced, causing Ben to chuckle for the first time since he'd arrived. A real, genuine chuckle that made her relax. He looked at her, immediately shaking his head at whatever expression was on her face. "Oh, don't look at me like that. You're lucky that I don't throttle you for the stunt you pulled."

From the softness in his gaze and touch, she knew there was absolutely zero validity to that statement, but it didn't stop her from letting a giggle bubble out of her. "I'll make it up to you later."

"Should *we* come back later?" Ryan teased, raising his eyebrows suggestively.

Hell, *let* them watch for all she cared. And she did just that when she kissed Ben once again. Neither caring that they now had an audience.

"Jeez, get a room," Brody called down at them.

"Yeah, like," Ryan added, "should we let them finish and come back later?"

With a laugh, Addie unwrapped her legs from around Ben's waist, taking his hand as the two helped one another stand. Everything else around them consisted of broken glass, shattered monitors, and the various gadgets and gizmos that had impressed her earlier that day but now sat completely useless at her feet.

That could've been her....

Before she could think too hard on that, Ben scooped Addie up by the waist and lifted her up to Ryan. Ryan seemed to be laying on top of what had once been the camper's front door, with Brody hovering nearby to keep him steady. His arms trembled with the effort as he pulled her up and free.

"I'd brace myself if I were you," Ryan said as Brody came to assist, grabbing her other arm, until she was finally out in the now bright afternoon sky.

Addie looked up, noting only a few traces of what had just happened in the clouds. "The storm's gone."

Another laugh as Ryan turned to help Ben next. "Not what I meant."

Brody turned his red baseball cap around and helped lower Addie over the side of the camper to solid ground. She honed in on the little college logo stamped onto it—an odd detail to focus on but better that than focusing on the couple of foot drop down to the ground below.

When her feet hit the ground, she had zero recovery time before the rest of the group swarmed her—now fully understanding Ryan's warning.

"How did you..." she started to ask before Evie poked her hard in the chest.

"You scared the bejesus out of me!" she scolded.

"I know. I'm sorry. How did you know where to find me?"

Grace pointed to Evie's phone. "You shared your location with everyone when we first started, remember? Your phone turned off after you sent Evie that message, but I checked to see where the last location it pinged from was."

Tony sidled up next to Evie with a grimace, his hand carefully resting on her hip. "Evie freaked out because you weren't answering her calls. Told us the whole story after sending the voice memo to your boss."

"Ben went off like a bat straight out of hell!" Ryan interjected as he landed on his feet nearby. "Tore off in his car before any of us could stop him."

"What the hell happened?!" a deep male voice boomed behind them. The instant flare of recognition coiled in Addie's gut, quickly replaced by a fiery anger that burned in her chest.

Billy stomped closer, his expression shifting between confusion, shock, and anger. "It's *wrecked*!"

It shocked her as he seemed to come out of nowhere in the chaos of wreckage strewn around them. Where the hell had he even gone? And why did he come back?

"*You're* about to get wrecked! You fucking *left* her in there, you son of a bitch!" Ben yelled somewhere behind her, followed by the accompanying thud as he landed on the ground. He raced across the field in their direction but was snatched back mere inches from Billy as he reached for him. Brody, Tony, and Grace all held him back, with Ryan rushing around to keep Billy back—animalistic sounds tearing out of him like he was a rabid coyote.

Shock rooted Addie to where she stood, watching mutely as Ben thrashed and clawed at his friends to get to Billy, who struggled almost as hard against Ryan to get to Ben. Evie remained next to her, a hand on Addie's shoulder and giving a reassuring squeeze.

"It wasn't fair!" Billy screamed. "You always get *everything*! I deserved something for once!"

"What the fuck are you even talking about?" Ben snarled.

Billy rushed over, but Ryan dragged him back, just out of reach.

"Dad chose *you* over me! The station chose you over me! My own fucking *sponsors* wanted you over me! It wasn't fucking fair!"

"D-Dad?" Ben sputtered, confusion overwhelming his movements as he froze.

"You're my half-brother, you fucking moron!" Billy exploded. "My mom finally told me about my dad on her deathbed, and guess what? Turns out he's also your fucking dad. Left my mom to cope with drugs and alcohol, while he ran home! Everyone *always* chooses you!"

Ben had paled a few shades, a mix of emotions so palpable that it damn near broke Addie's heart to see it. "I-I didn't ... Why didn't you tell me?"

"Why should I have?" Billy snapped. "I tried to confront our old man, and he *still* didn't want anything to do with me! Blocked me everywhere I tried to contact him. Slammed the door in my face. You're just an awful fucking reminder every time I look at you. It wasn't until I found out about the contract and my own fucking sponsors trying to go behind my back that I outright *loathed* you! My only regret is that it was *her* who came to confront me, or I'd have left your sorry ass in there!"

Any sympathy Addie might've had for Billy's situation was swallowed up in a millisecond when realization slammed into her. Billy had been keeping an eye on the weather. It was the whole reason he'd wanted to go to the camper in the first place. She hadn't had the presence of mind to check the storm's trajectory—but he had. He knew what was coming.

He hadn't left to *clear his head*; he'd left her on purpose.

Addie's hand coiled into a fist, adrenaline pumping static into her mind as she walked toward Billy. Blood roared in her ears, pulsing beneath her temples and deafening the screaming match taking place.

Her body moved on its own, propelling her forward, and she was powerless to stop it.

Billy turned, but as he opened his mouth, Addie reeled back and slammed her fist into his nose. A deep crunch reverberated around them, seconds before Billy squealed in pain and stumbled backward. Addie steadied herself as her breathing came in long, labored pants.

Whether from the adrenaline coursing through her veins or from the effort, she couldn't be sure.

But … it felt good.

Even as she saw shock on Billy's face as he held his nose, a drop of blood trickling down and splattering onto his white tank top. Her knuckles tingled, a purple bruise already forming on them. That would hurt like hell later. Later being the operative word and something she took advantage of as she reeled back to punch him again. This time, she was stopped, as Evie grabbed onto her from behind.

"That's my girl!" Ben whooped with laughter.

CHAPTER 34

*B*illy had been almost immediately loaded into the back of a police cruiser when more help had arrived. They hadn't needed to hear the whole recording to know what his intentions had been. The threats and ramblings he continued to hurl in their direction had just been the icing on the cake.

Addie's knuckles pulsed beneath the ice pack a paramedic had given her. It stung like hell, but that punch had been a hundred percent worth it in every regard. Yet it didn't aid the sting of the ice against her heated skin, now nothing more than a bag of melted water. It sloshed with each step as she walked into the motel room behind Ben. The one she and Ben had spent the entire night before making love in.

Her skin tingled at the memory, wanting nothing more than to feel Ben's body on hers after everything they'd been through. But that would have to wait. She realized by his stance, as he closed the door behind them, that she was about to receive her dressing down. He'd only heard the bits and pieces of what happened leading up to him showing up at the camper, as she'd explained it to one of the police officers. They had to have a conversation.

She remained rooted to her spot. Now that the imminent threat of danger was at bay, it was a consequence she'd prepared for. She'd have to live with whatever he had to say, even if it broke her heart.

"Say it. It's okay," she assured gently. "I know you're angry with me."

Ben huffed out a breath and placed fisted hands on his hips, bandages heavily wrapped around the hand he'd used to punch the window in earlier. "It's been a long day. You'll want to clean up a bit. I'll turn the—"

"Benjamin Borack not wanting to argue with me? Now, that *is* a miracle," she interrupted in a teasing tone, watching the warring emotions filter onto his face. He grimaced and rubbed his arms. A small smile stretched across his lips that didn't reach his eyes.

"It's okay," she assured.

If the roles were reversed, she'd be just as angry. She wasn't made of glass, and she knew to some degree that she deserved whatever he wanted to say.

"Do you know what it felt like to wake up without you in my bed?" he finally ground out, "Not knowing that you'd run off to do something so dangerous with no way for me to stop you?"

"I know. I'm sorry that I couldn't tell you. I wanted to protect you for a change." She took a step in his direction when he remained silent and continued, "And I won't lie, I'd do it again if I had to. I don't regret it. It *had* to be me to do it."

Ben's mouth opened and closed a few times, but he couldn't seem to land what he wanted to say. So, she continued, taking another step. "You've let me take the lead on things with our relationship. You've been incredibly patient, and I thank you for that. After everything today, I know you're probably angry with me, and I understand. But I won't apologize for doing it. If you need some space to sort out your feelings, I understand that too. I'll leave you be and go—"

At that, Ben took her face in one hand—the feeling surprisingly gentle against her cheek. "Addie, I'd rather argue with you for the rest of my life than spend another day *without* you. Don't you *get* that at this point?"

Addie bit her lip to prevent a sob from escaping. "I'm starting to."

"I understand why you did what you did. I really do. And you're damn right that I'm angry—but not at you," he said as his thumb swiped across her cheek in a move so tender and loving that it was in complete contrast with the dark expression he bore.

Addie cocked her head to the side reflexively. Why wouldn't he be mad at her? Not that she was complaining, but it was the complete opposite thing she expected.

"I'm angry that I'm just now finding out I have a half-brother, and it's fucking *Billy*," he continued. She laughed at that, seeing a genuine smile crack through the dark storm swirling in his eyes. "I'm angry that your boss didn't talk to *anyone* on my team before talking to you. He should have come *straight* to me if there were any issues. I'm angry that you were put into a position where you felt you had no other choice. I'm angry at myself for not telling you about my own suspicions before, so we could have faced this head-on. I'm *livid* at what Billy did and that I could have lost you today."

Ben paused to lift her chin. "From now on, anything comes our way, we deal with it *together*. Do you hear me?"

"Yes," she whispered, a tear trickling down her cheek.

Ben rubbed it away with his thumb, a soft smile playing on his lips. "Good. Then say it again."

What was he talking about? What had she said? In all the chaos, she hadn't the faintest idea what he meant.

"Say ... *what* again?"

Ben's expression softened further. "What you said in the camper. Did you mean it? True or False?"

What she'd said before?

I love you.

A blush crept up her face and burned in her cheeks as the memory hit her.

Normally, she'd push him away—make up some excuse so that she didn't have to feel so embarrassed and vulnerable. But after everything they'd gone through? She didn't have it in her to pretend she didn't want to say it to him over and over again until the world collapsed around them.

"True."

The smile on Ben's face deepened the dimples in his cheeks. "Then say it again."

She melted into his embrace. "I love you, Ben."

"Again."

"I love you."

Ben pressed a kiss to her forehead, so tender and loving that Addie's heart swelled.

"One more time," he pleaded, his voice so low and gravelly that desire burst to life. A sheer, blinding desire that drove her to grab Ben's clothes and begin ripping at them roughly. Her body already craved his touch.

With ravenous, greedy hands, Ben tore at her clothes just as hungrily, a growl emanating deep in his chest like a feral animal ready to devour its prey. Hard as iron beneath her trembling hands, she fought to find his zipper—a breathy moan whispered between them when she finally touched him.

The back of her knees hit the edge, causing her to stumble and land with a soft thud. She didn't have time to recover before Ben pressed her into the mattress, his mouth setting upon hers. There was no room for pleasantries this time—no time for soft touches and gentle exploration.

This was pure, blind need for one another.

She reached for his remaining clothing, but Ben stepped back and yanked at her jeans, causing her to fall back against the sheets. He fought against the fabric, urgent in his task. They flew across the room, along with the shirt as he practically ripped it off himself.

Addie needed to touch him, too, to feel his skin beneath her fingertips, but Ben shoved her hands aside. He brought his lips to her thigh, trailing a series of hot, hungry kisses north—and leaving behind a wake of fire as he went. Up her thigh, around the apex of her legs, where she so desperately needed him, up her stomach, to the bottom of where her shirt had ridden up.

He shoved the material above her breasts as he sought to continue his trail. She arched into his touch, to give him full access to her body, when he took a pebbled nipple into his mouth and lightly bit down.

"You taste so fucking good," Ben groaned against her skin.

This time, she managed to catch his face, so she could look into his eyes. His pupils were completely blown out, the pools of amber recessed to his desire. His mouth opened as gasping breaths wrung from him. Hair mussed from their hands on one another. He'd somehow managed to shed the rest of his clothing in the time he'd spent trailing up her body.

The picture he made—with hair mussed wildly and his cock twitching as it rested against her thigh— made for one of the most darkly sexy things she'd ever seen. She needed him in vastly inappropriate ways, though, and her patience had run out.

"Please, Ben..." she pleaded, needing to feel him inside of her.

Unable to deny her, or himself, any longer, he spread her legs further apart to make room.

He positioned himself at her entrance, trailing the length of her soaked pussy. Liquid desire coated the head of his cock as her fingernails formed crescent moons in his arm.

When he finally sank into her warm heat—inch by painstaking inch until he was fully seated inside of her—he threw his head back.

"Say it again, sweetheart," he demanded breathlessly. "I need to hear you say it while I fuck you." A soft whimper betrayed him when she clenched around him—pure music to her ears.

"I'll tell you as many times as you want," she managed before he experimentally thrusted to test the angle. "I love you, Ben."

"You better," he said before stealing another kiss from her—something she'd gladly let him steal from now on, whenever he wanted. "Because I'm so in love with you, Addie, that I'm never letting you go again. Prepare yourself."

CHAPTER 35

High heels clicked against the hard concrete floor and reverberated through the hallway as Addie made her way toward the staircase. The box of her belongings was surprisingly light considering how she'd practically lived there over the years, but it made today all the more easy. She was almost skipping as she rounded the corner.

John scurried to catch up with her, a stack of papers clutched in his hand as protests flew from his mouth. She'd tried her best to avoid him today, knowing this exact situation would happen, but there wasn't a single thing he could say to change her mind.

"Come on. Let's talk this through...." he pleaded for what had to be the hundredth time since she'd turned her two weeks' notice in. Two weeks to the day that she'd gotten back to the station from filming.

She adjusted the box she carried and continued. "It's not up for debate, John. I'm not—"

"But, Addie," he interrupted, "management is increasing their offer even *more* to keep you. We can't afford to lose you, too, after Sally quit. They want you to take over the weather side completely, and they even want to—"

This time, she finally did stop, the movement so sudden that John stumbled. "I don't care what management wants. I already told you, I'm done. My two weeks are up, and my ride is here."

"But just think if—"

"John?" Addie interrupted. She hadn't learned much yet, but she knew what the sign was that she gave John, as she flicked her palm from under her chin at him. "And I mean that from the bottom of my heart," she added, her voice sweet and thick with sarcasm.

Satisfaction sang throughout her nerves when she spun about, hearing John sputtering a response. One that would fall on deaf ears. It served him right, in her opinion. She'd been miserable for far too long—treated like dirt for far too long—to want to stay there for one second longer. The past few years had chipped away little pieces of her, and she was done letting that happen. For the first time in ages, she knew she was worth more than that.

She was *the* Adelyn Walters.

Up ahead, Evie waited for her by the staircase entrance—her own box of belongings in hand. She bounced up and down in excitement as Addie trotted over to her.

"Come on. They're waiting for us in the parking lot!"

Addie would've paid money to see John's reaction again when Evie had also handed in *her* two weeks' notice, later the same day that she'd turned hers in. They'd tried just about everything they could think of to keep the two, even offering to fire Frank for what he'd done to Evie.

Too little, too late.

Unfortunately for the higher-ups at Channel 5, they weren't the *only* ones that had been impressed by what Addie and Evie had ended up putting together for the documentary. The group that Ben and his team partnered with had taken note of how well it had turned out, coming out with rave reviews. Enough so that they'd made her an offer she couldn't refuse. The signing bonus alone had been enough that Addie was able to do the one thing she'd stayed all those years at Channel 5 to achieve.

She was now officially debt free. She'd cried the day the last bill was paid.

Addie linked her arm with Evie's as they burst through the back exit to the parking lot. They had started this adventure together, and they were going to continue it together as well.

The RV sat in the parking lot, a short distance from the door with a giant *"congrats"* poster dangling haphazardly off one side. Addie laughed as the team came into view, standing there like they'd been waiting for their arrival. Which, technically, they were. They started on their next documentary later that week.

Brody and Grace were perched atop the RV, party streamers popping as they lifted the sign higher up in the air. Ryan ran over with a party hat on top of his head. Addie couldn't help but laugh when he quickly placed a matching hat on both her and Evie's heads.

"Finally free!" Tony cheered as he pulled another party popper from his pocket with a laugh. It showered the two of them in brightly colored confetti. Evie dropped her things onto the ground and threw herself into Tony's arms, him laughing as he gave her a spin in the air.

"Great, we've got *two* couples to worry about now," Ryan grumbled.

Addie bumped her shoulder against his affectionately. "You know you love us."

A smile cracked through the frown. "I guess so, but just try not to rub it in our faces, huh? Just because you're the latest addition to the family doesn't mean you're exempt from ridicule."

That was fine with her. This team had become like a second family to her over the past few months—so much so that she honestly couldn't picture the rest of her life without all of them in it.

Particularly the man walking toward her.

Ben came around the side of the RV with a smile plastered to his face. He was wearing another graphic tee and jeans, the kind Addie had discovered hugged all of her favorite parts of him in the most delicious way.

"Glad to see you on time, Walters. I'd hate to dock you for being late to your first day on the job," he tutted, raising an eyebrow.

"Don't worry," she replied casually. "I have an in with the team lead. I think I'll be alright."

Ben took the cardboard box from her and set it aside. As he turned back, she began to move her hands, like she'd practiced. He watched, his eyes widening as she pointed to him, crossed her arms across her chest, palms flat against it, then pointed at him. She had no time to prepare as he lunged and swept her up into his arms. A giggle bubbled out of her as she wrapped her arms around his neck.

"Ugh," Ryan groaned behind them. "Do we have to start calling them Mom and Dad now or something?"

"Leave them alone. It's cute!" Grace shouted, throwing one of her party poppers down at him.

Ryan dodged the popper and rolled his eyes with a noticeable smile. "Yeah, but will it be *cute* in a week's time when they're arguing and at each other's throats again?"

Brody chuckled from where he sat next to Grace. "As long as they don't try to kill each other, I'm good."

Ben grinned. "Y'all might want to look the other way for a bit, then. I'm gonna kiss my girl."

Addie laughed when the rest of them turned away and pretended to engage in conversation. "Your girl, huh?"

"Yeah, my girl," Ben answered with a knowing smile as his arms tightened around her. "How'd you figure out how to sign that?"

She lifted a shoulder with a sly smile. "Brody may have helped. But more than that, mister, why didn't you tell me that it means *I love you*? You signed that to me when you told me you had feelings for me."

"I thought it would spook you if I said it outright, but I had to say it."

"So, you love me, then? True or false?"

The warmth of his smile as it overtook him was one of her favorite sights. "True."

THE PEN NAME PROJECT
FIRST CHAPTER EXCLUSIVE

Want to read more by Leigh Creek? Enjoy this first chapter sneak peek at her other book, "The Pen Name Project."

CHAPTER 1

SAM

Of all the things Samantha MacMillian expected today, getting pulled out of her writer's block by hearing the word "smut" was not one of them. But who was she to look a gift horse in the mouth? If it meant a light at the end of the tunnel for this predicament she was in, she'd take it.

She was set up in her favorite café a few blocks away from her apartment, her gaze fixed firmly on the blank page glowing at her from the screen. The relentless and much-dreaded blinking cursor taunted her with each passing second, a flashing reminder that if she didn't start coming up with something soon, she was in trouble.

She hissed out a groan as she rubbed the back of her neck to ease the tension there. Blinking a few times to shake the sleep out of her eyes, she began the torturous mental loop that had accompanied her every day the past few weeks.

How was she supposed to know that after publishing the last book, the well of ideas she'd had for something new would dry up?

Her popular detective mystery series had finally wrapped up last year with its final installment, a thrilling conclusion that had been well received by both critics and readers. But after she wrapped up the press releases and book tour for it, when her publisher had asked her what was next, she quickly realized that she didn't have anything planned next.

If only she could time travel and slap that stupid contract out of her hand. It had seemed like such a good idea at the time that she didn't even consider the scenario she would end up in.

While she was still in process of writing the fourth book in her series, her publishers generously offered her a brand-new contract for whatever else she wanted to write. After her mystery series had wrapped up with the planned ninth installment, she'd have free reign to write, well, anything she wanted. A creative person's dream come true.

She'd already expressed back then that once she was done with this series, she wanted to take a break from writing mysteries, and they had been excited about the prospect of her creative flair in a new genre. It was a smart business decision on their end. Sam was basically a guaranteed payout for them, as every single one of her books had hit the New York Times bestseller's list at least once.

That said, in her excitement about writing something completely new, she failed to realize what a creative slump she would enter immediately after publishing the last book.

Her book tour wrapped up just shy of a year ago, and she still had nothing to show for it in terms of her next project. Her publisher had been more than patient with her, something she was eternally grateful for. She'd told them that she wanted to take a bit of time off to decompress from the whirlwind that the past few years had been. She'd started writing her first book right before she'd graduated from college, and as she was now pushing thirty, she'd had little time for herself.

They'd extended the contract to allow for her to have a much needed break, but she knew that her grace period was swiftly coming to a close. She'd have to give them something soon, or she'd be breaching her contract. But the second she'd started to brainstorm ideas, absolutely nothing came. It was like she'd used all her best material on her mysteries, and now there was nothing left.

A reminder popped up on the screen, temporarily distracting her from her spiral and causing another groan to escape her. She had almost forgotten about the video call. Granted, it was a weekly occurrence, and normally she looked forward to it, but with absolutely nothing to tell her agent, Angel, she wasn't exactly leaping with joy.

She gave a languid stretch before getting up and walking over to the counter. Another cup of coffee might help wake her mind up, or at least that was what she tried to convince herself as she waited for her order.

The Oak House was her favorite coffee shop in downtown Durham. Not only was it one of the closest coffee shops within walking distance of her apartment, it was relatively quiet during the daytime, so she could work in peace. Plus, Sam couldn't help but adore the cozy atmosphere embedded into each inch of the space. Coffee shop during the day, craft beverage lounge at night—the ambiance alone was unmatched.

Sam collected her iced latte from the barista and went to sit back at her table, nestled comfortably in the back corner of the space. She allowed herself to sink into the comfortable leather seat as she gazed outside. Every time she came to work here, she always picked the same spot. It was far enough away that even the morning rush didn't disturb her, and it had the best ambient lighting of the entire space. It also didn't hurt that the floor-to-ceiling exterior window perfectly displayed the bustling downtown activity outside, currently showcasing the pitter-patter of a late spring shower as it created a sheen of water on the ground. It was the perfect kind of peace that almost made Sam forget her troubles.

Almost.

As she settled back into her seat, a familiar name popped up as a new text notification dinged.

> We still on for dinner tonight? I can pick you up from the complex if you want? 😊

Sam smiled involuntarily, the movement tugging at the freckles speckled across her nose. It wasn't like they hadn't just spoken half an hour ago—before he'd gone into the office earlier and about this very topic—but her best friend was anything but subtle when he had his mind set on something.

And though he would never find this part out, there was a high likelihood that her car would never leave the shop again after she'd taken it in a few months prior.

> Yes on dinner, no on the ride, I told you I'm fine to take the bus

She was in the process of saving up for another car, so the bus would have to do for now.

She could practically hear the groan from there when his response quickly came back, choking back a laugh as she read it.

> Ugh, fine, just sit FAR FAR away from the sniffer this time

Smiling at the inside joke, Sam set down her phone. She was jolted back to reality, however, when the tell-tale jingle of the incoming video call started blaring through her laptop's speakers. The suddenness of it caused her to nearly spill her coffee, an expletive leaving her lips as she placed the cup on the table and quickly placed her headphones on to limit the sound spreading to the rest of the building.

"You're early," Sam half-scolded as Angel's face lit up her laptop screen. Angel feigned shock as she placed a finely French-manicured hand on her chest, the subtle jingle of her gold bracelets accompanying the gesture. "Only by five minutes."

"That's five minutes I could've spent in peace and quiet," Sam teased, seeing the immediate frown appearing on the screen.

"Someone hasn't had enough coffee in their system yet, I see. Or do I sense bad news on my horizon?"

Sam sighed, rubbing the back of her neck before reaching for her coffee. "Both?"

"You're lucky I love you."

Sam chuckled. "You love me because I'm your best client."

Angel glowered at her. "Alright, I may be your agent now, but you forget I've been putting up with your antics for years."

This time Sam let out a genuine laugh. It was true, technically, Angel had first been her roommate back in college. It was only her good fortune that Angel had decided after graduation to move up to the Big Apple to work in publishing. The two of them had spent hours talking about books, Angel acting as a soundboard for the ideas Sam had for her first mystery novel, which she'd started working on at the time. It was sometimes hard, seeing Angel all prim and proper now, with her Manhattan-esque fashion sense and polished appearance, when a few of the memories Sam held dearest were the times when the two of them were sitting in their dingy little university student apartment, eating cup ramen.

"Still," Sam said as she leaned back in her seat, "it doesn't hurt that I'm also your bestselling client."

"No, it certainly doesn't," Angel conceded before quickly adding, "luckily for you, though, because any other agent would be throttling you right about now."

"I still have time."

"You have three months. To write an entire book. From scratch. And not a mystery," Angel reminded, a smile gracing her lips as she reached for the sleeve of her blush-colored blazer and deftly rolling it up to her elbows.

Regardless of the time of day, Angel almost never looked less than a million bucks. She possessed a sense of fashion that Sam couldn't help but envy, always appearing so effortlessly put together and professional no matter what she had on. She'd been that way since they'd met during their freshman orientation almost ten years prior, the only major change to her wardrobe now being a larger budget.

It was a far cry from the raggedy pajama set she often remembered Angel wandering around their old apartment in. A stark reminder of how different they were—Angel now all posh New York City girl who came from a rural town in North Carolina, while it felt like Sam had hardly changed at all. The same old type-A homebody who preferred the comfort of the local coffee shop down the street from her apartment over exploring most of the downtown area she lived in.

"Should we have another brainstorm session?" Angel asked as she leaned back in her office chair, the view of downtown Manhattan peeking in over her shoulder.

The claw-clip ponytail that Sam had haphazardly pinned up that morning finally relinquished the thick waves of rosy-blonde strands from its confines, unable to hold back another second longer. Sam groaned in frustration as she pulled the strands back, smoothing out the edges with her hands. "I don't know if another one is going to help. We tried that last month."

Angel shrugged. "Then what's the harm in trying again?"

Other than her pride, Sam couldn't think of any other good reason. "Fine, I guess we can attempt it."

"Alright, great," Angel said as she scooted forward in her chair toward the screen. "How about instead of trying to brainstorm story ideas right now, like we did last time, we just brainstorm a genre to try? It would be a bit less pressure and still at least gives us some progress for today."

"How very manager-sounding of you." Sam laughed.

Angel rolled her chocolate-colored eyes dramatically. "Did I also mention that because I've known you forever, you're also my biggest pain in the ass client?"

"Sorry, sorry, you're right. Let's brainstorm. Whatcha got?"

"That's more like it. How about fantasy? I remember you trying to write one a long time ago. Maybe that could be a good direction?"

Sam chewed on the idea for a second before shaking her head. While she did love a good fantasy, she wasn't sure if she could summon the kind of creative flare and worldbuilding needed to get through something like that.

"Historical fiction, then? It's a bit of a broad net but maybe something in that realm?"

Sam shook her head again. "I don't even really like to read those that much, so I don't think I'd enjoy the process of writing one."

"Literary fiction?"

"Same thing but also even broader of a net."

"Science fiction?" Angel suggested, a bit of impatience starting to creep into her voice.

"While I'd love to say I'm smart enough to come up with something ingenious for something like science fiction, I don't think I have that kind of creative brain power, either," Sam admitted, quickly taking another sip of her latte.

"Fair. How about a thriller? Your mysteries were all murder mysteries, so maybe something that leans farther into the thriller element?"

It was a tempting thought. It was familiar enough that she wouldn't have to venture too far out of her comfort zone to create something, and it would still technically be separate from the mysteries she'd been known for. It could work.

Then again, the whole pitch she'd given to her publishers when they came up with this arrangement was that she wanted to write something completely new and different from what she was known for. A thriller felt like a cop-out.

"Definitely something I'd like to circle back to, but I think it hits a little too close to what I've already done for it to be really unique."

"You're not taking this very seriously," Angel chided.

Sam laughed. "I promise I am."

"Alright," Angel said. "How about horror? It might reflect your love life?"

Sam scowled. "My love life isn't a horror novel, thank you very much."

Angel laughed. "I beg to differ. Do I even have to remind you of that terrible date you had with that guy a few months ago? What was his name again?"

"I'd rather not write something that you immediately associate my love life with," Sam quickly said, changing the subject. She already had enough things to worry about without having to add him to the list. "Besides, you're one to talk."

"At least I've been on more than one date in the past five years.

Though we both know your hang-up," Angel commented, looking narrowly down her slender nose at Sam.

"Oh shut up, are you going to help me, or are you going to just sit here and make fun of me?"

Angel's smile widened. "I rest my case. Though, with as many romances you read in your free time, maybe you could write a romance? Hell, you could even write a smutty romance. Maybe then you'd be getting laid, even if it's just in the book."

In that moment, it felt as if a lightbulb flickered to life—so much so that Sam felt stupid for not thinking of it already. Why on earth hadn't she thought of a romance?

It was her favorite type of novel to read when she needed to chill out and relax, but she'd never really pictured herself being able to write one herself. The series she'd just wrapped up had a minor romantic subplot, and even that had felt like she had no idea what she was doing. Her readers had apparently eaten it up with vigor, though, if the number of fanfiction stories and artwork she'd been sent over the past few years were any indication.

It would be another thing entirely, however, to write a book with romance at the forefront. And a smutty one at that? While the idea wouldn't have tempted her much at the start of her writing journey back in college, the thought was now titillating enough that Sam was practically drooling at the opportunity to explore.

It checked off so many different boxes that it felt like she'd be stupid not to dive into it. It was something she enjoyed reading for fun, so she wouldn't be forcing herself into a genre she wouldn't even pick up herself. And it was different enough from her other work that her publisher would probably agree that it met her contract. But, most importantly of all, it was the first time in quite a while that she felt genuinely excited to start writing again. She felt the spark that had so eluded her for the past year.

Angel was about to be very thrilled, especially since it was technically her idea.

"Hello? Are you still there?" Her agent's voice broke through

Sam's thought bubble, and she realized she'd been silent a lot longer than she'd intended.

"Angela Louise Smith, I could kiss you!" she declared excitedly, quickly suppressing her volume when a few other customers glanced in her direction.

"What? What did I say?"

Sam leaned back in her chair, her decision firm in her mind.

She was going to write smut.

ACKNOWLEDGMENTS

They say it takes a village to raise a child, and as this is a book baby of mine, I'd honestly have to agree with that. I'd like to take the time to thank just a few of the people in that village.

The first person will always be for my husband, Mike. You have been there for just about every aspect of this book, and have been nothing but supportive of me chasing my dreams. From being my sound board for ideas and talking through plot points, to reassuring me that I'm not crazy (for the most part) while I've edited it, and being my rock when I needed it most. I wake up every day with a smile because I get to turn over and see you there laying next to me, and I know everything is alright in the world. Every swoon-worthy MMC I ever write has a little piece of you in it because you set the curve. I love you peanut!

To my sister from another mister, Alex. There's only so many ways I can tell you how much I love you because let's be honest, our husbands know that we are each other's bae. But how lucky am I to have someone like you in my life? From being a beta reader for my books, buying them even though you *know* I'm gonna send you copies for free whenever you want, to watching my stupid butt on YouTube to the point that my godson, Theo, giggles seeing me because he thinks I dance like a psychopath (I do, but jeez at least let him get old enough for me to embarrass him with it first, come on that's my right as his godmother).

To my friend (and other beta reader), Sarah. I love that we can laugh about books, boys, and both in one. Please never stop messaging me when you find off-the-cuff romances because chances are, I've read it and am *desperately* needing to talk to someone about it.

To my mom, Michele—thank you for giving me my endless love of books and the creativity to bring them to life. To my dad, Lewis, for giving me the humor to make sure people laugh reading my books. And to my Aunt Ellen who cheers just as loud even if we're not related by blood, and takes my books on adventures with her. I love you all so much!

To my editor (and friend), Jamie—talking shop and laughing about the in's and out's of being an author has been a blast with you. You've helped to keep me sane in the editing trenches and reassuring me that it's okay that I keep using the UK spelling of certain words even though I've been in the US my whole life. And thank you for assuring me that my imposter syndrome is, in fact, wrong as hell.

To my readers, thank you for reading this far into the book! You didn't think you'd get a shout out, did you? Wrong! You guys are a big part of why I will continue writing for as long as ideas come to me. Thank you for embarking on this journey with me! 🖤🖤

ABOUT THE AUTHOR

Leigh Creek is the romance pseudonym for author Elizabeth C. Cabrera. She spends vastly too much time daydreaming about the movie version of her books, drinking ungodly amounts of coffee, and pretending like she has her life together. When she's not writing and reading vastly too much, she's spending time with her husband and two cats (Link and Luna).

Sign up for her newsletter for behind-the-scenes, sneak peeks, and more authorly chaos!

http://authorelizabethccabrera.substack.com/

www.ingramcontent.com/pod-product-compliance
Lightning Source LLC
La Vergne TN
LVHW030318070526
838199LV00069B/6499